Amanda's Civil War

IN THE GREAT SMOKY MOUNTAINS

Maggie MacLean

Jan-Carol
Publishing, Inc
"every story needs a book"

Amanda's Civil War
In the Great Smoky Mountains
Maggie MacLean

Published June 2021
Little Creek Books
Imprint of Jan-Carol Publishing, Inc.
All rights reserved
Copyright © 2021 Maggie MacLean
Front Cover Photo: © Farknot Architect / Adobe Stock

ISBN: 978-1-954978-08-9
Library of Congress Control Number: 2021939412

You may contact the publisher:
Jan-Carol Publishing, Inc.
PO Box 701
Johnson City, TN 37605
publisher@jancarolpublishing.com
www.jancarolpublishing.com

Though it has been many years ago, I am still inspired by my high school teacher through three years of French. We were both disappointed when I missed winning the French National Test by one-half point. The prize included a full scholarship to the Sorbonne in Paris.

Author's Note

While women's place in nineteenth-century society was strictly defined, some women transcended those boundaries. My fictional leading lady, Amanda Armstrong was one of those women.

Out of food and supplies, Amanda traveled to Knoxville, looking for a way to support herself until the war was over. Along the way, she encountered an orphaned black boy who attached himself to her and did not want to let go. When she returned home a few months later, he followed her.

After conquering her own fears, Amanda affected the lives of many people, including the women of her neighborhood who were also struggling to survive the war. Together they established a commune at her home.

Please visit *northeasttennesseecivilwar.com* where you can read passages from my book.

ONE

———◆•❖•◆———

Amanda Armstrong was trying to survive the Civil War at her home in the Great Smoky Mountains of Northeast Tennessee. The high ridges and dark shadows of those mountains had spawned not only Confederate sympathizers and true believers in the United States of America, but guerrillas and opportunists who held no loyalty to anyone or anything but their own greed. Like many civilians in their area of the state, Amanda and her husband supported the Union; however, their son Luke worshipped Confederate raider General John Hunt Morgan.

Sunday evening, April 26, 1863

"Luke's out late again," Amanda said. "Where could he be?"

"Don't know," her husband Jonathan replied curtly.

She stared out the glass in the sitting room's back door. The approaching darkness was at that moment when the twilight lowers its shade and turns the evening over to the night. The lack of light did not frighten her. There was no darker darkness than that left behind when the sun slipped below the mountains, but the thought of what—or *who*—might be out there caused a ripple of goose bumps to run up her arms. The war had brought untold dangers to the mountains.

Amanda stood at the back door for several minutes, trying to see beyond her own reflection in the glass. She did not recognize the woman looking back at her, with pinched face and furrowed brow. What happened to the girl with creamy skin and shiny hair? Her new hairstyle—parted in the middle, pulled back, and rolled into a bun at the nape of her neck—probably made her look matronly, but it was convenient.

It's not a good sign that convenience is suddenly more important than appearance. I think I still have a good figure, but I can almost feel my hips spreading into the shape of the middle-aged.

Her eyes met Jonathan's for a flash when she sat down in her rocking chair at the edge of the sitting room fireplace. It occurred to her how rarely they actually looked at each other these days. Why was that?

Jonathan's behavior on Sunday was unpredictable at best. He consumed no whiskey on the Sabbath—not that she knew of, anyway. He was probably hoping to atone for his nightly drunkenness the previous week. Now he was fumbling for his pipe. She pretended to concentrate on the novel she was reading.

She could see most of Jonathan's face above the newspaper he held. She hadn't noticed how deep the creases in his forehead had become—was her face that wrinkled? His hair was thinning in the front. He plastered it to his head with some sort of fixative, which created a harsh line across the top of his forehead.

"Could Luke be at the Crossroads?" she asked. Two miles away from their home, Cinnamon Hill (so named for all the cinnamon ferns that grew in the mountains) was Armstrong Crossroads, a small community established by Jonathan's grandfather.

"What would he be doing at the Crossroads?" Jonathan asked. "It's a bit far to walk, and there's nothing to do there since Bixby closed his store."

"Didn't he ride Lady?"

"Lady's in her stall."

"I don't know anything about my son anymore," Amanda complained. "'A boy has to turn away from his mother to become a man.' Isn't that what you tell him?"

Jonathan gave her a cold stare.

"What if the conscription agents got him? I've heard the Confederates are so desperate for soldiers, they're taking anybody who can lift a gun."

"That's just rumor, Amanda," he said, shaking his head.

"Didn't you hear what Tom Bennett said today?" she asked.

Their friends, Tom and Alice Bennett, had come for Sunday dinner after church. As usual, the war soon became the topic of conversation.

"I hate the draft," Jonathan had said at the dinner table. He and Tom had been eligible for the Confederate draft since the previous September. Union conscription laws had no authority over men who lived in the seceded states, even those men who were still loyal to the Union. "I would have fought to keep Tennessee out of the Confederacy, but the thought of being forced to fight for the Rebels, whom I abhor, is beyond words!"

"I thought you might be ready to ride up to Kentucky and join the Union army," Tom said.

"I am loyal to the Union," Jonathan said, "but that doesn't mean I'm ready to rush off and get myself killed. What's the Union army done for me? They've been promising for two years now to run off these Rebels in our midst, but I haven't seen them yet. And those poor fellows who burned the railroad bridges, hoping to make it more difficult for the Confederates to move more troops in here? The Union army promised to support them, but they never came. Those poor men were hanged!"

"Could we please postpone this talk of war until after we eat?" Amanda asked.

"If you enlist now," Tom said, chuckling nervously, "you won't have to worry about the Rebels getting you."

"Or I could get a phony medical exemption, like you did," Jonathan said, his voice cold, his eyes glaring.

"You know I'm disabled," Tom stammered sheepishly. The previous autumn, Tom had announced that he had been diagnosed with some sort of curvature of the spine that no one had heard about before.

"You're about as disabled as I am!" Jonathan shouted.

"The way I hear it," Tom said, braver now, "since your Daddy died, Amanda takes care of everything around here. Maybe you should stay at home, and send her to the army."

Jonathan's lips began to form a word, but froze in a half-pucker. His face glowed red.

All color drained from Tom's face. He grabbed Alice's hand, and they made a quick exit, leaving their plates almost full.

The only friends they had in all of Armstrong Crossroads were the Bennetts and the Cuthbertsons. Would they now have only the Cuthbertsons to socialize with? Franklin Cuthbertson was a brute. His wife, Emily, was quiet and withdrawn in his presence, but when she and Amanda took tea together on Saturday afternoon, she was altogether a different person.

* * *

"All this talk of conscription today frightens me," Amanda said, "especially when Luke's out there after dark. Knowing he's on foot worries me even more. I think you sometimes forget he's only fifteen. You have no idea where he might be?"

"You'd better go to bed, Amanda! Your disease is showing!" Johnathan shouted.

My grandmother whispered to me once that an ailment comes upon a woman after she can't have any more babies, and her whole personality can change overnight. This had come in explanation of my mother's behavior that day, crying fits and cursing over something my father did, or did not do. I guess I was too young to be told the full story, but I clearly remember that this horrible sickness was called the 'change of life.' Has that mysterious illness now overcome me? I think I'm too young. Until my dying day, I will regret telling my husband anything about it.

Jonathan rose abruptly, shuffled off to his study, and slammed the door.

We'll just see how he likes being ignored...but it's no use. I'm always too impatient to hold my silence, and I get no satisfaction after I express my feelings to him. He gives me nothing: *not one "I'm sorry," nor a single "I didn't mean it."*

Amanda's legs began twitching, itching to move. Pacing the floor was her worst nervous habit. She began to move slowly around the perimeter of the room, stepping as softly as possible. She remembered there was a loose board near the study door that creaked, but she didn't stop soon enough. The board screeched like a fingernail on a chalkboard. She held her breath. Jonathan cleared his throat with a loud and irritated "Uh-*umm.*"

Well, if he knows I'm up, why try to hide it?

She knocked softly on the study door.

"What?!"

She opened the door just enough to see him leaning back in his chair, his feet on the desk. Smoke from his pipe curled around his head. The study was a small room that contained some of Jonathan's personal possessions and a beautiful mahogany desk that had once belonged to his father, Charles.

"It's getting late," she said, looking through the window beyond the desk.

She used a conciliatory tone with him, all the while chewing the inside of her cheek until she tasted blood, attempting to keep the bitterness she felt from spewing out all over him. Only when he was drunk could she rail at him, but then he laughed at her. The angrier she got, the more he giggled. And the next day he remembered none of it.

"Please check the barn again," she finally said. "Maybe he went to do his chores before coming to the house."

"I did his chores."

"Well, he doesn't know that, does he?"

Why are you looking at your pocket watch? Have you and Luke made some previous arrangement? Have you known where Luke was all along?

"Please," she said.

"By the time I go to the barn again, he'll be here," he said wearily, but he stiffened his arms and forced his body erect. He carefully folded his newspaper and slapped her quite roughly across the face with it as he passed her. If she hadn't been leaning against the doorjamb, he would have knocked her down. The door to the back porch closed with a resounding thud.

It occurred to Amanda that only at church did they talk and laugh as if everything was fine in their family. How had this escaped her attention until now? The answer to that question came quickly to mind.

It hasn't. I've avoided looking at it for as long as possible.

She heard footsteps on the front terrace. Luke was halfway down the long center hall by the time she reached the sitting room doorway. His straight brown hair was in disarray, his cheeks pink from the night air, a cunning little half-smile on his lips. His jacket hung off his shoulders.

He stood almost a head taller than his father, and he probably hadn't reached his full growth yet. Where Jonathan was stocky, Luke was lanky, built like her father.

When she looked directly into her son's eyes, he assumed his guilty-but-will-never-admit-it face. He threw his jacket on the table. When she hung it on the hall tree, several slips of paper floated to the floor. She picked them up, and saw that they were newspaper clippings about the Confederate General John Hunt Morgan.

"Where did you get these?" she asked secretively.

"Mr. Crocker saves them for me." Crocker was their farmhand, a crude backwoodsman with a large and growing family.

"You'd better not let your father see these. You know how much he hates Morgan and his raids into Union territory."

Luke stuffed the clippings into his pants pocket.

Amanda entered the sitting room just as Jonathan opened the back door.

"I'm not going out there - there you are," Jonathan said when he saw Luke standing behind her. "Safe and sound as I predicted," he said, a smug look on his face.

"Lucas Cambridge Armstrong, sit down," Amanda said, motioning toward a chair at the walnut table in the center of the room. "This sudden habit of running off after supper is not acceptable."

"You go on up to your room, boy," Jonathan said. "I know you have reading to do." Luke, who was studying law under his father's tutelage, escaped with a grateful look.

"We have to discuss this," Amanda said. "I'm afraid it's Crocker's little gap-toothed girl—Lydia, I think her name is—that's keeping Luke away from home so much. She's only twelve or thirteen, but poor mountain girls marry young—as soon as they can find some fellow to provide an escape from the poverty and difficulties at home."

"That shouldn't be a problem," Jonathan said nonchalantly. "None of Crocker's children ever leave home. They just move their spouses in and start reproducing, and he adds another room onto the house."

"Luke would be a prize catch for a girl like her," Amanda continued. "You know as well as I do that she would not be suitable for him. A boy his age doesn't realize that one moment of pleasure can ruin his entire future."

"There you go again," he said, "off on some wild scenario that exists only in your head. If you don't have anything to worry about, you create something. The Crockers might not be ideal companions for Luke, but he'll figure that out in time."

"We are his parents," she insisted. "If we don't say anything, he might think we approve. We also have to make him understand that there are dangers out there on the road at night."

"He knows that."

"Well, he doesn't act like he knows it."

"Do you want him to shut himself up in this house and live in fear like you've done since the war started? I promise you there'll be no more coming home late," he said. His stern stare kept her from saying more.

Amanda excused herself and went upstairs. The day had exhausted her. She crossed the bedroom and sat down at her dressing table and took the pins from her hair, allowing it fall down her back. She washed her face at the marble-topped washstand in the corner and changed into a nightgown.

Jonathan soon came to bed. He leaned against the bolster pillows at the head of the bed and took her hand in his. She wasn't feeling particularly cuddly, but she went along with it. She still wanted to talk about Luke, but Jonathan quickly turned cold when she broached that subject.

"How dare you continue to question my ability to rear my son!"

"I raised him by myself from the day he was born until you decided I was to be completely shut out of his life! How do you think that makes me feel?"

"I don't care!" He stretched roughly across her body and doused the light. The candlewick sizzled when he touched it with his wet fingertips.

"You'd better let this go, Amanda."

TWO

———◆·❧·◆———

Monday, April 27, 1863

Amanda Armstrong groaned the next morning when she realized that Monday was not only laundry day, but the first day of spring cleaning—a week of total chaos. Amanda and her housekeeper, Barbé, worked from sunup to sundown. Before the week was out, they would clean everything and return it to its proper place.

Amanda was cleaning the parlor when she heard Jonathan shouting in the front yard. He had decided that the best contribution he could make to the war effort was to grow corn to feed the Union army and their horses if they ever arrived in Northeast Tennessee. Luke and Crocker were working in the northwest meadow, digging up the dried cornstalks from the previous year and readying the ground for planting.

Amanda went out onto the front terrace and called to Jonathan, "What's the matter?"

"Edgar just came to tell me that those damned Rebels have passed a new tax law. They think they're going to take ten percent of everything I grow this year to feed the Confederate army. Well, let them take ten percent of nothing!"

"You have to plant something," Amanda urged.

"We had enough food last year," he said, walking toward her.

"Barely. The garden was bigger then, and we grew extra potatoes in the back meadow, and extra corn. The pantry and the root cellar are nearly empty. You have no idea how much it takes to feed four people through the winter."

"If Juba [pronounced Joo-bah] ever makes enough money to feed his own, we'll have plenty," Jonathan said hatefully. Juba, Barbé's husband, was there helping with spring cleaning and undoubtedly heard Jonathan's remark.

"Then Luke isn't needed in the field anymore?" she asked.

"Nobody's needed in the field."

"Then tell him to help us with the cleaning."

"Luke, go help your mother."

"Do I have to?" Luke said.

"Yes," Jonathan yelled. "And quit whining. You sound like a girl."

Amanda told Luke to help Juba with the rugs and the upholstered furniture on the rear brick terrace. She returned to the parlor, where she was scrubbing the wooden floors.

"Where is my vinegar water?" Amanda called a while later, trying not to sound too impatient. She hadn't slept well and had been suffering with a headache all morning.

She had lost count of the number of buckets of water they had already used that morning. Every drop of water they used in the house had to be carried from the pump behind the summer kitchen. That didn't seem so bad until she carried several bucketsful, and her side began to burn.

"Here's your water, my girl," Barbé said breathlessly. As she hurried through the parlor door, a splash of water spilled onto the floor boards Amanda had just scrubbed and polished with beeswax. Her mournful eyes begged Amanda for forgiveness as she hastily mopped it up.

"Why isn't Luke carrying that?" she asked Barbé.

"You sent him to help Juba."

Amanda nodded. "Sorry," she said, "I forgot. Thank you for the water. I want to finish these windows before dinner."

"You best hurry," Barbé whispered secretively. She sat the bucket on the deep windowsill and left as quickly as she had come.

Earlier, when Amanda learned that Luke would be working with Crocker, she had begged Juba to help with the spring cleaning. She had put him on the spot in front of his wife, so he couldn't very well refuse, but he made it clear he didn't intend to stay long.

Juba was a big man—over six feet tall, with broad shoulders, long arms, and hands so large that he could pick up a rolled-up carpet with one hand. His skin color was almost black, much darker than Barbé's. He had come to live with Barbé at Cinnamon Hill after he bought his freedom. Prior to that, he could spend only a few hours with her after church on Sunday. Finding no other opportunities, Juba continued to work for his previous master for a pittance of a wage. Amanda saw his ego deflate as his hopes died. He had believed that the day he bought his freedom would be a magical time.

* * *

One morning a year earlier, Barbé had come crying to Amanda. "He'll get his heart broke," she said.

"What is it?" Amanda asked.

"Juba's going to see Mr. Bixby again about buying his old carriage house," Barbé said tearfully. "Says he's tired of being a fix-up man and waiting for something to make our lives better. Says he has to make it better, or it won't ever be."

"What do you mean he's going to Bixby again?"

"He's been there several times over the last few years."

"Why didn't you tell me about this sooner?"

"Because I promised him I wouldn't. You know he won't take help, especially from you."

Juba wanted to buy the old carriage house behind Bixby's General Store at Armstrong Crossroads and set it up as a blacksmith shop.

"Oh, Mandy," Barbé continued. "I know Mr. Lincoln wrote that emancipation paper to help us black folks, but it's got Juba so worked up I'm afraid for him. I keep telling him it just means slaves are free. It don't mean we can go down the road and buy a farm and some white man's gonna pay us a pile of money for our crops. He says, 'That's fine. I don't want to be a farmer. I want to be a blacksmith, like my daddy and granddaddy trained me for.'"

Amanda found Luke, who was still in the kitchen eating breakfast. "Ride as quick as you can to Mr. Bixby's," she told him, "and don't let Juba see you. Tell Mr. Bixby to come see me tonight after dark."

"This might work," Amanda told Barbé a few minutes later, "and it might be a good investment for the money I've saved from my father's trust."

"Really?" Barbé said, drying her eyes. "Don't give me hope if there ain't no hope."

"No, I'm serious," Amanda said.

"Oh, Dear Lord," Barbé said, hugging Amanda tightly. "If you could do this for me, maybe he'll stop thinking about moving to the North."

* * *

When Bixby came to the house that night, Amanda tried to make him see that his terms were unreasonable. The deposit he was asking for would take all of Juba's savings, and leave nothing for the tools he needed.

"That building has stood empty for years," she told Bixby. "I would think you'd be glad to be rid of it."

"It isn't costing me a penny sitting there," Bixby said smartly. "And I'm not so sure that man—that colored man—can make a go of a business here."

"So that's it."

"No, that's not it," he said haughtily. "I don't hold it against him that he's a Negro, but some folks around here will. I don't think they'll give him any work."

"You think they'd be stupid enough to travel clear to Greeneville, when there's a blacksmith right down the road?"

"Some would, yes."

"Then that makes me angrier than I already was," she said.

Bixby held fast to his original price. Amanda had to pay half of the deposit, and she agreed to pay the balance of the debt should Juba default on the monthly payments.

* * *

After many hours of backbreaking work, Juba opened the Armstrong Crossroads Blacksmith Shop. He smiled with great satisfaction. Amanda had never seen him so happy.

So, she was caught completely off guard when he stormed into the kitchen one Monday morning a few weeks later. Working in his spare time, he had transformed the big room above the carriage house into an apartment. He was bringing Barbé back to Cinnamon Hill after they spent their first weekend there.

"What have you done now?" he shouted at Amanda.

"What are you talking about?" Amanda asked. She looked to Barbé for an explanation, but she stood quietly by, eyes downcast.

"My wife won't come live with me at the Crossroads," he said angrily. "She wants to stay here with her precious Amanda." This last part he said mockingly, his lips protruding into a pout.

Barbé gave Amanda a sly sideways glance, and a slight shrug of her shoulders. Despite all the talk about the apartment and how nice it would be for Juba to have his own home for the first time in his life, Amanda had never thought about Barbé living there—apparently, neither had Barbé.

"And what would you have her do?" Amanda said.

"I would have her live with her husband, where she belongs."

"Wouldn't that be a hardship on you?" Amanda asked. "To have to bring her back and forth to Cinnamon Hill every day?"

"Who says she has to be here every day? Or at all?" Juba said. That remark got Barbé's attention.

"Juba," Amanda stuttered, "it's hard enough for me to get along with her here. "I can't imagine—"

"I just can't get away from you people," Juba said, shaking his head. "I bought my freedom from a man who treated me like a dog from the day I was born. I moved here, hoping I could be an independent man, to be respected. But all I got here was more bossing. Then, I'm thinking I've finally made it, with a blacksmith shop of my own. But all I got was another white man to order me around like I'm his personal darkie. If I'm lucky enough to get a job, Bixby takes me off it, puts me on another job for one of his friends, and my customer has to wait. But I carry on as best I can, because I have a goal. If this is what it takes to get my business going, then this is what I'll do. And I work every night to make a nice living space for my wife. I can finally give her the home she deserves—only to find out she don't want it!"

Juba left the kitchen and slammed the door closed.

"I don't understand why he's behaving like this," Amanda shouted. "I spent almost all my savings on that shop."

"But he doesn't know that," Barbé whispered, "and you can't tell him. I don't know what he'd do if he found out."

A compromise was eventually reached. Barbé would stay with Juba from Friday afternoon until Monday morning, and live the rest of the week at Cinnamon Hill. Amanda knew that Juba was disappointed, but she needed Barbé more than he did.

Business at the blacksmith shop did come slowly at first. It seemed that Bixby had been at least partially right. Some eastern Tennesseans had no problem with a black man working in a blacksmith shop, but to own one seemed to be another matter entirely. Even the most loyal Unionists weren't necessarily abolitionists. Even those who condemned a system that permitted one man to own another weren't sure how the freed slaves would fit into Southern society. Who could afford to pay the freedmen for their work? And who would house, clothe, and feed them?

Jonathan was sitting at his desk one day when Amanda withdrew a small valise from the safe in his office. She unlocked it with a key she wore on a long chain around her neck. There were only a few bills left, but it was U.S. greenbacks, not that worthless Confederate currency.

Jonathan moved his chair around, trying to look inside the case, but she closed it quickly. He chuckled as she put it back into the safe.

"What's so funny?" she asked him.

"Looks like you're down to your last dollar," he said, still smiling. "I told you that you'd regret the day you got involved with Juba and that business. I know you've done it all for Barbé, but he's got only himself in mind."

"He always cares for Barbé," she said firmly.

"Does he? It appears to me that you care for Barbé."

"What if I do?" she asked.

"How much do you plan to do for that n-?"

"Do not say that word in my presence!" she screamed.

"Well, that's what he is," Jonathan said hatefully. "He made himself that, not me. Don't rebuke me for calling him what he is. Some are Black folk; some are Negroes. Juba's a n-."

Amanda quickly put her forefinger to her lips before he said the vile word again.

"You know how disappointed your father would be to hear you say such words."

"Well, he isn't here to hear me, is he?" Jonathan said sarcastically.

"I know your attitude, Jonathan," she said. "The white man is king of the world; the black man is well beneath you."

"You're leaving yourself out," he said. "White women are next in line, then black men, black women, and then Indians of any description."

That last jab was directed at Galilani, Amanda's Cherokee friend.

"Do you remember what I told you the day Juba came here bragging that he was free, and could do whatever he wanted to do?"

"No, I don't," she said, "nor do I care."

"You disappoint me, Amanda," he said, slapping her on the back. "I thought you remembered everything I say."

She moved out of his reach.

"I told you that he'd become one of those uppity Negroes, who would expect the world to give him a living. You've paid him for every lick of work he's done here at Cinnamon Hill. Now you've set him up in business. When will it end?"

"It will end when I say it ends!" she shouted.

"Women shouldn't be allowed to have money," he said, leaning back in his chair. "They don't know how to handle it when they get it. That's why we men have to marry you and take care of you poor helpless creatures."

"I thought we agreed that you wouldn't bring this up again, and punish me with it," she responded. "It's my money, and you just can't stand me having it, can you?"

"Well, it was yours," he said. "Before it's over, you'll lose every dime."

"Next time I need confidential papers drawn up, I'll go to Greeneville," she said. "Then you won't know what I'm doing."

"Well, really, Amanda, what do you expect? Putting all your money into such a crazy venture—you might as well have burned it."

"I don't know if you noticed," she said calmly, "but I didn't ask for your opinion. I can't remember the last time I did ask for it, and I will have to be extremely desperate if I ever ask for it in the future."

"Oh, you'll come to me after this mess falls down upon you, and I'll try not to remind you of what you said here today." He giggled again.

She slammed the door as she left—but she still heard every word he said.

"You're quite a handful, Amanda," he shouted. "Old Alex Hunter knew just what he was doing when he set up that trust for you. He made sure I'd never have the slightest bit of control over his sweet little Amanda. All you Hunter women are arrogant bitches."

He has only recently begun to talk to me in such a manner, and I have no idea what to do about it.

THREE

⊛━◆━⊛

Monday noon, April 27, 1863

As Amanda wiped the last pane of glass, she noticed how far the sunlight had crept across the parlor floor. She had not made the final preparations for dinner—their noon meal. Jonathan would be coming in soon, and he expected his plate to be on the table when he sat down. As Amanda crossed the center hall, she heard his footsteps on the back porch.

It can't be that late.

Beyond the dining room through a narrow, enclosed passageway was the kitchen. It was sparsely furnished with a cupboard, a chest, and a large round table surrounded by six Windsor chairs in the corner. The floor was red brick.

Opposite the entry door was a huge brick fireplace. Pots and skillets hung from the ceiling. Dutch ovens sat around the perimeter of the hearth. The fireplace chamber had a spit for roasting meats and a crane that could be swung forward over the hearth to add or remove cooking vessels.

There was a new cast-iron cook stove in the opposite corner. It was a status symbol that Jonathan felt they must have. Amanda used it to heat water, but she still cooked in the fireplace. Cooking on the stove would be quicker and easier; but she still burned everything she tried to cook on it, and she never had time to practice.

Barbé was frying cornbread at the stove. Rivers of perspiration oozed down her honey-brown face. She constantly mopped her forehead with a linen handkerchief. An immense white apron enveloped her squatty body from chin to shin.

In the sidewall of the fireplace, a door about a foot square opened into a brick oven. Amanda peered inside, praying that Jonathan's hoecake wouldn't be too brown for his liking. As she retrieved the cast-iron skillet, a wave of lightheadedness swept over her. She had been rushing around too much this morning, but she couldn't slow down.

Jonathan insisted that his food be poured into serving bowls half an hour before mealtime, so it would be a comfortable temperature for eating, but the snap beans and meat were still boiling.

That morning, Amanda had put the beans and a piece of hog jowl into an iron kettle over the fire. She thought it was glorious to watch snap beans cook. They started out green as grass, smelling something like an old shoe. After two hours of cooking above the fire, they took on the hue of fresh sage leaves, and began to absorb the flavor of the smoked meat. Mid-morning, she buried in the broth some small potatoes and moved the kettle to the hearth. There they simmered slowly—the liquid barely rippling—for up to another three hours. She never stirred them, and they always came out tender and plump, taking on the brownish tint of the meat's juices.

"Amanda," came an impatient call from the dining room door. She had forgotten to set Jonathan's place. He came in for dinner at precisely twenty-five minutes past twelve o'clock, washed his face and hands, combed his hair, and was seated at the dining table at exactly half past twelve.

"Yes, Jonathan," Amanda said in apology, as she rushed to the cabinet for tableware, "I know I'm late."

"What's Juba doing here?" he asked.

"You've forgotten already? It's the first day of spring-cleaning."

"Why do you need Juba? You and Barbé and Luke did it last year."

"Yes, and we nearly killed ourselves," she said. "You seem to forget that your father is no longer here to help. Barbé and I can't drag the heavy furniture and the large rugs around. We just can't do it by ourselves anymore."

"If you did it last year, you can do it this year."

"Things were different then." She paused, eyes averted.

I was different then.

He glared at her. "Woman, you are the most exasperating human being ever born. To have to contend with you and the Confederate States of America on the same day is more than any man should have to endure!"

Amanda took his plate and hurried to the kitchen.

Luke and Juba had come in to eat dinner with Barbé in the kitchen.

"I hate when he talks to you like that," Luke said loudly.

Amanda touched a forefinger to her lips. "Don't make it worse than it is."

"He used to try to hide it, "Barbé whispered, "but he doesn't seem to care who hears him these days."

Amanda realized it was foolish to think that she and Jonathan had hidden their battles from the others, but she didn't like Luke knowing so much about it.

"Eat, "she whispered, after she filled Jonathan's plate from the bowls and platters on the table. "I'll be right back."

Jonathan was sitting at the dining table, a fork in his right hand, and a spoon in his left. It was his habit to shovel his food in with both utensils at once. After taking his first bite, he shrieked and covered his mouth.

"Now you've made me burn my tongue!" he shouted, then slurped down a glass of water.

Obviously not enough to shut you up.

* * *

An hour or so after dinner, it was apparent that Juba was getting impatient. "How soon do you think we'll be done here?" he asked. "I might be needed at the shop."

"That's fine, Juba," Amanda said coolly. "Your work is more important than mine. At least you're getting paid for it. Go on."

"You don't think I'll do it, do you?" he said arrogantly. He went out the front door and slammed it so hard her figurines in the étagère rattled.

"Why'd you do that?" Barbé asked.

"I'm tired of begging people to help me," Amanda said.

"We still have to carry the furniture in from the terrace," Barbé said.

"I know. Luke and I will do it."

"You're doing crazy things these days," Barbé said.

"I'm just so tired. My temper gets the best of me sometimes."

"I've never known you to have such anger. You're scaring me," Barbé said.

"I'm scaring myself."

* * *

Amanda cleaned Jonathan's study that evening, just in time to prepare for supper. Their evening meals were simple: leftovers from dinner, potato salad from yesterday's dinner, and some warm biscuits. Supper was soon on the table.

Soon after the war began, Jonathan had bought as much coffee, canned goods, and barrels of sugar and flour as he could find, knowing that the Union blockade of the Southern ports would soon make those items scarce. The last barrel of flour was almost gone, and she didn't know where the next barrel would come from—or if it could be had.

Jonathan came to the dining room table for supper at half past six o'clock. Amanda, Luke, and Barbé ate in silence at the table in the kitchen. As soon as Luke was finished, he hurried out.

"I'll be in the barn if you need me," he called.

"A load of wood for the sitting room would be most appreciated," Amanda yelled after him. He had stayed around the house that afternoon, willingly doing whatever she asked of him.

After she washed the supper dishes, Barbé retired to her little log cabin behind the house. Amanda fed the pigs and chickens. Back at the house, she carried her sewing basket to the sitting room. She must devote some time to the never-ending bag of mending: missing buttons, frayed hems, and ripped seams—clothing that she once would have donated to the church and bought new. But there was now no new to buy. The blockade of southern ports left very few goods to trickle down to their remote location.

Just as she was about to drop heavily into her rocking chair in front of the fireplace, Amanda realized she had forgotten to pick the peas she planned to cook for tomorrow's dinner. She had built a covered area at the corner of the barn for her precious baby peas.

Amanda pulled on a tattered shirt and an old straw hat that hung on a peg outside the back door and hurried across the rear terrace.

After Cinnamon Hill was built, Charles had built a brick terrace between the back porch and the outbuildings, and he expanded it several times, until it surrounded the entire house. It connected the group of white buildings behind the house into a picturesque unit and kept the mud from being tracked into the house.

There was a springhouse, in which perishables were temporarily stored. The summer kitchen was used for heavy kitchen chores, such as canning, making soap and candles, and preserving meat at hog killing time. They salted down and smoked the meat in the smokehouse. And there was the ubiquitous privy, which was beyond the terrace and connected to it by a stone walk.

Amanda stopped at Jonathan's office to ask if he would allow Crocker to plant potatoes in the back meadow. They would never have enough food to last through the winter if she didn't coax him into planting something more than just the garden. She peeked inside, but Jonathan wasn't there.

Where could he be?

Legal work hadn't been particularly active of late, but it would be dark soon and Jonathan's drinking companions would arrive. She crossed the footbridge over Bottom Creek that ran behind Barbé's cabin. A few yards downstream was a wider, sturdier bridge for horse and wagon traffic.

The kitchen garden was behind the two-story log house the Armstrongs used as a barn. All was quiet there. In the past, animals roamed the grounds as they pleased—ducks, chickens, goats, dogs, and cats. The dark figures who crept around in the dark of night had stolen every last one.

A few weeks earlier, Amanda had found their last dog with its throat cut, silenced by the same person who broke into the root cellar to steal food. Fortunately, the root cellar was empty.

Dew was already settling on the plants. Amanda squatted down and uncovered the short rows of peas, pressing every pod, searching for just the right stage of ripeness. Unripe peas would add bitterness to the broth. She cradled the peas in her apron, just enough to simmer slowly in cornmeal broth to which she would later add cornmeal dumplings.

She was moving toward the house when she heard voices. She sneaked up behind the barn. She could hear the voices more clearly there, but they weren't coming from the barn, but across the path at the stables. They had so few horses that the stables were no longer in use. There would be no reason for anyone to be in there.

The silliness of her skulking around in the half-light trying to eavesdrop on someone suddenly struck her as funny. Maybe Luke did have a female friend, who had been keeping him away from home at night, and maybe she had come to see why he hadn't called on her that evening.

A wide path of hard-packed earth ran between the barn and the stable. Amanda retraced her steps to a point where she was no longer visible from the stables and crossed the path. She walked past the pigsty and the two-story henhouse, creeping as close to the stables as she dared.

"You promised," a female voice said, obviously distraught. Amanda didn't recognize the voice, but she immediately knew the male voice that spoke next.

"How crazy you are to come here!" Jonathan said harshly. "You must understand. Things with Amanda are still very delicate. The loss of her father is still affecting her deeply."

"That excuse is wearing thin," the female voice said. "Well over a year has passed since then."

"Keep your voice down," Jonathan whispered. "Emily, I—"

Emily? Amanda knew only one Emily, and it couldn't possibly be her.

Amanda wanted to get a look at the female. She crept around to the rear doors, where there were narrow cracks in the weathered wooden boards. The female figure was only a few feet away, but the light was poor.

"I must go," the female said abruptly. "Franklin will soon be home. If I'm not there, he'll be suspicious."

It was Emily Cuthbertson! Her friend—the only white woman she considered a friend. Emily's back was to her, but Amanda could see the fine brown hair that created a halo of wisps around her head, no matter how much she brushed it, no matter how much dressing she applied to it. That was one of Emily's feminine insecurities, another being her poor complexion. Pockmarks marred her cheeks, but her beautiful green eyes made up for all that.

"Since when do you care what he thinks? "Jonathan said.

"Well, obviously you don't care anymore, "Emily whined.

Anymore?

"Emily, I'm sorry," Jonathan said.

"Let me go," she said fiercely, forcibly removing his hand from her arm.

"Did you hear something?" he asked suddenly. "I have to get you out of here."

Amanda decided it was time to make her escape. She crouched down, almost crawling through the stiff vines of the grape arbor. She skirted the field, and stepped out into the path at the same time Jonathan did, his paramour now clutching his arm. Emily saw Amanda, and with a horrified gasp she ran back into the stables and threw the rear doors open. She raised an awful racket as she crashed through the grapevines, sobbing loudly all the way.

Jonathan's face turned bright red, as if he had been in the sun all day, but Amanda didn't see. She had already turned away.

What a wonderful time to encounter my husband and his lover—when I look like a complete frump in a soiled and tattered dress, with a most unattractive hat shoved on my head. Yes, appearances are so important in these situations. I'd feel much better if I were wearing a Sunday dress and a jaunty little hat.

* * *

"Mother, what happened?" Luke was leaning over Amanda, who was sitting on the floor of Jonathan's study.

"Help me up," she said, leaning heavily on his arm.

"What happened here?" he asked again. "I heard you screaming—things crashing." He helped her sit down in the chair by the window. "I thought someone was hurting you."

"Me, screaming?" she asked, trying to remember.

Her hair was stuck to her face. She tried to push it back into its knot. Her hands worked quickly, pulling out and pushing in the pins.

"I don't know," she finally said.

"What do you mean you don't know?"

"Help me, Luke," she gasped, grabbing her chest. "I can't breathe."

"Take a deep breath, Mother," he urged.

"I can't."

He grabbed her shoulders and shook her, like one would shake a baby when it loses its breath. At last, she took a full breath.

Luke clutched one of her hands in both of his. She felt his hands trembling.

"Oh, no," she said, as memories came surging back.

"Did you do this?" he asked.

As she looked around the room, she saw that a flowerpot had been thrown against the wall. A glass kerosene lamp was in shards. Pictures of Jonathan's ancestors lay shattered on the floor. His pipe rack had been pounded into the top of the desk, leaving ugly marks in the mahogany wood. The desk chair had been smashed into the window. Every pane in the lower sash was broken.

"I guess," she said weakly.

It's like watching someone else's life.

"Why?"

"I was so damned angry I couldn't help myself," she said, and began to cry.

"Who were you angry at?"

"Your father," she said softly. "I was thinking about the times we stayed up nights talking about our future together. I don't know how things went so wrong." She couldn't tell him what she was really thinking about—Jonathan and Emily.

"Why do you and Father hate each other so much?"

"I don't hate him," she stammered, rubbing her eyes with both fists. "He exasperates me. It's just the way old married folks behave sometimes, I guess." She chuckled, trying to make light of it.

"You never tell me anything."

"Oh, my, your father will be livid," she whimpered as she rubbed her hand across the blemishes on the desktop. "Look what I've done."

"Wait," Luke said excitedly, "I can fix this."

"How?"

"Crocker knows woodworking. You should see the furniture he's made for his house. He just finished a canopy bed out of oak wood for his littlest daughter, Pearl. It's beautiful."

"He'll tell Jonathan!" she cried.

"Not if I ask him not to," Luke said confidently.

She touched a hand to her temple.

"You have a nasty bump on your head," he said.

What's happening to me? A total emotional collapse couldn't be much worse than this.

Luke helped her to her room. She brushed her teeth with a bit of sponge and homemade toothpaste, and slipped into a nightgown. As she slid her weary body between the sheets, she prayed that sleep would overcome her quickly.

* * *

Amanda knew when Jonathan was coming to bed, by his alcoholic shuffle. She listened to him climb the stairs and walk down the hall, clamoring around, bumping into walls. He had stayed at his office a long time after his companions left. Surely, he didn't want to explain to her why he and Emily were together. That was fine. She didn't want to hear it.

He flopped onto the bed with his clothes still on, and that's the way he would find himself in the morning. She was tired of undressing him. She could almost taste the whiskey that exuded from his body, oozing from every pore. The smell sickened her. She knew he had begun to sip it all day long; she smelled it on his breath when he came to the house to eat dinner.

She waited until he began to snore and then slowly slid out from under the covers, grabbed her slippers from the floor and her robe at the foot of the bed, and tiptoed down the stairs.

* * *

Tuesday morning, April 28, 1863

"So you're down here again, Miss Mandy," Barbé said.

"What?" Amanda was startled, and then realized that she was lying on the settee in the sitting room.

"You're killing yourself going without your rest," Barbé said patiently. "You hardly sleep in the bed anymore."

Amanda rubbed her eyes, then held her throbbing head in her hands. "I'm fine," she mumbled.

"So you say, but I ain't believing it," Barbé retorted.

Amanda tried to stretch the stiffness out of her limbs. When she sat up, she groaned and grabbed her lower back.

"See what I'm saying?" Barbé scolded. "We got lots more cleaning to do today."

"Don't say that word."

"And here you are, all worn out before we get started."

"I know." Amanda sighed. "When I think about all there's left to do, I feel like running away from home."

"Can I go with you?" Barbé asked.

Amanda groaned as Barbé helped her to her feet and held onto her while she took the first few steps. She felt like a mule had kicked her in the sacrum.

"It wouldn't hurt Jonathan so much to let go of some of that precious money of his and hire us some help, like Mr. Charles did when he wasn't able to help," Barbé said.

"You know that's not going to happen."

"Yes, I do, and it makes me mad," Barbé replied. "I don't know how much longer we can hold out, taking care of this big old house by ourselves."

Amanda enjoyed listening to Barbé talk, especially when she made two syllables out of such a simple word as *our*. Barbé's mother was a third-generation resident of the Tidewater of coastal Virginia, and she carried the accent with her to southwestern Virginia. Barbé picked it up from her, and brought it to Tennessee.

* * *

When Amanda entered the bedroom, Jonathan stirred but didn't wake up.

Shivering, she grabbed the clothes she had worn the day before—no need to put on fresh clothes until after she bathed. At the washstand, she splashed the ice-cold water on her face. Now she was awake!

On the chaise longue, she laid out Jonathan's clothes for the day: a loose-fitting black wool suit with vest, a white cotton shirt, suspenders, black socks, and a bow tie. Luke would clean his father's shoes and bring them up later.

When Amanda entered the kitchen, Barbé was cooking breakfast. Barbé had quickly become adept at cooking on the new wood-burning stove. She moved the pots and skillets around the top surface in an intricate routine: the eggs were too hot, the sausage was soggy, the oatmeal was getting lumpy...then slap, bang, and shuffle, and the pans were interchanged.

A blaze was going in the fireplace, and a large kettle of water was heating. The batter for griddlecakes sat in a bowl on the table. Amanda began to mix the biscuit dough Barbé had measured out in a wooden tray.

Luke rushed in with cold milk from the springhouse and an armful of wood for the cook stove. Amanda sent him upstairs with a pitcher of hot water for his father's bath.

There were no logs in the wood box beside the kitchen fireplace, and the fire needed to be stoked immediately. Amanda cursed under her breath as she hurried into the dining room and yelled for Luke to carry in some firewood from the woodpile behind the kitchen. When she returned to the kitchen, she saw that their farm hand, Crocker, had arrived and was feeding the fire and filling the wood box.

"Used up all that wood I brought in Sunday, did you?" he chuckled.

Crocker was a rude and crude backwoodsman with a round moon face. His jowls had begun to sag a bit, and they bounced when he laughed. He always wore overalls, and they were always tattered, torn, and patched. Amanda didn't know his age, but he looked to be at least sixty. Immediately after his first wife died, he married a young girl from the mountains.

After Charles died, Jonathan hired Crocker to help around the house and tend the fields. Since Jonathan hadn't allowed Crocker to plant much this spring, they no longer needed him every day.

Of course, Crocker jumped at the chance to spend the morning repairing the mess Amanda had made in the study. She would have to pay him out of her own money for that job.

She caught Crocker and Luke laughing and joking with each other, making her even more suspicious about Luke's relationship with Crocker's daughter.

Amanda followed Crocker out the rear kitchen door. "I hope my son isn't spending so much time at your place because of that girl of yours. Lydia, isn't that her name?"

"Yes," he said, dragging the word out.

"I don't want him around girls like her," she said flatly.

"I'd say that's up to him."

"It's certainly not for you to say!" Amanda shouted. "That's up to his mother and father."

"Then tell him," the old man said, grinning. She wanted to slap his smart face.

After breakfast, Barbé and Amanda cleaned up the kitchen and did their usual morning chores. Then Amanda carried a pan of water to the ironing table and began to sprinkle water on the clothes Barbé had washed the day before.

"Let me do that," Barbé stuttered, pulling at the clothes in Amanda's hands. "You can't do it as good as I can."

"It's just everyday clothes," Amanda said impatiently. "It doesn't matter if there's a wrinkle here and there."

"It matters to me," Barbé said.

"You make more work for yourself by being so perfect," Amanda said, pulling one of Jonathan's shirts from Barbé's hands.

"I don't care," Barbé argued. "That's the way I like it. I don't want to do it at all if I can't do it right!"

"We'll never get done with the spring cleaning."

"Go get your bath," Barbé said, finally wresting the shirt from Amanda's hands. "I'll have this done in no time, then I'll help you with the cleaning."

I'm a horrible person, fighting with a woman who loves me so much. And over laundry?

Amanda escaped to her room to bathe, standing on an oil-cloth in front of the washbasin. At home, she wore calico dresses with tight-fitting bodices. She shoved the long sleeves up above her elbows. Her skirts were full, and hung in folds to the floor, with only a cotton petticoat and stockings underneath. Her skirts swished here and there as she rushed around the house, always in a hurry.

"I'm sorry, sweetheart," she told Barbé in the kitchen. "I'm so tired—I don't recall ever being so tired."

Since it was already late, Amanda decided to clean the library, and leave the larger dining room for the afternoon. Glass-fronted bookcases lined the walls of the library and held Charles' book collection—everything from history to biographies to poetry. It should have been an easy room to clean, but she handled Charles' books with extra care, for she knew how much he prized them.

Luke stuck his head into the library around eleven o'clock and winked. After a while, she slipped into the study, and was relieved to see that they had rubbed out the scratches on the desktop, replaced the window glass, repaired the chair and the gouge in the floor.

* * *

Saturday afternoon, Luke went riding with the neighbor boys. Barbé was with Juba at the Crossroads, and Jonathan left for the Old Duck Tavern. He still spent Saturday evenings there as a convenience for his clients, or so he said. Amanda was glad to be rid of him. She had managed to avoid him since the incident with Emily.

FOUR

February 1841

Seventeen-year-old Amanda Hunter traveled to Cinnamon Hill for the first time as her father's emissary to attend the funeral of Jonathan's grandfather. Though their fathers had been friends for years, Jonathan and Amanda had never met. Her father, Alexander Hamilton Hunter, was preparing to leave for Richmond when the news of the death came.

"I must warn you about Charles' wife," her father told her.

"What about her?" Amanda asked.

"I'll just say she's strange," he replied, "and let you make your own judgment. Don't get your feelings hurt when she scowls at you. She does that to everybody."

Amanda's Uncle Teddy accompanied her to Cinnamon Hill. She had never traveled without at least one of her parents along, but the excitement of the trip and the rugged beauty of the mountains soon overcame her sadness at leaving home.

She had no great expectations of a house in an area as rustic as Northeast Tennessee. They had passed some beautiful homes in some of the small towns they traveled through, but the last leg of their journey had offered nothing of civilization except dogtrot houses: two separate structures of the same size connected by a roofed passageway. She was, therefore, unprepared for the beauty of Cinnamon Hill.

The Armstrong farm was tucked into one of the pockets of land—coves, as the locals called them. Beyond the house were fields of different sizes and levels, which rose higher and higher until they melted into the woods beyond. The lower hills of the Great Smoky Mountains rimmed the farm like a giant horseshoe.

Split-rail fences bordered a wide lane of hard-packed earth. The light dusting of snow from the night before had settled on the fence rails like icing on gingerbread. In the afternoon sun, the rails cast wavy gray shadows onto the pristine snow that covered the meadows in front of the house. Several swales in the land created subtle drops in elevation as the lane descended toward the house.

The lane ended at a white wooden entrance gate, which was attached to two red brick pillars. Fences intersected at right angles at the gatepost and enclosed the front meadows, where corn had been grown the previous season. The stubble left behind when the dry cornstalks were broken off looked like miniature tents under the snow.

Beyond the entrance gate, an oval carriage drive allowed vehicles to pull right up to the front doorstep. A creek meandered lazily through a line of very tall trees, their bare winter branches stretching skyward like bony fingers.

A brick chimney rose at each end of the house's most creative feature: a railed observation deck. It sat astride the center of the low-pitched roof. This was the sort of structure usually built atop a coastal house: a widow's walk, from which a nervous wife scanned the horizons for the return of her husband's ship.

The white two-story colonial house of frame construction had a brick terrace running the full length of its broad front. Four square columns stretched from the brick floor to the roof. At the right end of the terrace was a wrought-iron trellis that ascended to the roof and supported dozens of climbing rose bushes.

A carved oak door graced the front of the house. Handsome Ionic pilasters with brick bases supported the doorframe. Shutters flanked all of the windows, which had narrow panes of glass, nine to the sash, eighteen to the window. At the second-story level, a sizable balcony was suspended.

Jonathan's father, Charles Armstrong, Jr., came out to greet them. Amanda was just alighting from the carriage when Jonathan rode up on a beautiful and powerful roan mare. Introductions were made all around. Normally a conservative man, Charles Armstrong had been quite extravagant in building his house. He loved to show it off, and was delighted when Amanda commented on its beauty.

"Come in," Charles said, putting his arm around her shoulders. "It's a blustery day we're having."

Jonathan jumped right in and pulled Amanda away from his father, which she thought was rude, but Charles didn't seem to mind. Jonathan created quite a charming little ceremony of introducing Amanda to the house. He escorted her through the front door, which opened into a large rectangular center hall. The floors were made of beautifully-polished random-width pine. On the right of the center hall, an elegant staircase led to the second floor.

"I'm charmed to meet you, Evalinda," Amanda said, when she was introduced to Jonathan's mother.

"Just call me Eva," she replied coldly, and walked away.

The next morning, Jonathan chose a gentle bay mare for Amanda from their fine stables, and they rode together every morning. In the evenings they strolled through the woods, walking and talking, with an occasional respite for sweet kisses. Jonathan was impressed when she told him she fished and hunted with her brother at home and was an accomplished horsewoman.

With Jonathan, Amanda practiced her new mannerisms and melodious speaking voice, which she had acquired after many hours of rehearsal in front of a full-length mirror. She wanted to look and sound more like an English lady than a rural Virginia girl. At a very young age, Amanda had noticed that her mother spoke more elegantly in public than when she was at home with her family, and she intended to duplicate her mother's style.

Amanda and her uncle remained at Cinnamon Hill several days after the senior Armstrong was laid to rest, during which time Amanda and Jonathan had long conversations by the light of a blazing fire of hickory logs in the parlor. Their courtship officially began on Valentine's Day, 1841. By the end of that first visit, they had established a strong attachment to each other.

Everyone made a point of leaving the couple alone—everyone except Evalinda. When the clock struck nine, she appeared in the doorway and continued to stand there until Jonathan went upstairs to bed. She glared at Amanda all the while. The last night Amanda stayed there, Evalinda took the parlor lamp with her, which was the only light left burning in the entire house, leaving Amanda to find her way to bed in the dark.

Amanda wasn't accustomed to the strictness she encountered at Cinnamon Hill. Evalinda ran the household on a precise schedule. Everyone ate, worked, and slept when she said it was time to eat, work, and sleep. Charles and Jonathan tolerated it as if it were their duty.

Amanda immediately noticed the strangeness in Evalinda that her father had mentioned. It was something Amanda couldn't quite define, possibly a combination of coldness and aloofness. It seemed to Amanda that Evalinda just didn't want to be bothered with people. The longer Amanda knew her, the less she understood her. And she got the feeling that that was exactly the way Evalinda wanted it.

Back home at Hunter House in Virginia, Amanda's elation over the wonderful turn her life had taken was dampened by her mother's reluctance to have her youngest daughter become so obsessed so quickly with a man she hardly knew.

"You have many men to meet before you decide on a mate for life," Mother said.

"I must admit I'm a little flustered," Amanda said. "I didn't know people could fall in love so fast."

"Maybe you're the only one in love."

"Oh, no, he's just as much in love as I am."

She overheard an argument between her parents. Mother finally admitted that a union between their daughter and Charles Armstrong's son wouldn't be a step down for Amanda, socially.

Their courtship endured through long separations while Amanda fell more in love with Jonathan through his letters. He expressed beautiful emotions in his writings; when they were together, words seemed unnecessary.

Finally, on a warm and beautiful June evening in 1845, Amanda Belle Hunter and Jonathan Cambridge Armstrong were united in marriage. The wedding ceremony was held in the center hall at Hunter House, with family and many friends in attendance. Charles attended the wedding without Evalinda; she was spending the day in her bedchamber, Charles said.

The front and rear doors of the house were wide open, in hopes of catching a cool breeze to dissipate the heat from hours and hours of cooking. The pocket doors that separated the parlor from the hall were pushed back, and the band had set up in there. Across the hall, every inch of the eight-foot dining table was covered with a grand buffet.

Amanda wore an ivory hand-embroidered Indian muslin dress, trimmed in lace. Her sister Penelope served as her bridesmaid. Though Amanda knew that Penelope was mortified to see her younger sister married before she was even engaged, Penelope seemed to forget her displeasure for the moment and brought a pink rose for Amanda to wear in her hair.

The new Mr. and Mrs. Armstrong spent their wedding trip visiting relatives, which was the custom. After spending their last night at a hotel in Knoxville, Jonathan took his bride home, where Evalinda's strange behavior became stranger still.

On the day Jonathan and Amanda crossed the threshold at Cinnamon Hill as man and wife, Eva ceased to help with meal preparations, house cleaning, or any other chores. Amanda was soon bogged down with housework, and she was homesick. A tearful letter to Mother soon took care of those problems.

A few weeks later, Alex Hunter brought Barbé to Tennessee. "I don't wish to give the impression that I am overly concerned about Amanda's welfare," he told Jonathan, "but I will feel better if she has someone with her whom she has known all her life." Jonathan didn't object. Charles was an avid abolitionist and must have disapproved of the arrangement, but he never mentioned it to Amanda.

Jonathan agreed with Amanda that Cinnamon Hill needed to be redecorated, but what it needed most was a good cleaning. It appeared that it hadn't seen much cleaning in the two decades since it was built. The same draperies, the same furniture, and the same floor coverings remained. Amanda learned that Eva doted on her roses, but not much else. The draperies hung full of a moist, brown goop. The walls, once painted a soft gray, were an almost indescribable greenish color. The whole place reeked of tobacco.

Not only did Charles and Jonathan keep their pipes lit almost every waking minute, Eva also dipped snuff and kept a wad of it between her bottom lip and her gums all day long. There were spittoons everywhere, but Eva rarely hit them when she spewed an arc of vile brown liquid across the room. It appeared that she made a game of trying to hit the vessel farthest away from where she was sitting. If at the fireplace in the sitting room, she spat in the general direction of the spittoon located next to a chair at the window. She never aimed, nor did she actually look up. She just spat in that general direction. If the spittle hit its target, with a ping, she made not a sound. If it hit the floor with a splat or landed on the rug with a muffled thud, a loud cackle escaped from her lips.

Jonathan hired a group of cleaners to wash down every room in the house and then gave Amanda carte blanche to make the house the way she wanted it. She selected new carpets, furniture, and draperies. She went through the house room by room and changed everything, from floor to ceiling. She also bought new china, silver, and crystal for the dining room.

Charles was pleased with the improvements Amanda made, readily admitting that it needed a new look that was more in keeping with his son's new profession. Eva stayed with her sister in the mountains during the renovations. When she returned, she looked around, uttered a single grunt, and retired to her newly decorated bedchamber.

The refurbishing took months, but by winter, Amanda was bored and lonesome for the companionship of her husband. Jonathan began to spend an occasional evening at the Old Duck Tavern at Armstrong Crossroads, which left her feeling neglected.

Jonathan had passed the Tennessee bar before their wedding and made ambitious plans for his law practice. Charles jumped in and had a nice office built for his son on the rear terrace.

"I'll be able to help people in this community who have never had legal representation before," Jonathan said. "And, if I'm lucky enough to be elected, I'd like to serve in some capacity in the government."

Amanda looked forward to that lifestyle. She was excited at the possibility of becoming the wife of a senator someday, or maybe a governor. With a husband in political office, Amanda could continue the work her grandmother had begun. After she was widowed, Belle Hathaway Hunter had spent the last two decades of her life championing the rights of women.

Amanda waited for Jonathan one night until he returned from the Old Duck Tavern. He had spent two evenings there that week, and she was unhappy. And it was very late when he finally came home.

"I thought I knew you, Jonathan," Amanda said tearfully. "I never dreamed you drank, and certainly not in a vile, filthy place like a tavern."

"You do know me," he insisted.

"No, you've changed these last few months," she said. "And what's happening with your practice? I don't see anyone coming to your office."

"It's just slow in winter. And our neighbors who have attorneys in Greeneville... Once they realize they don't have to travel that far and pay those outlandish fees, they will bring their business to me."

"Really?"

"Things will pick up in the spring. Nothing for you to worry about."

* * *

But by the spring of 1846, Amanda was no happier. Life at Cinnamon Hill was nothing like she had thought it would be. She decided that if she were to have a social life, she would have to create it.

"It's dull here," she complained to Jonathan. "Don't you ever have company? Don't your friends ever stop by for a visit?"

"Absolutely not," said Jonathan. "Too busy."

"You head off to the tavern several nights a week, and I get lonely."

"You should be busy enough taking care of me and the house."

"That does not suffice. I need *people*," she protested. "Rarely did a day go by without someone stopping by for a visit at Hunter House."

"Charles had corn shucking, hog killing day, and such non-sense. I've put an end to that since I started my law practice. Can't have people underfoot all the time."

"Jonathan, I rarely see you these days. Doesn't it bother you that we spend so little time together?"

"Relationships change after marriage," he said. "Trips to the tavern are helping me attract new clients. Men are more likely to talk about their personal situations after they've had a few nips. It's only business."

"You have the companionship of those men at the tavern, while I'm left with your parents. I love them both, but Eva never talks. If Charles says two words to me, she gets angry. Then I just have to go to bed."

"Can't be here and there at the same time, Amanda," Jonathan said.

"Then let me have a little supper," she said. "I can get to know some of the women in the community. I could invite some of your clients."

"Not much for socializing," he said.

"Maybe you should be," she said, with a smile. "It might be good for your practice."

Jonathan relented.

* * *

Amanda invited the more prominent people around Armstrong Crossroads—there weren't many—to a casual Saturday night supper. She served ham, duck, and pheasant, several vegetables, and a selection of desserts. After supper, Amanda served wine and coffee to the women in the parlor. The men preferred whiskey, which Jonathan offered in the library. Amanda thought the occasion was a success and she felt more alive than she had in months.

"You're the talk all over the Valley," Jonathan said, the following night when he returned home from the tavern.

"Why?" Amanda said.

"People are saying that at your supper you flounced around and acted like you were better than the other women."

"I did not. You were there. You saw how I behaved."

"Didn't pay much attention to what you did," he said. "Trying to further my business interests."

"I was just trying to be friendly," she said.

"Tried to tell you people are different here."

"I'll do better next time," she said. "They just need a little more time to get to know me."

"No!" Jonathan shouted. "Men are afraid you'll influence their wives—who seem to think you have free rein to do whatever you want here. Don't want their wives demanding more freedoms at home. What'd you say to those women when you were in the parlor?"

"I just wanted to be interesting."

"You accomplished that. Didn't say you were boring!"

"It's not fair," she whined. "You have a party three or four nights a week with your friends at the tavern."

"Yes," he said, arrogantly, "I buy them a few drinks hoping they'll send some business my way."

"Isn't that expensive—buying all those drinks?"

"Not overly," he answered.

"Then I should be able to have a little party once in a while."

"No more parties!"

Amanda believed that it was essential for her happiness that she be the head of local society. She would just have to find another way to do it.

Mother had taught her that a true sense of self could only be achieved by helping others to lift themselves up from poverty and ignorance.

Maybe living at Cinnamon Hill would offer her the best opportunity to create a social life. In a larger community, she would have to compete with other women for the top spot. Cinnamon Hill was more isolated than she would have liked, but she vowed not to be disheartened.

A few nights later, while Amanda was getting ready for bed, she heard loud voices coming from Jonathan's office. And not just a few voices—several people, laughing and talking. Jonathan must have brought some clients home from the tavern. They should be leaving soon.

But they didn't leave.

She put on her robe and slippers and walked out onto the rear terrace, trying to get Jonathan's attention.

"Your wife wants you," one of the men said, laughing and pointing at her.

Jonathan rushed over to her and whispered, "Get back in the house. You're half-naked."

"Why are these men here?"

"I thought about what you said the other night; it is expensive buying drinks at the tavern. Much cheaper buying the whiskey myself and serving it here at my office."

"Well, I hope it won't happen again any time soon."

"I've ordered a whole case of whiskey, and I won't be drinking at the tavern anymore. I'll have my friends come here. It'll save me money, and you'll have no reason to complain about me being away from home so much."

"That's not what I meant!" she shouted.

"Keep your voice down," he whispered.

"How do you expect me to sleep through this?"

"It'll be over soon. Go back in the house."

She was shocked when she looked closely at the men who were there. They weren't anyone she knew—nor anyone she wanted to know. Their clothes were filthy. They chewed tobacco, and spat wherever they pleased. They were crude and unmannered creatures, from what she could see. She had no idea Jonathan knew such men.

And soon the men began to come every night except Sunday. In fact, Jonathan stayed up later and drank more because he didn't have to stay sober enough to find his way home. For the poor farmers who had been his most constant drinking companions at the tavern, it was a stroke of luck.

Amanda soon realized that the men of those mountains weren't interested in furthering the rights of their wives. They liked their women just the way they were, thank you very much! So, she would have to start slowly building her social life. She invited the wives of Jonathan's drinking mates to a Saturday afternoon tea. She gave several invitations to Jonathan, who would then choose which men to pass them to.

"Another disaster?" he asked.

"Just a quiet afternoon tea," she assured him. "I thought the women might like to see Cinnamon Hill. I'm sure none of them have ever been here."

"No, they haven't," Jonathan said emphatically.

Four poor women came, and one of those dragged six squalling children along with her; the eldest was only eight years of age. They ran through the house and grabbed everything that interested them. Amanda attempted to be a good hostess until she heard a crash in the dining room and ran to find that one of the boys had broken a plate of Grandma Belle's china.

Amanda had set up the dining room table prior to the women's arrival. After showing them how to serve tea on the small round table in the parlor, she intended to show them how to set a table for dinner.

After the mishap of the broken plate, she asked their mother if the children could play outside. Maybe they wouldn't find anything to destroy in the yard.

Eva came running into the hall and shouted, "My roses!"

Certainly nothing wrong with the old crone's hearing!

So, the children remained inside. Now that they were in the dining room, Amanda began to teach the women how to set the table. She set the first place with china, napkin, silver, and glassware in the proper places. The women took turns setting the other places, with Amanda calmly correcting their mistakes, until the table was completely set, except for the broken plate.

By the time they returned to the parlor, the tea was tepid and the teacakes were dry, but Amanda served them anyway. Her guests gulped it all down and prepared to leave. When the mother of the six children stood up, Amanda noticed that someone had spilled tea on her new red damask chair—at least she hoped it was tea.

The afternoon was a complete disaster, but Amanda was determined and invited the women to come back the following Saturday. "Without the children if possible," she said diplomatically. "I hope we can read some poetry, and the noise would be disruptive."

Two of the women giggled when Amanda mentioned poetry, but she paid no attention.

"I really want to come," the mother of all the children said, "but I got no one to leave them with."

"Maybe your husband will stay at home for a few hours with the children. You know, to give you some time away from them."

"He'll be where he is right now," the woman laughed. "At the tavern, drinking with your husband."

"Then bring them, I guess," Amanda said.

The following Saturday, at the appointed hour, Amanda carried three books of poetry from the library to the parlor: Burns, Keats, and Wordsworth. She planned to serve tea and cookies after the poetry reading, but left all of that in the kitchen where the children couldn't get at it.

She placed the poetry books on the marble-topped table in the parlor and waited.

No one came.

Still, Amanda was not disheartened.

"I want to have a picnic," she told Jonathan a few days later.

"What's this now?" Jonathan groaned. "Teas failed miserably—"

Charles cut in to say, "I think it's a wonderful idea. We haven't had a party at Cinnamon Hill in a long time."

"Longer still, if I have anything to say about it," Jonathan muttered.

"Please?" she said in her most pitiful tone. "Charles will help me with the preparations. Won't you, Charles?"

"I'd be glad to help," Charles said, though Eva was glaring at him. "I'll hire some men to set up the tables on sawhorses under the trees in the side yard," he said happily. "Like when we used to have get-togethers. You remember, Jonathan?"

"You know how I hate that sort of thing."

"We won't bother you one bit," Amanda promised. "You can go to the tavern as you always do on Saturday afternoon."

The following Sunday after the sermon at church, Amanda rose. "If I may have a moment, Reverend, before everyone scatters," she said. "I would like to invite everyone to a grand outdoor picnic at Cinnamon Hill next Saturday afternoon at two o'clock."

"Such a fool!" Jonathan shouted on the way home. "You should have told me you were planning to do that! Heaven knows what kind of people will show up."

"It's only the people from church, and I didn't want to play favorites."

"Believe me, they'll invite all their poor relatives!"

"It's the poor people I want to reach," she said. "I can teach them to live a better life."

"When are you going to give up on that stupid idea? These people are just as they want to be. You'll not change them as long as you may live!"

* * *

Amanda and Barbé cooked for three days. Four of the large tables under the trees in the front yard were covered with meats, vegetables, fruits, breads, desserts, and large pitchers of iced tea and lemonade. Amanda hoped to keep the mess to a minimum by serving foods that could be eaten by hand, such as fried chicken and fried cakes. Her neighbors' manners weren't the best, but she would watch over them to avoid any mishaps.

Amanda took the precaution of locking the front door so no nasty-handed children could wallow on her new furniture or break any more of her good dishes.

Charles assured her that everything would be fine.

At the appointed time, twelve families came. Some brought passels of children, aunts, uncles, cousins, and grandparents. One family even brought along a large, slobbery dog. Amanda had never seen most of these people, but she remained calm. Some ate their fill and left, without so much as a word of greeting, farewell, or gratitude.

People kept coming. It was all Barbé could do to carry more food and drink from the kitchen. Amanda busied herself serving people and urging some to sit on the wooden benches beside the tables, but most of them remained standing, grabbing handfuls of food from the tables.

Amanda noticed that the tables were almost bare, except for bones that had been licked clean and thrown back onto the serving plates. She ran to Barbé, who was standing on the front terrace, kneading her brow.

"Come on," Amanda said, "I know you're tired. I'll help you carry out the rest of the food."

"There is no rest," Barbé whispered. "It's gone."

"It can't be," Amanda said, looking back toward the tables. "Don't you know how much food we cooked?"

"Yes, I do. And I know it's gone."

Just then, several children emerged from the front door and brushed past her. "How did you get in there?" Amanda asked, frowning.

"The back door," one of them said. He giggled at his cleverness, as he rubbed his greasy hands on the front of his shirt.

"Out!" Amanda screamed as she walked toward the tables. "Time to go. Everybody. We have no more food!"

Charles ran up to Amanda, his face bright red. "What's the problem, Amanda? You're embarrassing me in front of my neighbors."

"The food's all gone," she whimpered.

"Well, you don't have to yell," he whispered.

"I'm sorry, Charles."

"I'll take care of it," he said.

"I've never seen such a mess," Amanda said after everyone had left. There were remnants of food everywhere—on the tables, on the ground, and spread all over the side yard. She sat down in a chair on the front terrace and wept.

Jonathan heard about the fiasco. When he returned that night, she pretended to be asleep. He leaned down and sassily whispered in her ear, "I told you."

FIVE

Amanda, as troubled as ever, suddenly sensed that she had lost Jonathan's adoration. Nothing she did made the slightest difference in his attitude toward her. One morning she followed him to his office after breakfast. While he worked, she talked about their future together, her hopes and her dreams for them. She cooed and complimented, coddled and cajoled, but in the end, she fretted and pleaded. And he lost patience.

"Told you time and again," Jonathan said, pronouncing every word slowly and succinctly, "there's nothing wrong between us. Stop this foolishness."

"You once looked at me as if you valued me more than anyone else in God's universe. Now your gaze slides right past me without so much as slowing down. What have I done to deserve that?"

"Don't see you falling all over yourself to shower me with affection these days."

"How can I? I never see you," she said tearfully. "Your life is totally separate from mine. I'm living the life you've made for me, and it is beginning to suffocate me!"

He looked at her as if she were speaking a foreign language, and she knew he had not the slightest idea what she was saying, that she might never be able to make him understand how she felt, but she couldn't stop trying.

"Many women would gladly take your place!" he shouted. "Some would give almost anything to have what you have, and live where you live."

"I don't even have pocket money, which I always had at Hunter House. Father made sure I did."

"Want money in your pocket? Will that make you happy? Here," he said, reaching into the safe. "Take it." He threw several bills at her.

"I'm leaving," she cried, picking up the money. "You'll be sorry when something horrible happens to me!"

"Good. Go!" he shouted, waving his arm wildly in her direction, not once looking up from his paperwork.

But where can I go? To Greeneville to buy a new dress. I don't really need one, but a new dress always makes me feel special, if only temporarily.

Charles joyously got the buggy ready and drove Amanda to the dress shop. He chatted with his old friends on the benches in front of the court house while she shopped.

While looking at some new fabric at the dressmaker's shop, Amanda overheard two women talking. Their conversation caught her attention when one of them said something about the snooty wife of that lawyer over at Armstrong Crossroads who invited everybody to a picnic.

"Of course, nobody of any social standing would ever attend such a gathering," one of them said. "And the only people who came were the white trash who get drunk there regularly and all their hungry relatives!" The women laughed raucously. They obviously had no idea what Amanda looked like; they walked right past her.

"The way I hear it," the woman continued, "she didn't like the people who came. So, she threw everybody off the property."

The other woman laughed so hard, she almost knocked the porkpie hat off her head.

"But that's not the worst of it," the first woman said, in a secretive tone, "I must tell you. Some people already know, and others soon will learn, about Armstrong's underhanded tactics in acquiring his new clients. My husband says he went behind the backs of some important attorneys hereabouts and stole their customers right away from them."

"No!" the other one said.

"Yes!" the first woman replied. "It's the worst scandal we've had around here in years!"

* * *

By the time Amanda arrived at Cinnamon Hill, she was hysterical. She didn't want to believe what those women said about Jonathan, and she looked to him for reassurance. He denied the charges, but she could tell he was lying and she couldn't control her anger. When she screamed at him, in words that were barely discernible, he slapped her across the face quite hard. Her first reaction was to slap back. But when she raised her hand, he caught hold of her wrist, and with a twist and a flex, he broke it, as neatly as he would have broken a tea biscuit.

Amanda lived in great pain for days. Charles finally stepped in and took her to his good friend, Dr. Jones. The doctor said it was too late to do anything, and it would never heal properly and would most likely pain her for the rest of her life.

The following day, Charles took Amanda to the high ridges beyond Cinnamon Hill.

The Great Smoky Mountains, part of the ancient Appalachians, extended through Northeast Tennessee along a northeast to southwest corridor. Millions of years ago, pressures inside the earth pushed the rocky formations up above the surface of the earth. Wind, water, and other forces of nature had rounded and eroded them. An almost endless variety of plant life thrived in the warm, wet atmosphere of the Great Smokies. The forests emitted a rich, earthy aroma.

"Go past that pine there, up the path on the left," Charles told her, "then straight on ahead."

"Where am I going?" she asked.

"There's an old Cherokee squaw lives in a hut up there. She collects herbs, roots, and medicinal plants in the forests. She'll make a poultice or mustard plaster to take the pain out of that wrist for you."

"Aren't you coming with me?"

"No," Charles said, shaking his head, "and you better never let anyone know I brought you here. Evalinda hates Indians more than she hates black folks. When I say hate, I mean *hate!*"

"You can't just leave me here," Amanda said, on the verge of tears. "How will I get home?"

"She'll show you. I'm sorry about all this, Amanda," he said, his voice softening. "I'm sure you've figured out by now that I'm a spineless old coward. It hurts me too much to go against my family, even when I know they're wrong."

"I'm sure it does," she said kindly. "Thank you for telling me that."

"Go on, now," he told her. "There's no danger."

Amanda suddenly passed from a dense wood into a small clearing. Directly in front of her, a sheer bluff stretched straight up to the sky. She didn't notice the log hut that was built in front of it at first.

A gruff voice greeted her, along with an old musket that protruded from a small opening in the front door of the hut. "Get away from here," the voice said.

Amanda stopped in her tracks. She walked backward a few steps. "I'm sorry," she called out. "I mean no harm."

The muzzle of the musket disappeared. After a few moments, the Cherokee woman appeared in the doorway of the hut. "Come," she said, motioning with her arm.

Amanda approached warily. "Mr. Charles brought me. You know, Charles Armstrong?"

"Yes, I do," she said. "He's a fine man."

A few strands of gray streaked through the squaw's black hair, which was plaited into two thick braids. Large haunted eyes dominated her face, but didn't hide the scar that ran diagonally across it. It had been a deep cut.

"Something troubling you today?" the woman asked.

"My husband broke my wrist," Amanda said. Then, she was suddenly embarrassed at having to tell a complete stranger that her husband had abused her. "Do you have a husband?" she asked.

"No, but I know such relationships are seldom easy."

"It's a lovely spot you have here," Amanda said, looking around, "but it's so small."

"It suits my needs. I have a garden back there at the edge of the forest."

"Have you thought about clearing away more of the timber?"

"Oh, I don't own this land," the woman replied without inflection.

Amanda was afraid she had offended her.

"I am called Galilani," the woman finally said. "It means 'friendly' in the Cherokee language."

Maybe not the best name for your strong personality.

Sit," the woman said, motioning toward two slat-backed chairs on the porch attached to the front of the hut.

"Thank you," Amanda said reverently and waited for the woman to be seated first. "My name is Amanda Armstrong."

Amanda was suddenly awed by the woman's presence, a feeling she couldn't explain. It had nothing to do with the gray in her hair, nor the calmness of her demeanor. She had no reason to believe this woman was any wiser than any other person she had ever met. But maybe that was just what she felt: a profound respect for Galilani's wisdom, suddenly wanting to know everything that lurked behind those dark eyes.

"You are a new bride?"

"Just over a year now," Amanda answered shyly. "I have a beautiful home. I don't know why I can't be happy."

"Possessions will never bring you happiness."

Amanda didn't know how to respond to that remark.

"No little ones yet?"

"No," Amanda said. "Do you have children?"

"No." The woman volunteered nothing more.

"You have no family?" Amanda asked.

"No more," she said, staring off into the distance. "My mother was stubborn," she finally said. "She refused to relinquish the old Cherokee ways. I love that way of life, and I continue it here, in her honor."

"It sounds like your mother was very strong."

"Women are revered in Cherokee society. Generations pass down from the mother's lineage, not the father's. My mother was the storyteller, the historian, of our clan. Once our people began to follow the ways of the whites, they lost interest in the old tales. But she taught them to me."

"Why didn't you go west with your people?"

"That's a long story I might tell you someday."

Amanda nodded.

"Would you like to learn about the forest?" the squaw asked. "So that you can travel wherever you choose and never get lost?"

"Yes, I would. That's exactly what I need right now: to be independent."

"I will also teach you to protect yourself. There are evil creatures living in these mountains."

"Bobcats?"

"No," the woman said ominously. "Men. Evil men."

"Please teach me," Amanda pleaded. "I can't be responsible for my actions if I'm forced to spend all my days with my mother-in-law," she said dramatically, clutching at her throat and crossing her eyes.

Galilani smiled.

"Would you mind if I stayed here a while?" Amanda asked. "I won't be in the way, I promise."

"Why would you stay?" the woman asked, a frown on her face.

"Mr. Charles asked me to. His wife would be very angry if she found out he brought me here."

"Yes," Galilani said, "I remember her. You can stay as long as you like. I have work to do in the cave if I am to make a bandage for your wrist. Come inside. Help yourself if you are hungry."

Amanda soon learned that there was always a small pot of beans or stew simmering at the edge of the fireplace in Galilani's hut, and a fresh loaf of bean bread made daily.

* * *

Amanda arrived at Cinnamon Hill just as Jonathan was returning to his office after supper. He stepped out of the back door as she reached the porch.

"Oh, there you are," he said. "Go tell my father and Barbé you're home. They've been worried about you."

Amanda seethed. How could he be so heartless? He denied her even the satisfaction of knowing that he was concerned for one minute during her absence. The more she pushed for his attention, the more he ignored her. It had become almost a game between them.

She was sure that Jonathan shared his mother's feelings about the Indians, but by the time he discovered where she was spending her afternoons, she didn't care if he knew, nor whether he approved.

The next afternoon Amanda made her first excursion with Galilani. It was only a rudimentary exercise, designed to teach Amanda to find her way through the forests, hills, and waterways that surrounded Galilani's hut. She learned to determine where she was at any given time by remembering certain landmarks, such as a tree, a rock, or a creek.

Then Galilani began to teach her about hunting in the mountains. She moved swiftly through the forest and along rippling streams, snipping wild herbs and pulling roots as she went, poking everything she collected into a large leather pouch draped across her shoulder. At the end of the day, she laid out the contents of the pouch on a ledge in the cave behind her hut: fruits and berries to be pickled, spiced, or dried; plants and herbs that she used to season food and to make medicines; and sassafras root for tea.

On her way home, Amanda listened to the language of the mountains: the twittering of birds, the chattering of squirrels, and the tinkle of trickling creeks. She found a spot where a little slice of sunlight peeked through the lush greenery of the trees and lay down on her back, the sun on her face, her arms and legs extended, and listened to the conversation.

* * *

When the full story of Jonathan's devious tactics became known, it was obvious that he had been worried about his lack of business. Amanda had been right; it wasn't going well. He had gone to every person he knew and told them he could handle all of their legal problems, and do so cheaper than their present counselor. He made many enemies, and it wasn't only the lawyers he alienated. Many people in the community shunned him and Amanda.

In time, Jonathan was excused for his bad behavior, but it seemed that Amanda would never be forgiven. Jonathan was tolerated because he was Charles's son. She was a stranger.

Jonathan soon lost most of the clients he had lured away from other attorneys. A few stayed with him. Their desire to save money outweighed their loyalty to their previous lawyers and the disapproval of their community. In the end, he was left with mostly poor farmers as clients, and they rarely paid their attorney fees.

Charles, who was loved universally, must have been crushed by the scandal, but people continued to greet him joyously at church and other functions. Those same people looked right past Amanda as if she didn't exist.

She had never been treated so badly. She wasn't sure if she could continue in her marriage. She went alone to Abingdon and talked to Mother and Father about her life at Cinnamon Hill. They advised her to stay with Jonathan and make the best of it. Divorcees were looked down upon, even if one partner was making the other miserable. Shortly after that trip Amanda's father set up a trust making sure she would have her own money.

One morning after church, Amanda was standing by the buggy waiting for Charles, who was talking to some local men. Jonathan was standing at the edge of the group but wasn't participating in the conversation.

The Widow Wilkes—that's the only name Amanda had ever heard her called—approached Amanda in the churchyard. The woman was tall and broad-shouldered with bright green eyes in a plain face that was just beginning to show its age.

"Good sermon this morning," the woman said in a strong baritone voice.

"Very fine," Amanda said politely.

"How is Miss Eva faring these days?" the woman asked.

"As well as ever, I suppose."

"Well, that's too bad." The woman laughed heartily.

"Oh—you're about as fond of her as I am, I see," Amanda said.

"She never did fit in down here."

"Down here?"

"People who're raised in the wild ways of the mountains don't usually survive well down here in the valley. They're taught no manners. Eva was very backward and hardly ever spoke when Mr. Charles brought her here as his bride."

"She still rarely speaks," Amanda said.

"Mr. Charles happened upon her on a hunting trip, the story goes. I've always thought that was the attraction for him—he got to show her a whole new world down here. It seems that the spell wore off after a few years, but to his credit, he is living out his commitment to her. She cemented her place in his life when she gave birth to Jonathan. He adores that boy, I'm sorry to say."

"Why do you say that?" Amanda asked.

"Jonathan's taken advantage of his father at every turn and has run his good name into the mire with each new so-called moneymaking venture. He'll put him in the poor house yet."

"Really?" Amanda was having a hard time believing what this woman was saying.

"I hear he's spending money faster than Mr. Charles can make it. A man his age shouldn't have to work as hard as he does. He should be enjoying the fruits of his labor, not still supporting his son by running that mill on Bottom Creek. If you think you've grabbed onto a rich one, honey, you are sorely mistaken. Once Mr. Charles is gone, there'll be nothing left but the house and the land."

"Oh, I'm sure that's not true," Amanda stammered. "He's doing much better with his law practice—or he was, until those rumors came out."

"See what I'm saying?" The woman put her head close to Amanda's and whispered, "The people around here think you're a big flirt. I shouldn't tell you this, but I know what it's like to be a pariah."

"A pariah?"

"I'm looked down upon because of me and Mr. Charles," the woman said secretively. "People always think they can hide their trysts, but someone always finds out."

When Amanda just stared at her, she said, "You didn't know?"

"What?"

"Charles Armstrong and I are keeping company," she said discreetly. "I don't know why I'm telling you this—and you mustn't repeat it, or things will be tougher for Mr. Charles.

"You and Charles are..."

"Lovers. Yes," the woman said, nodding. "Is that so hard to believe?"

"Well, no," Amanda said. "But I didn't think Charles was the kind of man who..."

"Who'd be unfaithful?"

"Well, yes," Amanda stammered.

"How do you think he's stayed with Eva all these years? Did she expect him to be celibate for the rest of his life? The man is a saint."

Amanda didn't respond. She stared at Charles and Jonathan, willing them to come rescue her from this creature.

"I'm sorry," the woman said, softening her voice. "I shouldn't have spoken so plain, but everyone knows Eva was so traumatized by the pain of Jonathan's birth that she never allowed Charles to touch her again."

"What did you say?"

"Charles and I are lovers," the woman said, becoming agitated.

"What did you say before? About me being a flirt?"

"This'll upset you, but you have a right to know."

"What, for Heaven's sake?" Amanda demanded.

"Everybody thinks you're a big flirt."

"Everybody flirts, don't they?"

"Not here, you don't," the Widow Wilkes warned. "Women look at you crosswise if you so much as say 'good morning' to their husbands. Especially me, since I been a widow all these years."

"They're coming," Amanda whispered to the woman. "Nice talking to you," Amanda said, loud enough for Charles and Jonathan to hear.

"And how are you today, Widow Wilkes?" Charles asked graciously, tipping his hat.

"As good as ever, Mr. Charles," she responded. When she looked at Charles, her whole face lit up.

"God grant that it will always be so," he said graciously. He climbed up into the buggy, and they were off.

Amanda looked back at the woman. She stood exactly where they had left her, with one gloved hand raised in farewell.

SIX

————◆»✦«◆————

May 1863

First thing after breakfast one fine May morning, Mr. Bixby came to Cinnamon Hill. Amanda knew it must be bad news for him to come in person. The telegram he brought was from Mother.

David killed at Chancellorsville. Come quickly.

Amanda ran immediately to Jonathan's office, weeping, crushed by the news of her brother's death.

"I want to leave for Hunter House today," she said tearfully.

"Can't," he said bluntly. "Have to appear before the magistrate this afternoon. First new case I've had in weeks, and I will not abandon it. We need the money."

"We're short on money?"

"Of course not! Meant to say I want the work," he stammered. "You'll have to go alone. I'll follow tomorrow."

"Barbé wants to go. She loves David as much as I do."

"Absolutely not. Can't leave the house unattended with hungry soldiers about."

"You can't leave her here alone," Amanda said, crying again.

"I'll fetch Juba," Jonathan said. "He'll have to stay with her until we get back."

"You know he won't want to leave the shop if he has work there."

"Then he'll come at the barrel of my gun!"

Before the war, Amanda would have just traveled to Greeneville and boarded the train, which ran straight up to Abingdon. But the war had threatened the safety of train travel, like everything else.

The railroad was of supreme importance to both the Yankees and the Confederates, especially the railroad bridges, massive wooden structures spanning hundreds of feet across valleys and streams. They were easily burned and took weeks to rebuild. Along those tracks, men, supplies, and critical communications passed from the main armies in Virginia to the troops west of the Appalachians. The army that controlled the railroad would control Northeast Tennessee.

Soon after Tennessee seceded from the Union, the Rebels rushed in and posted garrisons at all strategically located railroad stations and bridges. They retained possession in the spring of 1863, but the Yankees had twice burned the high bridges across the Holston and Watauga Rivers.

"Jonathan, I can't travel alone."

"You and Luke will have to go it alone. He's a strong boy. He can protect you."

"Then at least go rig up the horse and carriage while we pack."

"Roads are seas of mud this time of year. Better to go on horseback."

Amanda knew what she and Luke had to look forward to on their journey to Virginia and traveling without Jonathan only increased her anxiety.

Several times their horses' hooves were sucked in by the muck. Luke had to climb down and lead them out of the mire. At some spots the roads were impassable, and they were forced to detour on other roads or attempt passage through the adjacent fields. It was the worst journey she had ever undertaken.

Abingdon was a welcome spot of civilization in the wilderness, encompassing a few broad streets graced by large well-kept homes.

Amanda considered stopping at David's house there, but she was sure his wife and children would already be at Mother's.

Amanda was relieved to see Hunter House in the distance. The Georgian-style country estate was really a plantation mansion transferred west—along with all the customs and the slaves. The fifteen-room mansion was located at the center of a park of about twenty acres, surrounded by spreading trees, flowering shrubs, and borders of odorous boxwood. When Amanda was a little girl, she had thought it was a magical castle.

The house was constructed of soft red brick and had identical stone-pillared porticoes on the road front and the riverfront, looking the same to travelers on land and water. The house consisted of three distinct sections: a huge rectangular center block that rose three full floors above the high basement and symmetrical two-story wings on either side. From each portico, white marble steps led to a dark hall that ran the full depth of the house. Halfway down this hall was a cross hall that contained staircases to the upper floors and connected with the wings.

Amanda left the horses to be tended by one of the servants and asked Luke to take their bags upstairs. She gave her boots to a servant to be cleaned. Though she was a muddy mess and her hair hung in sodden strips on her face, she was anxious to find her mother.

She entered the center hall slowly, trying to prepare herself for the sight of a coffin containing David's body there—where her father's body had been laid out barely a year ago, on a day that seemed so painfully recent, and at other times, so long ago.

There was no coffin.

Life at Hunter House was one of simple elegance and comfort. A large army of slaves worked behind the scenes to make this life possible. The patina of antique furniture, the sheen of old silver, and a bouquet of fresh flowers in every room combined to create an atmosphere of charm and beauty as glamorous as any of the palatial homes in Richmond.

Mother wasn't in the Green Room. The servants were busy setting the tables. No one knew how many times the table might have to be set that night before everyone was fed. It was a sign of respect to allow the older and more important guests to eat at the first table. After they were finished, clean dishes and fresh servings of food were brought to the table, then the second table would begin.

Amanda found Mother in the kitchen and ran to her with arms outstretched, already wracked with sobs and buried her face in Mother's shoulder. The servants began to wail.

"They have been crying like this since the news first came," her mother said. "I simply must regain some control here, or no one will have anything to eat tonight. The parlor is already full of guests with more arriving by the minute."

"Where's Mattie?" Amanda asked. Mattie was Mother's head cook.

"She has run away from home with some slaves down the road. We are so scared for her."

Elizabeth Hunter was a strong and decisive woman. She hadn't been interested in her husband's businesses. Hunter House was her domain, but she was a kind boss. She worked with her servants. They didn't fear her, but they hated to disappoint her. A sideways glance or a stiffening of her already ramrod-straight back spoke volumes.

Amanda grabbed both of Mother's hands and promised to take care of supper.

"See to your guests in the parlor. You're much better at that than I am," Amanda said with a half-hearted smile.

Amanda thought Mother was looking older. She swore she weighed the same as always, but Amanda thought she looked thinner. Her hair had turned completely gray since Father was killed. Still, she was the most beautiful woman Amanda had ever seen. Her complexion was perfect, her eyes crystal blue. She still applied her makeup and dressed in fine clothes every morning, as if the Queen of England were coming to dinner.

Amanda's sister Penelope and her family had just arrived from Fredericksburg. Penelope was five years older than Amanda. They had never been close.

With meal preparations organized, Amanda escaped to the room she always occupied at Hunter House, the Rose Room. It had been her room when she was a girl, a beautiful chamber with quaint old furniture, spotless linens, and a glass bell on the bedside table to summon the servants. The four-poster was covered by a white canopy piped in rose pink with a flowered curtain draping down at the head. A pink and white calico quilt covered the bed.

On a small table by the window, Amanda found a book of poetry, which she suspected Mother had chosen especially for her. She wondered how Mother remembered all the little details of comfort most people overlooked, always doing a little special something for each of her guests.

After she had washed all reminders of the trip from her hair and body and changed into clean clothes, Amanda sat in the chair by the window and picked up the book. Some words of comfort might soothe the ache in her heart, but her mind couldn't grasp the meaning of the words.

She had thought she needed some time alone, but the room was too confining. Nor did she want to greet the visitors. Of course, their every word was of David. She decided to go for a walk.

Across the hall, the younger grandchildren would crowd into the large corner room, where their adoring grandmother had created their own private dormitory with six single beds. Amanda peeked into the open doorway and saw three little valises inside the door that belonged to David's children.

She passed the door to the room next to hers, the room that was David's when they were children. Her hand touched the knob, but she pulled back.

On David's last visit, on furlough, he had told the family that he planned to move back to Hunter House and to restore the farm to its original condition. The war, he said, had changed the way he looked at life. Mother had been elated. Now, that dream would never be realized.

Outside, the cool breeze felt good on Amanda's face. She entered her father's office in the carriage house. It had been maintained just as it was on the day he'd left to fight in the Confederate army. Amanda almost expected to see him sitting at the desk, pulling off his old straw hat, and mopping his sweaty forehead with a red bandanna.

Amanda couldn't visit Hunter House without spending some time in Father's office, touching his things: his accounting books, his field hat that was so worn it was shiny, the jacket he wore in cold weather. One of his soft flannel shirts still hung across the back of the office chair. She caressed her cheek with it.

A large map, yellowed by time, hung on the wall behind his desk. He had used that map to teach Amanda about the world, hoping she would be his traveling companion and would enjoy going abroad as much as he did. He already knew that Mother, Penelope, and David were homebodies. A tiny tack marked each place Father had visited. She went with him to New York when she was fourteen, but he must have sensed her homesickness. They stayed only a few days.

I should have offered to go with him again. I was the one he tried to instill with a sense of adventure and a hunger for knowledge. I was the one who disappointed him terribly. He was just too kind to say so.

They had talked frequently about her future. With Father's encouragement, she was beginning to believe that she could do whatever she wanted with her life, but it had all vanished like a wisp the moment she met Jonathan Armstrong.

To the east of the house was a hillside garden full of wildflowers. A network of walks and footpaths created intricate patterns. Being there only reminded her of David and the days they spent together. Time seemed endless then.

In good weather, she and David roamed the property. They played tag along these garden paths, pestering Mother while she worked in the flowerbeds. They suited their play to the seasons: made necklaces of jasmine in March, played hide-and-seek among the lilacs in May, watched the hummingbirds hover around the honeysuckle in June and July, stole fruit from the orchards whenever available, and swung on stripped grapevines in the fall. They fished, hunted, built forts, and rode horseback, always trying to get the better of each other.

In very hot weather, Mother kept them inside. They took their toys and books to the central hall, where there was usually a breeze blowing up from the river below or drifting down from the cool woods to the west. They learned hymns and Bible verses during morning prayers at the dining room table, and on Sunday mornings, the whole family sat together at Old Christ Church down the road. They were taught to be clean, polite, and well mannered, especially when away from home or in the company of visitors. They studied their lessons at night in the library. Amanda often nodded off over her books, exhausted by her wanderings through woods and field with David that day.

She recognized early on how lucky she was. Not everyone, not even many of her friends, had the things they had: a wonderful home in which to grow and learn, an almost endless array of material possessions, an appreciation of books and nature, their parents' kind and gentle voices, gardens and woods to run and play in, and cornbread baked in an iron skillet.

Hunter House was famous back then as a highly productive wheat farm. She and David went with the women in the afternoon to take pieces of pie to the workers in the field. They followed the slaves as they cut the grain, swinging their cradles in perfect rhythm, and delighted in their singing—mellow voices raised in rich African rhythms. The binders followed the cradlers, and tied up the bundles of wheat; next came the men who formed the shocks of grain.

She and David romped through the tall golden wheat at sunset. With closed eyes and arms outstretched, they fell backward on the springy stalks of wheat and watched the lightning bugs circle overhead. At those times, giggling with her brother, Amanda experienced complete joy.

* * *

Amanda could think of no more heartwarming sight than looking into the family parlor at Hunter House and seeing the massive fireplace ablaze. The walk through the gardens had improved her mood, but she returned to the house knowing that her brother's body had been delivered while she was gone. She had caught sight of a military ambulance headed in the direction of Abingdon.

She returned to her room after supper to read the letter that had arrived with David's body. It was written by his commanding officer. The letter read:

> *This place called Chancellorsville, where the Yanks have set up their headquarters, consists of one large brick house at a crossroads about ten miles west of our lines at Fredericksburg. It is located a mile or so within a forest known as the Wilderness, a twisted mass of immature oak and vine-covered pine that stretches across many acres.*
>
> *David read his Bible by the first ray of light every morning, then placed it in his pocket over his heart. He waited patiently for his orders, which he performed with diligence and care. A finer man I know I will never meet. A bullet through the head took him down.*

When Amanda read that last sentence, she dropped the letter and screamed. The words were so...well, abrupt. She realized that the painstaking description of the forest were the meanderings of a man who was avoiding the task before him. Then, those eight little words. The loss of a life should take longer than that, especially one so full of love and kindness. She would have admired David even if he hadn't been her brother. They had talked for hours about what life really meant.

David told her once that human beings would be more than arrogant to think that we could make the slightest difference in a world so big, but we must still try. For in the trying, we might touch each other, and maybe that one tiny fingerprint wouldn't fade after we're gone. Nobility was to be found in the effort, he said, not the result.

As she bent to pick up the letter, Mother and Penelope came running through the door.

"Are you all right?" they asked in unison.

"I'm sorry to frighten you," she said softly. "I'm fine."

"Are you sure?" Mother asked.

Amanda nodded and wiped the tears from her face with the backs of her hands.

Alone again, she laid the letter aside and held her hands straight up at shoulder height, as a mime might do in trying to escape from an imaginary box. She had almost forgotten this. After running all the way home, she and David would stop and press their hands together, palm to palm, fingertip to fingertip. And if they stood very still, they could feel each other's heartbeat. Now she sensed David's hands pressing against hers, and she was at peace.

She would cry, of course, and she would miss him always. But her tears would be for her family, for the void left in all their lives by his death.

She picked up the letter and began to read again:

I have previously thought myself hardened to war, but the events of this day have left me to wonder whether any cause can justify such loss. I am sure you are aware of the exceptional man your son was, and you can be assured that he was as loved here as he was at home.

We have sent the men under his command to the rear for the time being. They are so shocked and heartbroken we doubt that they are capable of defending themselves.

I will try to visit Hunter House after the war. David talked of it so often I almost feel like I have already been there. I have never met a man so completely devoted to his family. I hope you can find solace in knowing that he did not suffer.

Brigadier General Albert Sommers
Chancellorsville, Virginia
May 2, 1863

* * *

Downstairs, Amanda found Jeremy, David's youngest child. The boy didn't understand death, but clearly understood that Daddy wouldn't be coming home ever again. She lifted his little body and carried him to a chair in the corner of the parlor.

"Daddy asked me to tell you that he is with God in Heaven," she whispered, "and when it's your turn to go, he will be there waiting for you."

"I want to go now," Jeremy sobbed.

"Only God can decide when it's your time to go, so you have to wait. Do you understand?"

He nodded his dear little head and soon fell asleep in her arms. She wouldn't give him up to be put to bed for hours. He was a part of David she could still hold on to.

* * *

The following afternoon David was buried with great military flair. Confederate soldiers from local garrisons marched in the procession from the church to the cemetery. Amanda led David's horse with its empty saddle. Mother and Penelope walked beside her.

Amanda had never seen Mother so utterly crushed. That evening, at her request, everyone gathered in the family parlor, the Blue Room.

"Tonight, we should remember David. His goodness..." Mrs. Hunter paused, her thoughts seeming to stray. "He fought in twelve battles for his country. His courage, I am told, was the finest ever known, and we are proud. We know he loved us, and he wouldn't want us to suffer at his passing. We must remember that through the difficult days to come," she managed to say before her voice gave way.

Seeing her so broken down, the servants began to wail, especially David's servants, who had come with his wife and children. Jonathan, who had been standing at the very back, had pushed through the crowd and left the room during Mother's speech. Amanda followed him to the music room across the hall.

"How rude of you to leave while Mother was talking," she said, trying to keep her voice down.

He had arrived barely in time to attend the funeral, leaving her to worry about his safety—and to wonder if he had decided not to come at all.

"What is the matter with you, Jonathan?"

"You buried the man," he said. "Can't you let him be?"

"And you would have us do what? Act as if he never existed?"

"Better than continuously talking about him. You hunters have to wallow in your grief, expressing your every little emotion beyond the limits of human endurance. And," he continued, flinging his arms, "God forbid you should become overwrought! For then you're too agitated to make any sense whatsoever. But you repeat yourselves, and say the same thing over and over."

"Like you're doing right now?" Amanda said. "I guess it's better for everyone to keep their mouths shut like you and Eva, so everyone around you can be uncomfortable all the time and wonder what it is you're feeling. You might as well have stayed home, for all the help you've been to me since you arrived."

"That can be easily remedied," he said.

"Go ahead!" she shouted. "I can't stand the sight of you right now."

When Amanda saw him later, he had been into the drink—he always carried whiskey in his saddlebags—and was in a mellow mood, but she went to bed without him.

* * *

Mother stood on the back portico, trying to say goodbye to Amanda. "I thought burying your father was the most difficult task I would ever face," she said. "Now I pray that losing one of my children is the worst pain I will experience in this world. If there is a greater hardship, I will not survive it."

"I can't believe that God would allow another member of our family to be sacrificed to this horrible war," Amanda said.

"Please stay on with me a few days more," Mother begged. "Everyone is leaving me at once."

"Penelope said she would stay on a few days."

"She's not strong like you."

Amanda was overcome.

I'm strong? My Lord! Where did she ever get such an idea?

"I'll ask Jonathan," she finally managed to say.

"If he's concerned about your welfare, please tell him I will send one of the servants to deliver you home safely."

"How can I refuse her?" Amanda told Jonathan, who was standing nearby, waiting impatiently for Amanda to say her good-byes.

"Just say you can't stay," he said.

"I've never seen her so shaken."

"Who'll take care of me if you stay? Of Luke?" Jonathan said.

"Barbé is capable of—"

"No," he said resolutely.

"Please," she begged, "I can't leave her in such a state."

"Come home now, or don't come home at all," he said, and mounted his horse.

What an ass! I am so tempted to call his bluff, but I worry too much for Luke's safety to be away indefinitely. Luke thinks staying at Mother's is boring—so I have no chance in trying to get him to stay with her. And who knows what new rumors might begin to surface about the Armstrongs?!

* * *

The night before the last leg of their journey home, the Armstrongs stopped to stay with their friends, the Andersons. Jonathan didn't care much for the Andersons—he suspected they were Confederate sympathizers—but Amanda begged, and he finally relented. The Andersons served them a wonderful supper, and Amanda enjoyed a few hours of conversation that had nothing to do with death or war.

Maybe Amanda and Luke lingered too long at the breakfast table the next morning, or maybe he was still angry with her. Whatever the reason, as soon as he gulped down his breakfast, Jonathan went to make sure the horses were ready for their departure.

Mr. Anderson asked Luke if he was still following the activities of General John Hunt Morgan. Luke's eyes lit up at an opportunity to discuss his hero. Jonathan came in to hurry them along, and soon discovered the topic of conversation.

"Stupid to admire such a murderer," Jonathan taunted Luke.

"He's not a murderer!" Luke shouted, his face turning bright red. "He protects civilians and doesn't allow their homes to be burned or sacked. He's the finest gentleman I know."

"You don't know him," Jonathan said.

Normally, Luke would back down, but Amanda saw a fire in his eyes she hadn't seen before.

"This is neither the time nor the place for this conversation," Amanda interjected.

"Morgan doesn't kill," Luke said defiantly. "He has done a great good for the Confederacy. He has burned bridges, blown up tunnels, tore up railroad tracks, and captured supply depots, but nowhere have I heard of him murdering anyone." Luke was seething.

"Son, you are just being naive," Jonathan said in a superior tone. "He's a lying, thieving, low-down Confederate rat."

"You take that back!" Luke screamed.

"Jonathan, please," Amanda begged, pulling on his arm.

"Settle down now, son," said Mr. Anderson. He put one of his large hands on the nape of Luke's neck, the other on his arm, and walked Luke out to his horse. He didn't release his hold on Luke until he had calmed down a little.

Luke spoke not a word all the way home. Amanda tried to turn her thoughts away from her family's troubles, from Luke's stony silence and the sure knowledge that this was not just another father-son spat and would not pass quickly.

Amanda thought Luke's hero worship could only lead to disappointment. She realized, as most people seemed to have forgotten in their romantic notions about the war, that these were only ordinary men who had been thrust into a place of prominence by unusual circumstances. Some would succeed; many would fail.

Passing through Greeneville on their way home, Amanda admired the town. Its appearance hadn't changed much since the beginning of the war, but many businesses had been forced to close. The cool waters of Big Spring in the heart of town had first attracted settlers in the 1700s. Lovely homes, churches, and places of business bordered its tree-lined streets.

As they passed the Williams house, Amanda was tempted to stop and spend a moment with Catherine, now a widow, but decided against it. They who had been acquainted for many years.

There was discomfort in the town regarding the politics of the members of that household. Catherine, now the head of the family, was an avowed Confederate and didn't care who knew it; one of her sons was in the Union army, and his wife lived there with his mother.

* * *

About a mile from home, Luke urged his horse forward and rode ahead of Amanda. Jonathan had ridden so far in advance that she hadn't seen him for hours.

When Amanda arrived at Cinnamon Hill, Jonathan and Luke were shouting at each other on the front terrace. Luke stood beside his little mare, Lady, the reins still in his hand. The horse was frightened by the loud voices and reared up, trying to break free of Luke's hold on her.

"You can't see anyone else's point of view, can you, Father?" Luke shouted. "Your opinion is always right."

"Yes," Jonathan said after a moment's pause. "I've lived much longer than you, and I know a good deal more than you will ever know."

"If it means I'd turn out like you, then I don't want to know it. I'm ashamed you are my father!" Luke jumped into the saddle and took off in a rush of pounding hooves.

Jonathan grabbed at the reins, but he couldn't hold onto them.

Luke didn't come home that night.

SEVEN

———◆◆◆———

By dawn the next morning, Amanda was on the verge of collapse. She had slept little, only short naps in her rocker by the sitting room fire, which she kept burning brightly through the night. Once, she awoke abruptly to the sound of horses' hooves, but soon realized she had been dreaming.

The remainder of the night she paced around the sitting room, running to the window when the slightest noise broke the silence. She hadn't seen Jonathan during the night. She sometimes heard his footsteps in the hall and the parlor. By midnight, his shuffling steps had stopped altogether.

When the first thready light of morning crept over the high ridge, she found Jonathan asleep in a high-backed chair he had pulled up to the front window in the parlor. She pressed her hand on his shoulder and shook it.

"I'm going to look for Luke. With you or without you," she said in a voice made gruff by inhaling the smoke from the fireplace all night.

"I need coffee," he said, pulling his stiff body out of the chair.

"We haven't had coffee in months. Let's go."

They saddled their horses, Bean and Jody, and rode off. At the main road, Jonathan told Amanda to ride in the direction of Greeneville. He would head toward the Crossroads. But Amanda already knew where her first stop would be.

The path that led to Crocker's cabin was almost directly across the Greeneville Road from the entrance to Cinnamon Hill, but it went on for what seemed like a mile before the house came into view.

Amanda slowed her horse to a walk, trying to approach undetected, but she was soon met by a passel of barking dogs. They nipped at Jody's hooves and spooked her. Crocker slipped out the front door and hustled to meet her. A napkin was tucked into his shirt collar, its tattered edges stuffed behind his suspenders.

"Have you seen Luke?" she asked, watching his face for any evidence of deceit.

"Not since last night," he said, that sick grin she hated so much on his face. There were biscuit crumbs in his beard.

Luke could be staring at her from that open window in the hayloft right then. Her eyes searched that opening, the barn door below, and the cabin's windows for movement, but saw nothing.

"What time last night?" she asked.

"About ten, I suppose," he said, scratching his head. "When I went to bed."

"He left then?"

"Yeah," he said noncommittally. "He left the house about that time."

"Is he still here—somewhere?"

"Not that I know of."

"Could I look around a bit?" she asked impatiently.

"We're still having breakfast," he said, fluttering his napkin toward her, in case she hadn't noticed.

Her eyes burned, her head ached, and at that moment, she hated that old man more than she had ever thought herself capable of hating anyone. She suspected he was deliberately being vague.

"Will you tell him I'm looking for him?" she said angrily.

"If I see him," the old codger said, so obviously enjoying watching her twist in the wind. He went tripping back into the house, his napkin still flapping.

Amanda met Jonathan back at the barn at the appointed time, nine o'clock. He hadn't found Luke. Nor had anyone seen him.

"I'm going back out to look," she said, not bothering to dismount.

"Where? Do whatever you want," Jonathan said, shaking his head. "I'm having breakfast."

Reluctantly, she followed him to the house and ate breakfast with Barbé in the kitchen, what little she could keep down.

Later in the day, she rode to one of the high ridges behind the farm. As one of Jonathan's manhood tests, Luke had built a lean-to and had spent the night alone there a few times. She didn't remember exactly where it was, but eventually found it. The fire ring, enclosed by a circle of stones, was cold. Nothing had been disturbed. Nothing indicated that anyone had been there for weeks.

Amanda was losing hope. A thought had nagged at her all day: Luke might have gone off to find General John Hunt Morgan, who had been recently reported to be at Liberty, Tennessee, one hundred and fifty miles west. Was he angry enough with his father to undertake such a journey? She prayed not.

Another restless, sleepless night left Amanda almost helpless. The throbbing pain behind her eyes and forehead, the sick feeling in her heart, would be enough for any average Southern lady to stay abed for the day. But she couldn't be still.

Jonathan ate breakfast and went to his office, as if nothing was wrong.

Don't you care at all that your son has been gone for two long, frightful nights? How did I ever come to avow my love and life to such a man as you?

Amanda saddled Jody and made a roundabout trip from Cinnamon Hill to the Crossroads. She traveled the old farm roads and Indian trails, searching anywhere she could think of that Luke might be. She stopped again at Crocker's cabin. He was as noncommittal as he had been the day before, but again she had the strange feeling that Luke was nearby. If he was planning to run away to join the army, she desperately wanted to see him one last time.

"Still ain't seen him," Crocker said.

"Would you tell me if he was here?" she shouted.

"Course I would," he muttered.

"Listen to me, old man," she said vehemently, "if I ever find out that you've been harboring my son and lying to me about it, I will put a bullet between your eyes!" She couldn't believe such words had come from her lips, but she meant every single one.

"You couldn't find my eyes down the barrel of a cannon," he scoffed with an evil grin.

"My father taught me to shoot when I was a girl," she said coldly. "I abhor guns, but you'd be surprised what a good shot I am."

For the first time since she had known Crocker, she saw a flash of fear in his eyes.

"I happen to know that one of your sons is in the Confederate army. I wonder how your Unionist friends will feel about that when I tell them," she said hatefully.

"You wouldn't tell such a lie," he stammered.

"You keep my son from me, you might be surprised what I'll do."

"Your boy ain't here," he said in a strong voice. "Don't come back."

* * *

"If you could come to the table just once without complaining..." Amanda mumbled. Jonathan had returned to his normal schedule, and she was supposed to do the same. She stopped scurrying and took a deep breath. It was suppertime, but she couldn't eat a bite.

And Jonathan is being his normal, hateful self, complaining that the potatoes are cold.

"What did you say?" Jonathan asked, his voice full of contempt.

"Nothing," she said without looking at him, which always made him angry.

"Finish your statement, woman!" he bellowed.

She flung the clean napkin he had requested onto the table in front of him, and said, "I will never forgive you for hurting my son."

"What are you talking about?"

"Luke ran away because you never listen to his opinions, and you made a fool of him in front of the Andersons."

"Did not," Jonathan said.

"Then why has he been gone for two days?"

* * *

It was early, not quite five thirty. The rooster had yet to announce the coming dawn. This was the third day of Luke's absence, and Amanda's fear for his safety was almost more than she could bear. She had learned the previous day that without breakfast, she had no energy. So, she was hurrying to cook, eat, dress, and make the rounds again, looking for Luke. What else could she do?

She and Barbé shuffled about the kitchen, doing their breakfast dance, which was so precisely choreographed they could have done it blindfolded. Thus they were when they heard someone calling their names from the dining room. The voice sounded like Luke's. They ran to the dining room, and there he was.

"Where have you been? Are you all right?" Amanda and Barbé were talking at once.

Luke grabbed Amanda and hugged her like he never had before.

"Get to the barn, boy," Jonathan said, startling Amanda. She didn't know he was standing behind her.

"Let him stay a minute," Amanda begged. "He just got here."

"Go on," Jonathan said, roughly pushing Luke toward the back of the house.

"Jonathan!" Amanda said.

"Stay out of this!" he shouted.

Amanda and Barbé went back to the kitchen. A few minutes later, they heard a scream. They looked at each other, startled. When the second scream came, they left the kitchen as it was—food cooking on the stove, biscuits baking in the oven—and hurried outside.

"No! Please don't!" they heard and broke into a run.

Amanda reached the barn several yards ahead of Barbé. She ran inside, but saw nothing. Then came another plea for mercy. "Daddy, don't!" Luke cried.

Amanda found Luke and Jonathan in a horse stall in the back of the barn. It was hard to see in the half-light of early morning but her eyes soon adjusted to the darkness, and she looked upon a scene for which nothing could have prepared her.

"What's going on here?" she asked nervously.

Luke lay on a pile of hay in the stall. His face was red, and it was beginning to swell. Jonathan stood over him, his fist raised to strike another blow. Amanda grabbed Jonathan's arm but he threw her off as if she weighed nothing. She fell back heavily, striking her head on the stall door. She heard the thud when Jonathan's fist struck Luke's head. She lay there for a minute, waiting for the vertigo to pass.

In the meantime, Barbé arrived and discovered what was happening. She grabbed Jonathan's right arm and pulled back on it with all of her weight. Even that didn't keep his fist from striking Luke again, but it lessened the blow a little.

"Don't, Daddy," Luke continued to beg. "I'm sorry I ran away."

Amanda finally regained her feet, but she had to lean against the post behind her to remain upright. Jonathan soon managed to fling Barbé off his arm, and she fell on her backside in front of Amanda.

Amanda had never seen a human face more frightening than Jonathan's as he continued to strike blows to Luke's head and body with his fists. Amanda went at him again, jumped up on his back, and locked her hands around his neck. As Jonathan leaned forward to hit Luke again, her feet left the ground and she hung helplessly on Jonathan's back. She tried to lock her legs around his waist, but that only angered him more. He wrenched her hands apart and lunged backward. She fell on top of Barbé, who was still struggling to get up.

Amanda helped Barbé to her feet, and they attacked him at the same time, one on each arm. Even that wasn't enough to stop him. He grabbed the front of Luke's shirt, and when the women finally managed to pull him out of the stall, he brought Luke with him. They held onto Jonathan's arms and tried to loosen his grip on Luke's shirt, but they were no match for the adrenalin that was coursing through Jonathan's veins. He began to walk backward quickly, trying to shake them off, but they held on until he slammed them into the wall of the barn. They cried out in pain, but continued to hold onto his arms.

Jonathan finally let go of Luke's shirt, and he fell to the ground. Jonathan began to kick him, first in the back, then in the head. Luke lost consciousness and flopped around on the ground like a rag doll as his father continued to kick him with the toe of his boot. Barbé and Amanda cried and begged Jonathan to stop, but he didn't seem to hear them.

"That'll teach you to stay away from home and worry your mother to death," Jonathan shouted, "because when she's worried, she makes my life hell!"

Jonathan's right leg was in midair, prepared for another kick to Luke's torso. Amanda and Barbé caught him off-balance, and they all went tumbling backward onto the hard-packed earth of the barn floor.

As if the fall jarred him to his senses, Jonathan sat up and looked at his bloody, swollen knuckles. "What have I done?" he whispered.

"What do you mean, what have you done?!" Amanda screamed. "You have beaten your own son half to death, you bastard!"

"Somebody's got to teach the boy a lesson," Jonathan stammered.

Amanda rushed to Luke, who looked lifeless lying on the ground.

"Let me," Jonathan said, reaching out.

"Don't you dare touch him ever again," Amanda said in a voice as cold as stone.

Luke stirred, beginning to regain consciousness. Amanda helped him to his feet. Barbé reached to help him stand as well; he leaned on her as he took his first faltering steps.

"I could kill you for this!" Amanda shouted at Jonathan. She grabbed a hoe that was hanging on the wall nearby and swung it at Jonathan. His face again filled with rage.

"You want to fight?" he asked, taunting her.

"Get Luke out of here," Amanda told Barbé.

"Then let's make it a fair fight," Jonathan said. He picked up the shovel they used to muck out the stalls. He came at her, swinging the shovel wildly. Just the sound it made as it sliced through the air frightened Amanda to her senses.

"Please, Jonathan," she begged, "I don't want to do this."

"You should have thought of that before you swung that hoe at me." He came closer. She raised the hoe in front of her face in self-defense. Time after time, he whacked it with the shovel. Then, with one sideways blow, he knocked it from her hands. She sidestepped his next blow, and ran after Barbé and Luke.

After they laid Luke on the bed in Barbé's cabin, Amanda went barreling back through the door and stuck her fist in Jonathan's face. "If you don't want to die today, I'd suggest you get out of here. Get *out!*" she screamed with all her might.

"You can't run me off," he said hatefully. "This is my farm!"

"Barbé, get your gun," Amanda said, her voice calm.

Jonathan ran off toward the barn, and Amanda heard his horse trot off a few minutes later.

After Barbé and Amanda cleaned Luke's wounds, he finally fell into a fitful sleep.

"I must get Galilani," Amanda said. "She'll know how to treat his wounds."

Leaving Luke in Barbé's care, Amanda and Jody sprinted toward the mountains that the Cherokee called *Shaconage,* the Place of Blue Smoke. This was the place where their tribe had found game, medicinal plants, and all of life's necessities, long before the white man came to this place.

She tethered Jody to a strong tree branch so he could roam about and nibble on the fresh new shoots of grass. Breathing deeply, she tried desperately to regain some control over her emotions. Galilani—whose name Amanda had shortened to Gali [pronounced galley]—didn't handle tense situations well.

"What is it, my friend?" Gali asked when Amanda called for her.

"My family is destroyed," Amanda sobbed. "I can't live with this. I'm not strong enough."

"You are stronger than you know," Gali said. "You have made a good life in this unforgiving country with a man I would have killed in his sleep long ago. What is wrong?"

"Jonathan has beat Luke terribly," Amanda finally told Gali.

"I will kill him and save you the trouble," Gali seethed, running into the hut for her gun.

"No!" Amanda shouted, running after her. "No more violence," she begged.

"Luke is like my own son," Gali said, clutching at her throat. "Is he hurt badly?" Gali paced about the clearing, her anger still fresh.

"He's bruised from head to toe, and he desperately needs your help," Amanda sobbed.

"I hope the Creator will help me through this," Gali whispered. Amanda had never seen her so shaken.

"Barbé and I cleaned his wounds as best we could," Amanda said. "His chest and back are covered with bruises. Jonathan hit him so hard in places he broke the skin, and I think his collarbone is broken, maybe some ribs, too. His face is cut in several places. His lips are split and bleeding. Both eyes are swollen, the left one completely shut."

"How could a man do such things to his son?" Gali shouted. "The Cherokee never strike their children."

"Luke was gone from home for three days because he was angry at his father. I was scared nearly to death."

"We must focus our attention on helping Luke now."

"He looks so pitiful."

Luke was delirious when Amanda and Gali arrived at Barbé's cabin. The swelling had increased. He cried and begged someone to end his pain. "Just let me go, Mama," he pleaded. "I can't take this like a man."

"You're not a man, Luke," she said softly, wiping away his tears. "You're just a boy, and I think you're incredibly brave."

Barbé heated water at the fireplace while Amanda went to the house for a piece of fabric for bandages. She knew it should be free of dyes, which might infect the wounds. She could find nothing suitable.

The dress! The white linen dress Mrs. Bixby had been making for her in 1861 should work. It was to be trimmed with lace or embroidery of some kind, but after the war began, the materials ordered to complete the dress had never arrived.

She ran up the stairs and flung open the doors of her armoire. The skirt was wonderfully gored and unadorned. It hung fold upon fold and would be large enough to wrap around Luke's torso, binding his open wounds with the pastes Gali made from medicinal roots. She didn't bother to remove the dress from the peg upon which it hung.

With a few deft strokes of the scissors, she separated the skirt from the bodice, petticoat and all.

Gali had brewed an herbal tea and was helping Luke drink it when Amanda returned. His breathing soon slowed, and he closed his eyes. Gali was hoping the tea would help him sleep; the binding of his broken bones would be excruciatingly painful.

As Barbé cut wide strips of cloth, Gali soaked roots and herbs in hot water which she then mashed and spread onto the fabric to make poultices for his open cuts. With continuous strips of cloth Gali and Barbé bound Luke's chest as tightly as he could tolerate to help the broken bones heal as straight as possible. Amanda held his head in her hands and spoke soothing words of poetry and prayer. He cried out in pain and begged them to stop.

When they were finally finished, they hoped Luke would sleep, but he sat up suddenly in the bed, his eyes wild. "I have to leave here so he won't hurt me again."

"I promise you," Amanda said calmly. "I'll never let him hurt you again."

He flailed his arms and tried to stand, but they held him down. Soon a blessed unconsciousness overtook him, and he slumped back onto the pillow.

They carried Luke to the house. Barbé had a fire going in the sitting room and had pulled the settee close to the fire. He didn't groan or cry out, which frightened Amanda.

"Be thankful he can sleep," Gali said. "The more he sleeps, the less he will hurt, and the faster he will heal."

* * *

Jonathan returned to the house the following day, eyes downcast, and asked sheepishly to speak to Amanda on the front terrace. Barbé went to the sitting room, where Amanda was resting in her rocking chair; she had two black eyes and cuts and bruises on her face and arms.

Amanda thought she might as well face the confrontation that had to come sometime. As much as she wanted to tell Jonathan to get out and never come back, she had to be practical. Would she and Luke have enough resources to continue to live at Cinnamon Hill if Jonathan left?

Jonathan backed up several steps when she opened the front door. He gasped when he saw the condition of her face. She knew he was probably incapable of comprehending that her internal pain was far more hideous.

He seemed to be genuinely remorseful, but he would have done better to remain silent. Amanda was far from being ready for excuses.

"That's the way I was raised," he mumbled. "If I was bad, I could expect to be punished."

"That wasn't just punishment you gave Luke. You almost killed *your own son* with your fists!" There was a cold restraint in her voice.

"Did not," he said firmly. "That's exaggeration."

"Do you want to see him—to look at what you did?"

"N-no," he stammered.

"I didn't think so."

"It's your fault I beat him!" he shouted suddenly.

"What?"

"Your endless complaints about him staying out at night and running away. I just can't take it," he said, shaking his head.

Amanda was speechless.

"You told him yourself that his absences would no longer be tolerated," he said. "You told me to make sure it never happened again."

"You do that with words, Jonathan," she said, her voice getting louder. "Not with fists!"

"I should have beat you!" he screamed, his face reddening.

"I wish you had!" she cried, all control gone now. "I couldn't possibly suffer more than I am suffering right now. To watch my husband beat my only child almost to death. To see with my own eyes the monster you have become."

Jonathan opened his mouth to speak, but closed it quickly.

"All the times you were cold, inflexible, and overbearing. Your aloofness, your infidelity!"

Jonathan looked down at the ground.

"All of that pales compared to laying your fists on my son. Even I didn't believe you were capable of such cruelty!" She leaned against one of the stone columns that supported the terrace roof. It was surprisingly cool against her cheek.

"I swore I'd be different," Jonathan said after several minutes had passed. "I never wanted to be like her."

"Her?" Amanda turned to look at Jonathan's face, to see the insincerity she expected to find there.

"Evalinda," he whispered.

"Your mother beat you?"

He nodded slightly, eyes averted.

Amanda couldn't stifle the laugh that came up in her throat. "Eva weighed all of a hundred pounds. What could she have done to you?"

"I was a little boy," he said. "Anyone who's ever been beat with a willow switch knows how bad it hurts."

"Surely Charles would have stopped her."

"She made sure he wasn't around, and I was afraid to tell him."

Amanda pressed her hand to her lips. "Even if that is true," she said, calmer now, "it does not excuse your behavior. It makes your actions all the more despicable, if what you say is true."

"It's true," he whispered. "I swear it."

"But Eva didn't beat you with her fists, did she, Jonathan?" Amanda said, her anger rising again.

"I was scared Luke had been kidnapped or killed. When I saw that he wasn't at all concerned that he had worried us so, I lost control."

"That's not all you've lost here today," she said coldly.

* * *

The following Sunday, Jonathan was sitting in the family pew when Amanda entered the church. He had left just enough room for her to sit next to him, near the aisle. But she surprised him by passing in front of him and taking a seat at the opposite end of the pew. Heads turned. People whispered.

After the sermon, she stopped to talk to some of the congregation, hoping Jonathan would be gone when she exited the church. But he was waiting for her, holding Jody's reins.

"I'm coming home," he said nonchalantly.

"I don't want you there," she said, trying desperately not to raise her voice.

It was evident that his intention was to address her in the presence of others so she wouldn't cause a scene. He didn't seem to realize that his actions of the past few days had irrevocably changed their relationship.

"It's my house," he whispered into her ear. "You can't keep me away."

"Maybe not," she shrieked, "but I can sure make it hell for you while you're there!"

Everyone in the churchyard turned to look.

Amanda climbed into the saddle, prepared to tell everyone what a bastard Jonathan Armstrong was, then ride away. She pulled on Jody's reins, but Jonathan still held them tightly in his hand—which was fortuitous. It gave her a moment to realize that her son also bore the Armstrong name, and she should not besmirch it.

"Then, when can I come home?" he asked sheepishly. "You'll have to forgive me eventually."

"There is no forgiveness in my heart for you," she said under her breath.

"Then I shall proceed as I have planned," he said arrogantly.

"Planned?" she asked, wondering what he meant. "Planned what?"

"You'll know soon enough."

Just like Jonathan to leave me wondering.

She jerked the reins from his hand and rode away, but he followed her to Cinnamon Hill and accosted her at the barn when she dismounted.

"This is going to be settled right now!" he said, tightly gripping her arm. She wrenched it from his grasp and ran toward the house. He was right on her heels.

"You can't do this to me," he shouted, trying unsuccessfully to grab her arm again.

"Grab this arm, Jonathan," she shouted, shoving her elbow in his face. "It doesn't have as many bruises as the other."

"What have I ever done to you to deserve such treatment?" he shouted. "Let's leave Luke out of it for now. What have I done to you?"

"You really want to know?"

"Yes, I do. Let's get it all out in the open, once and for all."

"It isn't just that you treat me like hired help, nor that I have to constantly walk on tiptoe to avoid upsetting your delicate system, nor that your attention is taken up by everything in the world but your family."

Her voice grew louder with every word, and she could do nothing to stop it.

"It's all the little indignities you've shown me since I married you that have combined to form a lump in my throat that I can no longer swallow. I can't live like this anymore, and if you feel the need to beat me for speaking so plainly to you, then go ahead!"

* * *

Jonathan appeared at Cinnamon Hill again. He sat on his horse in the front yard and called for Amanda to come out. Jedediah Palmer, Jonathan's best friend since childhood, sat astride his horse at Jonathan's side. Amanda had assumed that he had been staying with Jed the past few nights. Jed was a widower and had no family.

"What's going on?" she asked nervously.

"Jed and I are off to join the Union army," Jonathan said. "I'm doing my civic duty. We'll ride for southeastern Kentucky, where there is a large Union camp and training area. It's said that General Ambrose Burnside is assembling an army there to invade Northeast Tennessee."

"You're leaving me?" Amanda asked.

"It's what you want," Jonathan said.

"Well, you can't take Bean," Amanda stuttered, reaching for the horse's reins.

"If I am to be a cavalryman, I must furnish my own mount."

"I'll never make it here by myself," Amanda said, hating herself for panicking.

"Luke can take care of you."

"Luke is barely able to take care of himself after what you did to him," she said hatefully.

There was a long, dead silence.

Jed Palmer frowned. "What's she talking about?" he whispered to Jonathan.

"Not your business, Jed," Jonathan answered quickly. "Go to your mother's," he told Amanda. "She'd be glad to have you."

"How will I get there? You have to take me before you leave."

"If I don't go now, there's a good chance I'll be forced to serve as a Confederate, and I would sooner die."

"Then how can I go to Virginia with Rebels everywhere?"

Jed sat silently on his horse, staring out across the fields as if he had just stopped by to enjoy the view.

"I have taken care of you all these years, Amanda," Jonathan stated flatly. "For once, you can take care of yourself."

"What if the Rebels come after me?" she asked, frightened by that thought. "They know you're a Unionist and will assume I am, too."

Suddenly her hands began to shake. She gritted her teeth, determined that the tears so close to the surface would not betray her.

"How will I live?" she asked.

Jonathan looked at her and calmly said, "You'll survive."

"Then I'll not be here when you come back!" she shouted.

"Just stay in the house," he said.

"Then go!" she shouted, fumbling for her apron pocket. No handkerchief there.

She marched across the terrace and into the house. "You can burn in hell's fire for all I care!" she shouted in farewell.

EIGHT

Amanda feared that Luke was forever changed. Even after his external wounds began to heal, his emotional health didn't improve. While in the presence of others, even with her and Barbé, he was skittish and distrustful. Amanda spoke softly, remained calm, and tried in every way to avoid provoking him.

One morning, Amanda overheard part of a conversation between Luke and Barbé in the kitchen. She was ready to intervene, but thought Barbé might be able to make him understand where she had failed.

"Your mother loves you," Barbé said patiently. "She's doing all she can for you. She'd go back and take that beating your father gave you if she could. Your being mean all the time is killing her."

"It's none of your business what I do," Luke said hatefully.

"You're right. It's not my place, so I won't say no more. But while you're here, I'd sure appreciate it if you'd fill the wood box."

Then Amanda heard crashing and banging and rushed to the kitchen.

"What's going on here?" Amanda asked, looking directly at Luke.

"The helpless old darkie wanted wood, now she's got wood," Luke said hatefully.

Amanda could hold her tongue no longer. "Luke, don't you ever call Barbé that foul name again. You know better than that."

"I should have known you'd take her side. You've always loved her more than me."

"That's not true," Amanda said softly. "I love you equally."

"I'm your son!" he shouted. "You should love me more."

"Listen," she said patiently. "No one knows better than Barbé and me how horribly you suffered at your father's hand, but you can't continue to quarrel with us. Your father did you wrong, not us."

"But he's not here for me to take it out on, is he?!" Luke shouted. His eyes were filled with rage.

"What is wrong with you?" Amanda said, much louder than she had intended.

"Some days I'm just so *angry*," he said. "I go to bed angry, I get up angry, and I'm angry all day long. I can't help it," he said, pacing the floor, repeatedly running his fingers through his sandy brown hair.

"I have tried in every way I know to make you feel safe again," Amanda said. "I've told you that I will kill your father if he ever tries to hurt you again. What more can I do?"

"Nothing," he mumbled. His face softened. Tears welled in his eyes. "And I hate myself when I treat you like this. I just don't want to be here anymore. Everything I see reminds me of him."

"Where else would you go?" Amanda asked, frightened of what the answer might be.

"The army," he said quickly. "Maybe if I get away a while, I'll feel different."

"Give it a month," she begged. "If you don't feel any better, we'll see. Please," she begged.

"All right," he nodded and headed up the stairs.

* * *

Crocker continued to stop by Cinnamon Hill from time to time, as he had done before Jonathan left. Amanda made it clear that she had no work for him or any way to pay him if she did, but he continued to stop by.

Amanda talked to him on the front terrace one afternoon. He came to tell her about a raid in the Valley. A large party of Union cavalry had come down from Kentucky, and were on their way to Knoxville, wreaking havoc as they went. "I hear they're just scouting the area to see where might be the best place for an invasion. Maybe the Yankees will do better by us than the Rebels."

"It's all well and good", Amanda replied, "if General Burnside is truly coming and if he can run the Rebels out of the Valley. My fear is that it will only cause more fighting and more trouble for us civilians. Just when Jonathan deserts me, the Yankees finally decide to make a fight."

"Where's Luke?" Crocker asked suddenly. "I haven't seen him since Mr. Armstrong left."

"He hasn't been feeling at all well," she said. "A spring cold it probably was to start with, but it's really got him down. He keeps to his room most of the time."

"Well, you tell him I asked about him, and would like to see him sometime soon."

"I'll tell him."

When she stepped through the front door, Luke was standing right in front of her.

"Why'd you tell Mr. Crocker I've got a cold?"

"So you've taken to eavesdropping now?"

"I have the right to know what you say about me."

"I didn't say anything wrong."

"Yes, you did," he insisted. "You lied. Don't you think he's going to figure it out eventually? Some of these scars won't ever go away completely, Mother," he said, touching his face, which was still scabbed and swollen in several places.

"Crocker's the last person I'd want to know about this," she said firmly. "He tells everything he knows, and sometimes what he only surmises. If he finds out about this, he'll tell everyone from here to Knoxville. It would be just too good to keep to himself—another scandal in the Armstrong family!"

"He won't tell if I ask him not to."

"Oh, Luke, you're so naive." She sighed.

"Don't you think people will ask me what happened to my face?"

"Sure," she said, "but that doesn't mean you have to tell the whole sordid story. No purpose will be served by telling everybody what a monster your father has become. I'm not asking you to excuse him or what he did, but if word of this gets out—well, it would be embarrassing."

"Mother, it seems to me you've spent your entire life trying to hide things Father's done—you, Grandma, and Grampa—but you haven't hidden a thing. Even those men who come and drink his whiskey know what kind of man he is. They pretend to like him, but behind his back, they laugh at him."

"Maybe you don't care right now, but when you're a grown man, you'll want a name you can be proud of."

"Not if it's a lie!" he yelled. "If anybody asks me what happened to my face, I'll tell them the truth. Maybe if all of you hadn't lied and covered up everything Daddy did all along, he might have been a better man."

"I know." She nodded. "I just meant that at some time in the future you'll want a family, a wife and children, and you'll want a respected family name to give them."

"Why would I want a family?"

"Well, I assumed… Everybody wants a family."

"You assumed wrong."

"Well, I guess we'll have to deal with this when your father gets back."

As much as I hate myself for it, I've decided there's no way I can survive in this hostile place without a man. From what I've seen, Jonathan is about as good as any. At least, I'm familiar with his foibles. God help me, I hope he comes back soon.

"He's coming back?!" Luke shouted. "You said he was gone!"

"He is gone," she said. "He went to Kentucky to join the army."

"But you don't think he'll really do it, do you?"

"I don't know," she said reluctantly. "He likes his comforts too much."

"You let me believe I was safe here."

"You are safe here."

"Not if he's coming back!" Luke shouted. "You don't care any more for me than he does."

"How can you say such a thing?" Amanda rushed at Luke and wrapped her arms around him before he could pull away. "Baby boy, don't you ever think for one second that I don't love you more than anyone on God's green earth, and I will die trying to keep you safe," she said. "Barbé and I would have saved you that morning; but with all that anger rushing through his body, your father was just too strong." Tears of anger and regret streamed down her face.

Luke stopped struggling to get away, buried his head in his mother's shoulder, and wept in heartbreaking sobs.

"I love you, Mama," he said, pulling away from her, "but I have to get away from here."

"Please wait awhile," she begged. "Now that your body is healing, your emotions might improve faster than you think."

Luke shrugged.

"Well, I have to be practical," Amanda said. "If your father never comes back, that will be fine with me, but I don't know how we can continue to survive here. With no income from Jonathan and only my small monthly check from Father's trust—that Confederate money gets more worthless by the day—"

"Then having one less mouth to feed will be a blessing," Luke said and rushed up the stairs.

Amanda called after him, but he did not respond.

* * *

"Luke, breakfast."

After Amanda called again and got no response, she began to feel uneasy. She went upstairs. After knocking on his door, she opened it. The bed was neatly made, and most of his clothes and boots were gone. She hoped this was just another adolescent rebellion. Maybe she should just give him a little time to figure things out.

"If he thinks he can run away every time something happens that is not to his liking, he is sadly mistaken," Amanda told Barbé.

Amanda was so sure she knew where Luke was that she waited three days before she went to see about him.

Crocker came to the door when she knocked.

"Luke's not at the barn," she said with a sigh. "Is he in the house?"

"I've not seen Luke but once since Mr. Armstrong left."

"Old man," she responded. "I don't have the time or the patience to play your silly games today. Where is he? I just want to talk to him and make sure he's all right."

"Luke is not here," Crocker said emphatically.

"Where else could he be?" she asked.

"The only thought I have is that he might have gone off to enlist with General Morgan, but the way he's been beaten... How could you let that happen?" he accused.

"I tried to stop Jonathan," she said.

"I would have died before I'd let someone beat my child like that."

"It's so easy for you to judge when you weren't there!" she shouted.

"Well, right or wrong, he blames you just as much as his father."

"Why would he blame me?" she asked.

"A mother is supposed to protect her child."

August 1863

Amanda had been frantic for a month. Not even Crocker, who seemed to know everything, could discover where Luke had gone. Her nerves assaulted her hourly, even in her dreams. She ate and slept little. Dresses that were once snug at the waist now hung loosely on her frame. She felt compelled to find Luke, to make sure he was safe, but she had run out of places to look.

One Sunday evening, she was in the sitting room reading. She had suffered a long and lonely weekend with little sleep, awakening at every little sound. Every day was lonely without Luke, but especially so when Barbé was at the Crossroads with Juba. Amanda had long suspected that Juba made Barbé feel guilty every time he brought her back to Cinnamon Hill.

Amanda was expecting Juba to bring Barbé home at any minute. In fact, they were later than usual.

Someone was calling from the rear terrace. It was a male voice. She jumped up and ran to the window. Barbé was standing on the back terrace, and Juba was leaning against the summer kitchen.

Amanda opened the door. "What are you doing out there?" she asked. "Come in."

"We want to talk to you out here," Juba said.

"Are you on foot?" Amanda asked. "I didn't hear you come up."

"Wagon's broke," Juba said.

Amanda walked slowly onto the porch. "What's going on?" she asked Barbé.

"I can't be your slave no more," Barbé mumbled so softly that the only word Amanda heard was "slave."

Juba noisily cleared his throat.

"I can't be your slave no more," Barbé said louder.

"You're not my slave," Amanda said. "Remember the papers I signed?"

Juba frowned and looked at his wife. "What's she talking about?"

"You didn't tell Juba?"

"What papers?" Juba asked.

"I gave Barbé her freedom years ago," Amanda explained. "The papers are in the safe in Jonathan's office."

"How did you pay for your freedom?" he asked, turning to his wife.

"There was no money involved," Amanda said.

Juba shot a nasty look toward his wife. Barbé began to sob uncontrollably.

"I can't believe this," Juba said.

"I thought if you knew, you'd take me away from here," Barbé said through her tears, but Juba was now fixated on Amanda.

"That's just another way you've shut me out of her life," Juba shouted, "another case where you can give her what I can't." He extended his index finger and with every word, he jabbed it toward Amanda, coming closer and closer. He didn't stop until his finger was almost in her face. "You even make her feel guilty when she's not here."

This time Barbé responded. "It's my fault for that," she sobbed. "I don't want to hurt your feelings, Juba, but I can't wait to get out of that stuffy little room above the shop."

Juba looked at his wife, dismayed. "Well, that decides it," he said. "We're going to the North. The Union soldiers tell me what a good life we could have up there. Blacksmithing jobs are plentiful. I could charge higher prices for my work, wouldn't have to take all this worthless Confederate money. We could own our own home, our own land."

"What about the shop at the Crossroads?" Amanda asked.

"I've worked myself nigh to death for over a year, and I still can't make a decent living. Ain't enough business around here. After the war's over, I'm afraid it will dry up to nothing."

"It takes a long time to establish a business. You're giving up too soon." Amanda then turned to Barbé. "Is this what you want?"

"No-o-o," Barbé sobbed.

"Enough of this!" Juba shouted. "You tell my wife to leave with me."

"What?" Amanda's head was reeling.

"She won't leave Cinnamon Hill unless you tell her to go, and you know her heart will be broke if I leave without her."

"And how will she feel if I throw her out of her home?" Amanda said angrily. "Juba, it's time you knew how ungrateful you're being."

"Please, don't!" Barbé screamed, but Amanda couldn't stop herself.

"I made the deal with Bixby so you could buy the carriage house. I paid half the deposit, so you would have enough money left to buy tools."

Juba's jaw dropped. His face went blank as if his brain failed to comprehend what she had said. If he hadn't been such a dark-skinned man, his face would have paled. He turned around and walked slowly back to the summer kitchen. He braced his arms against the doorway there, as if his legs alone couldn't hold up the weight of what he had heard. He stood in that position for several minutes, shaking his head slowly from side to side.

"Is this true?" Juba asked, turning toward his wife.

"Yes," Barbé whispered.

Juba grabbed Barbé's arm roughly and pulled her away. When they reached the corner of the house, he turned and looked at Amanda, pure hatred in his eyes. "Her things are packed. We'll be back for them when I get the wagon fixed. And you can do whatever you want with *your* blacksmith shop!"

As soon as they were out of sight, Amanda ran to the little cabin on the creek bank. Just inside the door, she found a small suitcase bulging at the seams with clothing, an old knapsack filled with various household items, and a large roll of bedding. There was nothing else in the cabin to suggest that Barbé had ever lived there. Amanda slumped to the floor beside Barbé's things. She wanted to cry, but not a single tear would come.

A while later she went to Jonathan's office to retrieve Barbé's papers. If Barbé was really leaving Cinnamon Hill, she should carry them with her.

Jonathan's father, Charles, had convinced Amanda to give Barbé her freedom. "No matter how well a white man treats a slave, she's still a slave. She eats when her master says eat, works when her master says work, stops when her master says stop. If she can't legally marry the man she loves, can't buy a piece of land, can't go visit her relatives on a whim for fear she'll be stopped and questioned, and Lord knows what else, no matter how much you love her, she's a slave."

Amanda hadn't looked in the safe since Jonathan left, and was shocked to find only a few dollars in Confederate money. No Federal greenbacks at all. Her brown leather valise was empty. The little money she had saved from Father's trust was gone.

* * *

Two days later Barbé and Juba returned to Cinnamon Hill in the wagon, which was almost full of his blacksmithing equipment. While Juba loaded the bags from the cabin, Barbé went to the house to see Amanda. They quickly said their farewells and turned away from each other.

Barbé managed to control her emotions until her hand touched the doorknob. "I don't want to go," Barbé said, sobbing. Barbé ran to Amanda, and they held onto each other tightly.

"Tell him I can't go," Barbé sobbed.

"It wouldn't do any good," Amanda cried. "You have to tell him."

"I can't," Barbé said, pulling away from her.

"You have to!" Amanda shouted. "If you leave me, I'll be completely alone here!"

"He's my husband," Barbé said. "I have to do what he says."

"Barbé," Juba called from the rear terrace.

"Go then!" Amanda shouted. "Desert me, like all the rest!" She walked quickly to the back door and pushed Barbé through it.

Amanda stood in the center hall, where she wouldn't be able to see them leave, but she heard Barbé's heart wrenching sobs as the wagon pulled away. Though it was only a few minutes, it seemed like forever before she heard the wagon's wheels rattle across the wooden bridge over Bottom Creek.

When the full impact hit her, Amanda ran to the family cemetery on the hill and fell down beside Charles's grave.

"Why is everyone leaving me?" she whispered.

She soon noticed that the dampness of the wet ground had soaked through her clothing. She wore no coat. Night was coming on. A cool wind had kicked up after the rain showers that passed through earlier. Finally, the last light of that dreary, sunless day crept over the high ridges.

She remembered as the darkness settled around her, that there was not a candle or lamp of any sort burning in the house.

It doesn't matter. No one is waiting for me. What if I lay exactly where I am and gave myself up to the cold and let the last, deepest warmth seep from my body?

* * *

Her spirits lifted a little when Crocker came the following morning with news of Luke.

"This isn't fresh news by any means," he said, "but it's all I can find out at the moment. He was over in Middle Tennessee with General Morgan, as I have suspected all along. I couldn't get any specific details about his health or condition, but at least we know he made it that far."

"Amen," Amanda sighed.

"They are readying for another raid into Kentucky."

"I don't like the sounds of that."

"This is what Morgan does best," Crocker said.

"I owe you a debt of gratitude," Amanda said, "and I won't forget it." *No matter how much you frustrate me.*

* * *

Crocker came again. News of Luke was more troubling this time.

"General Morgan rode north and invaded Indiana and Ohio."

"Good Lord, what's he doing way up there?" Amanda asked, already anxious.

"I'm afraid it only gets worse from there."

"Tell me, then!"

"General Morgan was overtaken by a bigger Union force and was forced to surrender. They threw him into a penitentiary up there. I can't ascertain if Luke was with him at that time or not."

"Oh, no! I've got a bad feeling about this," she sobbed.

"Now, don't go slobbering all over yourself there," Crocker said impatiently. "Some of Morgan's men got away. Maybe Luke did, too."

* * *

Amanda and Gali were walking along Bottom Creek, on the way back to her hut after a successful day of collecting roots and herbs for

Gali's cave. Amanda had needed a diversion from her worries about Luke and Barbé.

As they strolled along, a gang of grimy bearded horsemen burst out of the woods and onto the trail in front of them. One of them, a particularly obscene animal, jumped from his horse and pressed a long knife at Gali's throat and shouted at her in short, clipped sentences.

"Hard of hearing, squaw?" he shouted.

Gali didn't speak.

"Told you before. Get off that land. It's mine." He pressed the tip of the knife harder into Gali's neck.

Amanda expected to see blood spurt out at any minute. She had been so startled when they jumped out in front of them that she truly could not move.

"White people told me where I can live all my life," Gali said calmly. "I will not run again."

A stubby cigar protruded from the corner of the man's mouth. Brown drool ran down his chin. "You will leave, with or without my assistance," he said. "Don't make no difference which."

He shoved Gali so hard she fell to the ground.

"I know where you live, too, Indian lover," he said abruptly, turning toward Amanda. She gasped.

Laughing raucously, he quickly mounted, and they rode away.

"Who was that?" Amanda asked.

"A no-account bushwhacker who lives a few miles to the north. They call him 'Judie' Baker. His birth name is Judas, which tells you all you need to know about his character. He was a liar and a thief before the war. Now he thinks he has legalized his rampaging by wearing that dirty old Union jacket. He is not a soldier, never was; just looking to take from others what he's too lazy to get for himself."

"You've got to leave," Amanda said.

"He came to these hills long after I did, laid claim to acres and acres of land around here, and ran almost everybody off."

"He scares me to death," Amanda whispered, still reeling.

"He is just full of wind, likes to feel important. It galls him that I am still here. A woman—and a squaw at that. Maybe one of these days, he will believe me when I say I am not leaving."

"What right does he have to evict you?"

"He says he has papers of ownership from the courts, but he will not let me see them."

"Please, Gali," Amanda begged, "promise me you'll hide in the cave if he comes here again."

"He hates all Cherokee—what did the whites expect us to do? They moved onto our land and took it as their own. The government sent men from Washington, who managed to find the weakest and most immoral chiefs and plied them with liquor. They signed away our land and got nothing for it. *Nothing!*"

Amanda had never seen Gali so agitated.

"The Cherokee moved farther south, and farther west. But the whites kept coming, pushing us away from the mountain country we love."

"How did you come to be on this land?" Amanda asked. "I've asked a dozen times, but you've never told me."

"It is hard to talk about."

"Maybe it's time you did."

"I do not know if I can," Gali said softly. "It has been inside me so long."

They stopped. Amanda sat down on a boulder at the edge of the trail.

Gali was silent for a long time. Her eyes became very intense. She stared off into the distance while she told the story of running from the soldiers in her village at Tellico. Her voice took on a secretive quality, as if she were still that young girl, in that place, and couldn't speak in a normal voice, or she would be taken.

"The soldiers began to capture the Cherokee and lock them in stockades, to force us to leave our homeland and march west. My family made a pact that if the soldiers came for us, if one of us was able to escape, we must do it at all cost. I saw the soldiers at our hut, heard my mother cry, and knew what must be happening. I ran from the field where I was hoeing the corn, but I stopped for a moment and looked back, and saw my parents and my brother being removed from our home. One of the horse soldiers saw me and caught up to me at the edge of the woods. Bending down from his saddle, he struck me with the flat of his saber, then he turned it and dragged the sharp edge across my face."

Gali touched the scar on her face as if she had just discovered it. It began on the right side of her forehead, from hairline to eyebrow, across the bridge of her nose, down her left cheek to her jawbone.

"I fell face first in the mud. The soldier rode away, leaving me for dead. I was bleeding badly. I packed the mud against my face to hold back the blood. If my mother had not taught me which medicinal plants to use to staunch the bleeding, I would have died. I traveled through the woods all the way here, living on nuts and berries. I followed the streams when possible in order to leave no trail. The soldiers were still everywhere. I lived in the cave behind my hut for many weeks before I began to feel safe.

"My mother and father died in the stockades before the march began. My brother escaped before they reached the Indian Territory. With the help of others who had run away, he found me here. He died soon after, from fear and exhaustion."

Gali's voice softened and turned melancholy. "Every day I live, I ask myself if I made the right choice."

Late August 1863

A loud knock at the front door woke Amanda from a light sleep on the settee in the sitting room. She shuffled down the hall, wondering who might be calling at such an early hour. Fear jolted her mind awake. Who could it be? What could they want? She began to sidle along the wall, looking through the sidelights at the front door, trying to see who was knocking.

But they were standing too close to the door.

"Who's there?" she called in her gruffest voice.

"It's Bixby."

"Oh, thank God," she muttered.

"What can I do for you?" she asked, opening the door a crack.

"I've come for my monthly payment, of course," he said nonchalantly.

"But Juba's gone," she said, trying to clear the cobwebs of sleep from her mind.

"Precisely," he said, "and you promised to make the payments if he left."

"Oh, no," she sighed. "I only have a few dollars in Confederate money," she said, reaching into a small pocket at the waist of her skirt.

"Well, that won't do."

"It's all I have," she replied.

"That can't be," Bixby stammered. "You're the richest folks around here."

"Not anymore," she sighed.

"You're lying!"

"Pardon me, sir," she responded. "I do not lie. I know I promised to pay you, but Jonathan took all my money."

"Then, I'll sue you for it."

"Feel free to do so," she shouted. "Now get out of here!"

Amanda was anxiously anticipating her monthly check from Father's trust fund; maybe she could buy some food. If any were to be found, it would undoubtedly be outrageously expensive.

September 1863

"I have news of Jonathan, Mrs. Armstrong," Crocker said.

"What of him?"

"I couldn't care less myself," Crocker said, "after what he did to Luke, but I thought you might want to know. He's at Strawberry Plains between here and Knoxville, guarding the railroad bridge there. If he comes up this way, he might decide to pay you a visit."

"Really?" Amanda muttered.

"And I have better news. At long last, General Burnside has arrived!" he shouted. "You might want to stay real close to home, and indoors as much as possible. The Union troops are trying to capture the Rebel soldiers General Buckner left behind when he pulled out of Knoxville. Since you're way off the Greeneville Road, they might not find you back here, but you never know."

"What would they want with me?"

"Shelter, food, money, anything that might make their lot easier. I certainly hope they wouldn't...assault you," he mumbled.

"Do you have to scare me to death?" Amanda said, her voice trembling.

"It's for your own safety," he said impatiently.

Amanda's mind was racing. How could she remain at home with such dangers nearby?

"I hear Burnside will make his headquarters in Knoxville," Crocker continued," and the town will soon be safe for Unionists. You're a Unionist, aren't you, Mrs. Armstrong?"

"What I am is none of your business."

"I guess you'll be going on down there to Knoxville to be with your kind. Us non-partials will be staying at home." He laughed at her with a wicked leer. Every conversation she had with him, no matter how benignly it began, eventually led to some sort of teasing or taunting.

"You expect me to believe you're impartial." She was tempted to laugh at that thought, but she couldn't even muster up a smile.

He had no trouble producing a big belly laugh, leaning back, and pulling on his dirty red suspenders for effect.

"One of these days, old man," she spat at him, "you'll get your comeuppance, and I hope I'm there to witness it when you do. Do you know what *karma* is, Crocker?"

His smile faded, and he shrugged his shoulders.

"I didn't think so," she said smartly. "Karma means that someday you'll get slapped with the same treatment you've given others."

"Now you're just being devilish," he said in disbelief. "There ain't no such thing, and you know it well as I do."

"You want to take that chance?"

He stuck his pipe in his mouth and shuffled off up the lane.

Why do I allow that man to make me so angry? I would enjoy never having to look at his sickening face again, but if there were ever any news about Luke, Crocker would likely be the first to hear it. I wonder where he gets his information, how he seems to know everything before anyone else does.

The following day, Amanda received a letter from Mother.

> *It is my sad task to inform you of the failure of the bank that administers your trust fund. They wired me, saying that there will be no further payments coming to you. Because Father and I were so extravagant over the years, my financial situation isn't the best either. And, of course, our savings in the bank in Abingdon were converted to Confederate currency with the onset of war and becomes less and less valuable every day.*
>
> *I can't believe everyone has deserted you at once, but there are so many women in your situation. Come to Hunter House. We'd love to have you here. Our gardens produced well this year, and we have enough vegetables to last the winter if we can keep the thieves from getting it. The servants and I try to carry on with life as it was, though it will never be as it was. It amazes me that many of them are still with me, as loyal and true as ever.*
>
> *Be careful, and know that I love you always, and I will pray for your safety every moment until I see you again.*
>
> *Love, Mother*

NINE

Late September 1863

"How will I live without the money from my trust?" Amanda asked Gali. "I'm scared to death at home. I rarely sleep."

"So that is why you look so frail," Gali said.

"My preference would be to go to Mother's. If I can go the back way, the way Jonathan and I went before the main road was built, I think I can make it. I'll have to travel through some rugged terrain, but I think it will be safer than traveling the main road for a woman alone. Crocker says Burnside has already run the Rebels out of the northeastern counties where I will be traveling."

"What does he know?" Gali said impatiently.

"I don't like him much either, but he's the only source of information I have. Gali, when did I become such a coward?"

"You are stronger than you know," Gali said emphatically.

"That's not true," Amanda said. "I know myself better than you."

"I am not sure you do. Your life has not been easy, and yet you are still here. When I first met you, I did not think you would last another year married to that man."

"He wasn't like that before I married him. He wrote me beautiful letters."

"Love is easier when you do not have to prove it every day. Now you must make your own life, as I have done here."

"And where do I begin?"

"Only you can know."

"Well, I know I can't stay in that house anymore," Amanda stated flatly. "My food is almost gone. Somebody raided the garden again, dug the potatoes right out of the ground—where I buried them last week. Last night, someone brought a wagon and loaded everything they could get their hands on. Someone walked up onto the back porch. I huddled in the corner, hoping they wouldn't come into the house. When I went out this morning, Jody was gone. They took my only horse, tackle and all!"

"You walked here today?" Gali asked.

"Yes," Amanda said. "Wherever I go, I'll have to go on foot."

"That would be an arduous trip to Virginia."

"I know, but I'm barely surviving on raw carrots and green apples. And it's killing my stomach."

"I have food aplenty," Gali said. "I will gladly share it with you."

"I can't take your food. You'll need it for winter."

"And I offer my home, if you will have it."

"I'd go crazy out here, especially now that I know Judie Baker's always lurking about." Amanda sighed deeply. "Then, that's it. I'll go to Mother's—if I can summon the courage. I have a thought: Why don't you move to Cinnamon Hill with me?"

"I will do almost anything for you, my sister, but I must live here," Gali said, spreading her arms wide to include earth, woods, and sky. "I am not a social creature, and I am too old to change."

"You're barely ten years older than me."

"Yes," Gali said, nodding her head, "but my soul is very old."

"How can you choose this over the warmth and protection of a house? I've often thought over the years that we would outlive Jonathan and Luke would be off somewhere with his own family, and you and I would live out our days at Cinnamon Hill together. I sometimes wonder how we have remained friends for so long. We're so different."

"But in some ways, we are almost identical. We both need a strong sense of who we are and where our place is in the world."

"I'm not so sure I know who I am anymore," Amanda said, standing up and stretching her arms. "But I do know I can't stay at Cinnamon Hill any longer."

* * *

In the armoire in Charles' bedroom, she found some old trousers that were large enough to shove a dress and petticoats into. And some boots that required only one sock stuffed into the toe to fit pretty well. Several old shirts were hanging on pegs inside the armoire. They would be sufficient to cover the bodice of her dress. Thus outfitted, she could change identities quickly. She made a bedroll with some old blankets and an oilcloth to keep the dampness away when she slept on the ground, then made a sling so she could drape it across her shoulder.

Amanda pinned her hair up high on her head and shoved an old slouch hat on top, pulling it down as far as possible. Its wide, flexible brim hid much of her face. Looking into the mirror, she decided she made a convincing-looking man; walking through the forest for long distances would be much more comfortable in her disguise than constantly getting her skirts caught up in brambles. Someone would have to get mighty close to see that she was a woman, and she didn't plan on letting anyone get that close.

Gathering the few valuables that were worth taking on her trip—the amethyst ring Father gave her on her sixteenth birthday, the marcasite brooch that Grandma Belle once wore, and a silver necklace—she packed them in an old canvas knapsack she found in the attic. She might find it necessary to trade those items for food or supplies.

Amanda added two extra shirts and two pairs of pants, carrots, apples, a few pieces of dried beef, and a biscuit made from the last scrapings of the flour barrel to the knapsack. The biscuit was three days old, and so hard it could kill a chicken at twenty paces.

She went to sleep at dusk and awoke shortly after midnight. Leaving under the cover of darkness, she believed, would attract the least attention. She would have to travel the main road to Greeneville, but soldiers should be encamped and asleep by that late hour. If pickets were posted to protect the troops from surprise attack, their campfires should be easily spotted from a distance.

Thus accoutered she stepped off shortly after midnight, but quickly realized traveling at night might not have been such a good idea. The sliver of moon gave little light. The stars could be used to plot direction, Amanda knew. Was that the North Star? She had no idea how to locate a single star.

She belted Charles' old field coat tightly around her. The air was cold, and a strong wind had begun to blow.

At Greeneville, Amanda made her way to the eastern edge of town, where she would pick up the back road. When she took a shortcut across the lawn of a beautiful antebellum house, a large dog came running after her, barking viciously. She ran as fast as she could for at least a mile before she realized the dog had stopped chasing her. She stopped for a moment and rested her hands on her knees, unable to breathe deeply for several minutes.

And she had wet her pants.

After trying several streets, she finally located the one that connected to the old road, where she headed northeast. She remembered a few landmarks to watch for and sometimes followed the old Indian trails she knew. Relieved to have reached the outskirts of a village called Limestone Station before dawn, she found a dry ditch concealed from view by the low branches of a large oak and bedded down for a few hours of sleep.

The sun was still low in the east when Amanda awoke. She tried to rest longer but was awakened by the slightest sound, even the songs of the birds in the tree above her. Eating half of the biscuit and some of the dried beef reduced the growling in her stomach to a whimper.

She traveled through rough terrain that day, attempting to keep the road in sight to be sure that she was still traveling in the right direction. At times, she was unable to see it and would have to find her way to it again. She skirted the edge of the woods near the road wherever possible, which made her feel safer than walking out in the open. There was more traffic than she had expected; twice she had to duck down and lie flat on the ground when she heard horses approaching on the road. She suspected that they were cavalry patrols, though she didn't raise her head to look at them.

Clear mountain streams were plentiful, and Amanda drank the delicious liquid until she had her fill. Splashing her face with it kept her awake and moving when she thought she had no energy left. She was constantly hungry. When she found homesteads that looked deserted, she scrounged for any crumble of food. Sometimes she found only a few ears of dry corn, but it kept her going.

* * *

By dusk, her energy was totally depleted. She was hoping to find a nice barn or some sort of dry, warm place. Her body had ached all day from sleeping on the hard ground the previous night. The last light of evening was growing dim. She was traveling much too fast for safety when she suddenly entered a clearing and didn't see the low fire until it was too late. Amanda had happened upon a small band of Rebel soldiers.

She turned to run, but one of the men grabbed her by the collar and pulled her backward, dropping her on the ground near the fire. When she held her head up to get a look at her captors, the flames singed her hair. She soon found her legs and sat up quickly.

"Looky what I found for you, Sergeant," the soldier huffed.

"Them Union boys think they're so clever," said the sergeant. "They think we won't suspect a woman, but I'm not so easily fooled. Put her in the wagon, boys. I think we've got ourselves a real-life Union spy. And tie her down. She looks like a slippery one."

Before she could think of anything to say, they led her away. "Wait," she cried, but no one would believe she was a Rebel in this neighborhood of Unionists.

The most unpleasant-looking soldier tied her hands behind her back and yanked her arm violently as he pulled her up into a covered wagon. The other one put his hands on her buttocks and pushed her hard. She fell on top of the soldier in the wagon.

"Oh, you want to play, huh?" he said crudely, fondling her breasts.

"You'd better hope I don't live through this," she said through clenched teeth, "because if I do, I'll be back to take care of you, you ape." She spat in his face as he bound her feet in front of her. He slapped her so hard her vision was temporarily impaired, and that took all the fight out of her.

He yanked her arm again as he tied her hands to a wooden post at the corner of the wagon. "You'd better watch your step, missy," he whispered, his foul breath in her face.

He then jumped down from the wagon, leaving her alone.

Amanda expected one of the soldiers to assault her at any minute. All night she tried to free herself, but the rope around her wrists was too tight. So frightened she would do anything to get away, Amanda rubbed the rope against the sharp edge of the wooden post, and it eventually began to fray. Just before sunrise she managed to get her hands loose and untie her feet, but not before the soldiers were up and about. Their canteens clinked together as they filled them at the creek nearby.

She slumped forward and pretended to be asleep when the corporal looked in on her. He said not a word. She hoped they were preparing to leave and she could slip away.

Before she had time to decide her next course of action, she heard the pounding of horses' hooves entering the clearing. She soon realized that the Rebels were being attacked, probably by some of General Burnside's men. In the confusion of smoke and gunfire, she managed to escape and ran far into a deep dark wood. She hid out there all day, listening to the sounds of people and horses coming and going in the distance, too frightened to move. She would have run back home right then and locked herself inside—if she only knew how to get there.

* * *

Three roads converged where she stood. In the process of escaping from the Rebels and running through the woods, Amanda had lost all sense of direction and was compelled to come out of hiding and try to discover where she was. She thought she was still on the old road headed for Virginia, but she couldn't be sure. Thus far, no house or landmark had struck her as familiar.

If not for a sharp curve in the road and the sound of loud voices up ahead, she would have walked directly into the midst of a small cavalry detachment who had stopped to feed and water their horses. She climbed a steep embankment and hid behind some shrubs, watching them from a safe distance.

She had no idea if they were Union or Confederate. The ones she could see from her hiding place were dressed in homespun clothing, which gave her no clue to their identity. Listening to their manner of speech, she was fairly certain they were Union men.

When they finally resumed their journey, they walked their horses for some time, allowing them to rest and digest the corn they had been fed. She followed along the embankment above them until the land flattened out in front of her, level with the road.

She had to decide quickly whether to trust them or to let them pass. The experience with the Confederates had left her badly shaken, but she realized she would have to trust someone in order to find her way again. She stayed hidden in the underbrush until she saw the portly Major's blue Union coat. Feeling better about her decision, she stepped out of the bushes and was instantly met by six or eight guns, all pointed at her head.

"Don't shoot," Amanda said nervously, holding up her hands. "My husband is a Union soldier. Uh...Jonathan Armstrong. Do you know him?"

"It's a woman," one of the soldiers said.

"It don't look like a woman," another said.

"No," said the major, rubbing his scruffy beard, "I don't know anyone by that name."

"I'm a Unionist from over in Greene County. My husband's in the cavalry somewhere between here and Knoxville," she stammered. She couldn't remember the name. "Strawberry Plains," she finally said, "that's the place."

The major took her aside and questioned her thoroughly about her loyalties, and what she was doing on this lonely mountain road alone.

"In the short time we've been here," the major said kindly, "we've already learned that you can't trust civilians around here. They'll lie right to your face."

"I'm trying to get to my mother's," Amanda said, "near Abingdon, Virginia."

"You're not headed for Virginia, ma'am," he said, shaking his head. "You're going south, on the road to Knoxville." He invited her to sit down on some grass and take a drink from his canteen, while he drew a crude map on the damp ground with a stick.

"Towards Virginia," he said, "there's Rebels everywhere. We're headed back to our headquarters at Knoxville to report what we've found up here. Best thing you can do for yourself, ma'am, is to go back home. You're safer there than you'll be out here."

"I'm beginning to realize that," she said with a sigh. "Well—can you help me find my way home? It's over east—yes, east of Greeneville." Her voice took on a plaintive quality she hadn't noticed before. "Can you take me there, or point me in the right direction?"

"Which way is Greeneville from here?" he asked.

"I'm so turned around I don't know." She heard the fear in her voice.

"This way is north, more or less," he said, pointing to the direction from which they had come.

"Then Greeneville has to be that way," she said, pointing toward the southeast.

"Then you can't go home neither," the major explained. "We're running the Rebs out of here as fast as we can, but they're a feisty bunch and don't give up easily."

A large Rebel encampment was now somewhere between their position and Cinnamon Hill, the major said. They had met up with some of them the day before.

"I don't know how many," he continued, "but it's more than a few, are holed up between here and your home."

"What am I to do?" Her voice quivered. She was on the verge of tears.

"I can take you to Strawberry Plains," he offered. "It's not too far out of our way. Maybe your husband can help you from there."

"I don't know," she said, her mind racing. She wasn't anxious to see Jonathan, but he might be able to take her back home or someplace safe if any such place could be found.

"That's all I can do for you, ma'am. I hear Knoxville is full of refugees from the valley up here," he said. "Maybe you can find work there and support yourself until the war is over."

"I pray so," sighed Amanda. "Thank you, major."

* * *

It was dusk when they reached the bridge near the town of Strawberry Plains. The major spoke to a soldier on duty and ascertained that Jonathan was encamped with a small garrison nearby. The major pointed Amanda toward some tents near the other end of the long bridge.

"I have to get going before I'm court-martialed," he said as he helped her down from the saddle. "Good luck to you, ma'am."

"God bless you, Major," she said. He and his men took off in a flash of hooves.

The first soldier she encountered was still some distance from the bridge. She explained the purpose of her visit—which she had to repeat to several other soldiers before she actually reached the bridge. The soldier who guarded the other end of the bridge called for his superior, to whom she explained again why she was there.

"You're Armstrong's wife?" the sergeant asked. He grinned sheepishly as he pointed out a tent that sat a short distance from the others. "Go on," he snickered. "I'm sure he'll be glad to see you."

She walked across the bridge as quickly as she could and hurried to the tent, wanting to be away from the soldiers' prying eyes. The anticipation of a good night's sleep in warmth and shelter—even if it was with Jonathan—and maybe some food, as well, were the only thoughts in her mind as she approached the tent.

Amanda quickly pulled back the tent flap and stepped inside. A small desk in the center of the room partially obscured the far corner of the tent, from where she heard voices. She took one step forward and waited for her eyes to adjust to the soft light. She saw two bodies on a large mattress, barely discernible in the low flame of the oil lamp on the desk.

A woman, totally naked, was giggling and riding a man as if he were a bucking bronco. The man, Amanda soon realized, was her husband. A loud gasp drew attention she didn't want. She stepped out of the doorway, hoping to sneak away unnoticed, but Jonathan was running

after her, his drawers flapping, trying to get his pants on and his suspenders onto his shoulders. His pant legs soon tripped him up. She
looked back and saw him fall face first in the dirt. Under other circumstances, it would have been a comical sight.

"Please, Amanda," he called, up and running again. "Wait."

She stopped suddenly, and he almost ran into her.

"You should have posted a lookout," she said without emotion.

He appeared to be tongue-tied after running all that way to catch
her. "What're you doing here?"

"There's only one thing I want to know from you, Jonathan," she
said, a tremble in her voice. "Where is my money?"

"What money?" he said, not at all convincingly. "Had to have some
traveling money, and knew you'd be getting money from your trust."

"The bank failed, Jonathan," she said, seething. "I won't be receiv-
ing any more money from the trust."

"You and Luke have vegetables from the garden if nothing more."

"The garden's been picked bare, and Luke is gone."

"Where?"

"To serve with General John Hunt Morgan."

"How could you let that happen?" he asked angrily.

"You ruined any control I ever had over him, remember?"

Jonathan sighed heavily, but said nothing in rebuttal.

"Where did the money go, Jonathan? The money Charles left us."

"How do you think I bought the precious flour and sugar and
coffee you couldn't live without? On the black market, that's how.
Hundreds and hundreds of dollars."

"How many hundreds went for the whiskey you and your cronies
drank? And how many hundreds went uncollected for legal services
rendered to those same men? Men who are, in case you have been able
to delude yourself completely, a bunch of black-hearted Confederate
sympathizers who have now taken to the hills to hide from the conscription agents. Too lazy and no-good to fight for their country."

"Not true," he sputtered.

"Oh, it's true, all right. I always suspected it. Now everyone in Armstrong Crossroads knows it."

"Don't have to listen to this," he said.

"No, you don't," she shouted. "And if God is kind to me, I will never have to look upon your sorry face again."

"There is no money left," he said. "Paid off Confederate conscription agents so I could stay at home and take care of you."

"Hah! Then you turned around and left anyway."

"You threw me out."

"No, *no*," she protested. "You left because you couldn't face what you did to our son. You have done exactly as you pleased your entire sorry life. Now get away from me!" She began to run again.

"Where are you going?" Jonathan shouted.

She didn't answer.

"Come back," he called. "I'll take you home." That was the last thing she heard him say.

She ran ahead, hoping to catch the major and his men.

But they were nowhere in sight.

TEN

—•◦━━━◦•—

October 1863

Amanda had been to Knoxville on her wedding trip, but she hadn't paid the slightest bit of attention as to how to get there. She knew the general direction, but there would be towns and roads that she should avoid—because she was a woman and she was alone There would be creeks and rivers to cross, as well as gaps in the mountains to be negotiated. She finally decided that, though it wasn't the most direct route, following the East Tennessee and Virginia Railroad was the only way to avoid getting lost again.

She started out moving fast, walking from one skirt of timber to another—while avoiding all roads. Traveling during the day was danger-ous. She feared that she could be spotted from the foothills, could be tracked and hunted down like a dog, without ever knowing someone was after her, until it was too late.

She had eaten nothing for two days. With every step she took, Amanda blamed herself for not at least getting some food from Jona-than. Gali had warned her many times about her pride. She finally found some berries and ate them voraciously, though a thought nagged at her brain. Gali had taught her about wild berries a long time ago.

Were these berries poisonous? She couldn't remember. She couldn't stop eating them, regardless; her hunger took over.

Within two hours, it all came back up, leaving her weaker than before. She lay on a secluded ridge for two days, munching on basil leaves, before she could move on. She parched some corn she had stolen from a barn and finally regained a little strength, but she was running out of the one commodity she needed most: hope.

About mid-afternoon one day, heavy clouds rolled in quickly. The sky became as dark as night. She could barely see her hand in front of her face. The wind whipped up fiercely, knocking her off balance when she tried to walk. Rain came down punishingly hard, pelting her face; it was followed by hailstones almost the size of hen's eggs. The rain and wind assaulted her eyes so violently she couldn't keep them open. Amanda fumbled around and finally found a shallow ditch where she could at least hide her face from the onslaught. The storm lasted for what seemed to be an hour before she could continue her journey. She was soaked to the skin and shivering, but she trudged on.

Amanda was traveling in an open area, with no woods on either side of the railroad. So, she walked on the west side of a ridge that ran parallel to the tracks and climbed to the top from time to time to make sure she hadn't veered off course. After one such exercise, climbing back down from the ridge, she stopped abruptly. One more step and she would have tumbled down a fifty-foot ravine. At the bottom was a dilapidated hut.

The setting would be idyllic, if the dwelling wasn't so shabby. The site was protected from bad weather and sheltered from the hot sun. The stream that flowed past the dwelling was probably full of fish; the surrounding forest likely full of game. She could see the remains of a small vegetable garden; there were probably only potatoes left in the ground now. Large sheets of flattened tree bark covered the exterior of the hut and a good portion of the roof. She couldn't imagine what the interior might look like.

She argued with herself for several minutes, her mind bringing up advantages and disadvantages of stopping at this place: What kind of people might live in such a dwelling? Could they be dangerous? Considering the condition of the house, would they have anything to share with a tired and hungry traveler? That pretty much took care of the disadvantages.

There was only one advantage, but it was an important one: It was the only structure of any sort she had seen in hours. The thought of spending another night in the forest hungry and cold, and now wet as well... It didn't take long to decide it was worth the risk. If the place was empty, she could investigate the garden; her mouth drooled at the thought. And there was an old wooden bucket hanging on the side of a well. Springs of cool clear water hadn't been so plentiful in her recent travels.

She summoned the courage to call out as she slid down the steep ridge on her backside. It wasn't a good idea to approach a residence without first announcing your presence. Doing otherwise might get you killed.

"Hello!" Amanda shouted. "Is anyone home?"

A slender woman with perfectly white hair came around the corner of the hut, wiping her hands on an apron. "I'm here," she said, squinting at Amanda. "Do I know you?"

"No, ma'am. I'm just passing by and was hoping you might let me dry myself by your fire. I was caught in the storm, as you can see," Amanda said, self-consciously trying to straighten her mud-caked clothes. "I was almost too afraid to call out—half expecting a large, gruff mountain man who might feed me and then make me his slave."

"There's only me here," the woman said, laughing.

"I've never seen anybody as skinny as you are and still breathing," Amanda marveled.

"Always was thin—runs in my family." The woman smiled and showed four large brown teeth. "When you live in a glen," the woman said, motioning upward, the skin on her bony arms flapping, "there's too much climbing to get fat. Why's your face so red and splotchy?" she asked.

"Hailstones got me pretty good," Amanda explained.

"Well, where are my manners? Come in," the woman said. "Just because I was born in the woods doesn't mean I should act like it." She stopped and extended her hand to Amanda. "I'm Dolly Harper." She opened the narrow door and motioned for Amanda to follow her in.

Inside, there was a warm candlelit interior a thousand times more beautiful than Amanda would have ever imagined. "My goodness," she sighed. "What a lovely place."

"If I kept the outside looking as good as the inside, I might have more company than I want," Dolly said.

The glow and warmth of the fireplace almost brought Amanda to tears. If Dolly had nothing more than the fire to share, she would have been very grateful. But there was more.

She served Amanda collard greens, cornbread fried in bacon grease, and potatoes baked on the hearth. The potato peeling was so crunchy and tasty that there was no trace of a potato left on her plate when she finished.

Amanda ate too much and too quickly for her shriveled stomach to digest. She barely slept that night. The nausea was all-consuming. Dolly brought a slop-basin to her bedside and bathed her feverish forehead with a cool cloth most of the night.

"You're too sick to travel today," Dolly said near dawn.

"I'll be fine," Amanda whispered. But she wasn't fine; when she tried to stand, weakness assaulted her limbs and she had to lie back down. She stayed there for two days before continuing her journey.

"It seems to me you haven't had much luck finding your own way," Dolly said at breakfast on the day that Amanda was determined to leave for Knoxville.

"I'm terrible with directions," Amanda admitted.

"I'll draw you a map so you can go across lots and enter the city at an inconspicuous place. I wish I knew someone there who could help you out, but I haven't been to Knoxville in years. The people I knew there are most likely dead and gone."

Thanks to Dolly's map, Amanda made good time the first day. Thanks to the food Dolly packed in her knapsack, she was able to travel longer.

* * *

They saw Amanda before she saw them, and she soon realized they had planned it that way. She was walking along the edge of a wooded ridge. As she approached a hilltop, two black women stepped out from behind some trees, startling her. Then the others showed themselves.

They were a family of ex-slaves, ten of them, all women and children. Amanda soon learned that they were refugees on their way to a contraband camp near Knoxville that had been set up to care for fleeing slaves. Two of the women were breastfeeding infants. They immediately accosted her for food, but she told them that she had none.

Amanda hurried on, quickly moving across an open field to the edge of the woods beyond when she sensed a presence behind her.

What a shock it was to encounter a pair of huge dark eyes bulging from an angelic brown face, which was covered with some sort of white powder. It was a very small black boy, barely the size of a toddler.

"What are you doing here, child?" she asked.

"Cold, Misty," he said softly, "and hungry about to death."

He wore only an old flannel shirt that was too big for him, and a pair of pants that were so worn that the fabric was unraveling at the hem. He crossed his arms and held them close to his body, and began to shiver.

"What's that on your face?" she asked him.

"Flour. I licked every bit of it out of the wood box we brought from home."

"It might have been better if you'd mixed some water with it."

"I did," he said, "on my tongue." His mouth was a white gooey mess.

"Doesn't it make your throat dry?"

"Terrible dry," he said, coughing.

She invited him to sit down on a nearby log and offered him a drink of water from her canteen.

"Where are your folks?" she asked him.

"They's the only folks I got left," he said, pointing to the group on the hill. His breath puffed out white in the cool morning air.

"They say I'm too slow," he said sadly, "I'm gonna get us caught. They can't carry me all the time, and my stubby legs can't walk fast enough. They're looking for a man named Burnside. They say he's a Union man and he'll protect us from the Southrons. Do you know him?"

"He's an officer in the Union army."

She didn't have time to be encumbered by a child, but he looked so pitiful.

"Here, wipe your face. It's as white as mine." She handed him a handkerchief.

"Thank you, Misty. I'll be clean, I promise.

"Don't call me 'Misty.' I'm not your mistress."

"What do I call you?"

"Amanda is fine."

"You a Rebel or a Yankee, Misty—I mean, Amanda?" It came out sounding like "Abanda."

"Neither," she said, after a long pause.

"You got to be one or the other," he insisted.

One of the black women was walking toward them. She pulled the boy's arm, rather roughly, Amanda thought, and shoved him behind her.

"I was just talking to him," Amanda told her. "I mean no harm."

The woman stared at Amanda.

"Are you his mother?"

"His mother's gone," the woman said flatly.

"Gone where?"

"You know—gone."

"Leave us alone for a bit," Amanda told the woman. "He's perfectly safe." The woman stepped aside but glared at Amanda as she returned to the group.

"Yankee or Rebel?" the boy asked again.

"Why is it so important to you to know what I am?"

"I don't know," he said, shrugging his shoulders. "Everybody's got to be one or the other."

She handed him a small piece of cornbread.

"You said you didn't have no food."

"Shh," she said, watching the group. "I don't have enough for the others, and don't let them know I gave you this."

"Why won't you tell me what you are?" he asked, savoring his cornbread.

"I'm not sure what I am."

"I think you're a Rebel. Rebels don't like black folks."

"I'm a dove," she said abruptly. The word left her lips before the idea had formed completely in her mind, but it sounded good when she said it.

"What's that?"

"You're awful smart for such a little fellow," she said, smiling.

"I listen to grown folks a lot."

"I can see that. I'm a dove because I hate the war and the killing. Nobody will be better off when it's over."

"Mama said we'll be free when we get to Knoxville, where the blue soldiers are, and we won't have to work for white folks no more."

"What happened to your Mama?" Amanda asked, still watching the black women.

"Died," the boy said. The corners of his mouth turned down, but not a single tear filled his eyes.

"I'm so sorry. When did she die?"

"Four days ago," he said.

"What happened?"

"Froze to death," he said, nodding his little head. "This big storm come up, and we were caught out in the open field, no barn or shelter nowhere close by."

"I got caught in that storm, too, but I was lucky enough to find shelter for the night."

"We all climbed in this big ditch beside the road. Mama laid her body across me to protect me. When I woke up, she was froze."

"What do you mean, froze?"

"She had little pieces of ice froze in her eyebrows," he said, pulling at his own eyebrows.

"My word," Amanda whispered. She reached out and took his little brown hand in her own and rubbed it gently. She was touched by this child's innocence. Surely, he didn't comprehend the meaning of the words he spoke.

"They left me there, under her," he said. "I guess they thought I was froze, too. But I caught up to them."

"What's your name?"

"Josiah Turner," he said, extending his little hand to shake hers.

"Aren't you sad? Don't you mourn for the loss of your mother?"

"Yes'm. Every day, but I have to keep my pain in my heart," he said, laying his little hand on his chest.

"Didn't you cry?"

"For two solid days," Josiah said sadly. "But Vinie said, 'If you don't quit that crying, you'll die, too. None of us have the energy to take care of you, so you'll have to take care of your own self.'"

He was the biggest of the children. There were three others, five grown women, and a girl who looked to be in her teens.

"How old are you?" Amanda asked him.

"My birthday is on the Fourth of July," he said proudly, puffing out his chest. "Just like Uncle Sam. July past I was five years old."

"Are you sure? You must be mistaken."

"No'm," he replied, "I'm five."

"My, you're small for your age."

"My Papa was small, but he was brave and strong. No shame in being a small man, Mama said. My papa died before I could remember him. Killed over a dollar bill he won in a card game. Some said he cheated, but Mama said my pa would never cheat. He was just trying to win some money for us."

"Don't you have any family left?"

"Vinie's my aunt," he said, pointing to the tallest of the women, "but she loses patience with me. Says I talk too much and ask too many questions. Says it'll get me into bad trouble someday if I don't quit it."

* * *

At Knoxville, Amanda learned that—after taking the oath of allegiance to the Union, which she would gladly do—she should be able to draw food and other necessities from the Union Army, which had recently occupied the town. However, the streets were packed with refugees who had arrived ahead of her, and the food supply was not always plentiful. Some days she had to beg on the streets in order to survive another day. Finding a warm place to sleep was a daily battle. Cold weather was setting in.

Life was hard in the alleys of Knoxville. Nights were cold. Hundreds of refugees had traveled there hoping to find some protection, only to find that they had to beg on the streets for the basic human needs in order to survive another day.

Amanda slept wherever she could find a bare spot on the ground, and her limbs ached so badly that it took her an hour to stretch them out after she woke up. She became very depressed and constantly berated herself for ending up in such a hopeless place, for being too proud to accept Jonathan's help, for leaving home at all. She cried constantly and couldn't believe people walked right past her without offering any assistance. She soon realized that they were in the same situation she was.

She finally found a place at the back door of a shoemaker's shop that opened onto the alley. The doorframe was about two feet deep, and if she pressed her back against the door, she could get a little heat from inside. When she spread her oilcloth there and pulled the blankets over her, it was the most comfortable place she had found so far.

Her problem then was trying to hold onto that spot. Squatters' rights prevailed in the alleys of Knoxville. She had befriended the old man who owned the shoe shop, and he tried to keep the space cleared for her. But if she didn't get back by the time he went home, it was very likely that someone else would be sleeping there when she returned. And, she had to leave every day to look for work and scrounge for food.

Any jobs that might have been available to outsiders had already been taken by the time she arrived. There were so many vagabonds that every little corner of the city was full of them. They huddled together in their makeshift tents to keep warm. Amanda found it strange how quickly people can become accustomed to almost any way of life.

She had been to the Brandywine Hotel several times looking for work. On one particular day the man at the front desk didn't even look up at her, but he suggested that she speak with the manager of the dining room. "His office is behind the kitchen," he said.

Amanda allowed herself to be hopeful for only a moment. He was probably just trying to be rid of her. The only door she found behind the kitchen looked like a closet door, but she opened it anyway, startling a man who was sitting at a desk, which took up most of the cramped space.

"Excuse me. Sir, are you the kitchen manager?"

"Yes," he answered reticently, concentrating on the paperwork spread out on the desk. "What can I do for you?"

"The man at the desk said you might have some work for me. I'll do anything—dishes, laundry, whatever."

"Sorry," the man mumbled, "I don't have anything right now."

"Sir, I don't mean to be pushy, really, and I'm ready to cry—it's a miracle I'm not crying already. Listen, I've been sleeping in a dirty alley since I arrived in Knoxville," she said in a plaintive voice. "I'm sure you get all kinds of hard luck stories these days, but please, don't you have something I can do for a little pay?"

"Well, I promised a young lady I spoke to yesterday that she could serve breakfast for two hours this morning, but she didn't show up. It's a little extra service we offer to the people living at the hotel. We serve them in a small room off the dining room at a lower cost than the public pays. It's mostly men, and you're pretty enough."

"What have my looks got to do with it?" she said, suddenly panicked.

"I've learned it helps to have an attractive waitress."

"All right," she said excitedly. "I'll be here in the morning, I promise you. You'll have no trouble from me. And might I bother you for some information about the hotel. Do you suppose they have any rooms—small rooms—available?"

"I wouldn't know," he said, looking back at his desk. "You'll have to check at the desk."

"The man at the front desk is a bit tired of me. I thought you might know of something—a place to sleep would be a Godsend. Even if it's just a closet."

"Sorry, can't help you there."

"Well, thank you for the job, sir. I'll be here in the morning. Good day to you."

The man caught up to her in the kitchen. "I will—let's step back into my office," he said secretively. "I'm fairly certain they have nothing available in the hotel, but I'll let you sleep here, in my office, if you want to."

"Where?" she asked, looking around. "There's no room for a bed."

"I happened to think maybe you could sleep on my desk, and I would use it during the day."

"Well, I don't know..."

"It was just a thought," he said. "At least it's shelter. Better than sleeping on the ground, I should say."

"You're right," she said quickly.

"There's no heat in here," he explained, "but if you leave the door open, the warmth from the kitchen keeps it quite livable. I'll find some quilts and blankets—you know to make it more comfortable for you. And I'll throw in a biscuit and sausage for your breakfast."

"God bless you, kind sir."

"Then, including the food for breakfast and the sleeping quarters," he said, counting on his fingers, "and the short time you'll be working, I'll give you a dollar a week."

"A dollar?" In her excitement, she had forgotten about her wages. And she knew that people could charge almost any outrageous price for shelter of any sort in Knoxville.

"Take it or leave it," he said angrily.

It was still better than anything else she could foresee, so she took it. And she felt the safest she had felt since she left Cinnamon Hill. The job wasn't so bad, carrying trays of food and pouring coffee, but people who could afford to live in a hotel could be very demanding.

Amanda was more tired than usual one morning when the manager knocked on the door—her signal to dress and get ready for work. She was serving a table of businessmen. They were particularly obnoxious, having no patience whatever. She was glad her shift would soon be over. While she was replenishing their coffee cups, one of the men patted her on the behind. She thought at first that she must be mistaken, but when she looked at him, he smiled at her, obviously proud of his deed. Without thinking, she poured the entire pot of hot coffee in his lap.

He yelped and screamed, and tried not to touch himself, but finally shoved his hand down his pants and pulled the hot clothing away from his private parts.

Amanda was fired.

"You'll have to vacate my office as well!" the kitchen manager yelled. "You'll have no money to pay for it."

"How can you do that?" she whined. "You know I have no place to go."

"You should have thought of that before you poured hot coffee into that gentleman's lap."

"He had no right to fondle me."

"Get out!"

As Amanda was leaving the hotel, the man at the front desk, asked why she was crying. She explained the situation to him.

The man said in a comforting voice, "I don't think that's right."

"I don't either," she whimpered, "but what can I do?"

"I think you should speak to the hotel owner."

"Really?" she said, drying her eyes. "Where can I find him?"

The man directed her to his office. Johnson, he said his name was.

"Mr. Johnson?" she said, tapping lightly on the door.

"Yes," a voice said, "come in."

"Mr. Johnson, my name is Amanda Armstrong, I have just been fired from the kitchen, and the man at the front desk thought I should speak to you."

"Yes," he said kindly. Please, sit down."

The man looked a little seedy, like his hotel, but he dressed fairly well and was well spoken.

"I have one room left on the second floor, in the very back, at the end of the hall."

"I have very little money."

"We won't worry about that right now. Here's the key," he said, reaching into the top drawer of his desk. "You take your things on up and have a rest. I'll come up later and we'll talk."

"Wonderful!" she cried. Then she thought a moment. "Why would you do this for me? I have nothing to give you in return," she said suspiciously.

"Is this the way you treat people who offer to help you?" he asked.

"I just don't understand why—"

"Please, Mrs. Armstrong," he said patiently, "go rest. We'll talk later."

* * *

"Hello?" a man was saying at the door, waking her.

It was dark outside, and Amanda couldn't remember where she was.

"Mrs. Armstrong?" he said softly. "It's Mr. Johnson. May I come in?"

"I'm sorry," she said, opening the door. "I must have dozed off."

"That's all right. I'm glad you could rest, but I need to clarify our arrangement here."

"Yes?" she said cautiously. The hair on her arms stood on end.

"What do you expect me to do?" she asked cautiously. "In return for this nice room?"

"You're a beauty," he said, looking her over. "You'll bring a good price. It's not my taste, you understand, but some men prefer the slim uppity type. Me, I like some flesh on my women."

"What are you saying?" she asked in a raised voice.

"Well, we have gentlemen who come here for a little companionship. I'm sure you understand what I mean," he said, smiling at her. "I'll let you keep half the money. I can tell you it's the most generous offer you'll find in Knoxville."

"That might be true, sir," she said haughtily, "but I will not prostitute myself for any reason!"

"Do you really mean that?" he asked angrily. "Those alleys are colder than they were a few weeks ago. Do you really want to put yourself back in that situation?"

"If that's my only alternative, then yes, I do."

"Then back to the alley with you!" he shouted.

* * *

Amanda saw the little black boy she had met on the way to Knoxville on the street. "Josiah, how are you?"

"Starving, Misty," he said sadly. "Vinie sent me to beg something for the babies, but nobody won't give me nothing."

His large plaintive eyes touched her heart.

"I'd share with you if I had anything myself." She didn't think he could be any thinner than he was when they met on the road, but he appeared to be. His round little cheeks were sunken in now.

"Josiah, I'm on my way to the hotel," she said kindly, "and I have to go. Take care of yourself."

"Yes'm," he said. He stood in the alley and watched while she walked away.

"All right," Amanda said when she reached Mr. Johnson's office. "I don't like this one bit, mind you, but I'm ready to do whatever it takes to keep a roof over my head and food on my plate."

Oh my, I said that so easily.

"Do you really mean that?" he said, smiling.

"Yes."

"You're not meant for this work, Amanda," he said.

"I left my husband up at Strawberry Plains in a tent with a whore," she yelled, "and I don't have one shred of dignity left!"

"I didn't mean to upset you."

"I apologize, Mr. Johnson," she said. "I've forced myself to face the reality of my life. My legs are arthritic from sleeping on the cold ground. I've got a nagging cough I can't get rid of. I've probably lost ten pounds since I arrived here, and I was too thin already."

"You're only upset because you've discovered that you're just like everybody else."

"How so?"

"In the end, we'll all do just about anything to stay alive."

* * *

The first time Amanda was with a man, it made her ill. She excused herself and ran toward the washroom at the end of the hall. Her client was left unsatisfied and didn't understand that she was sick. Still in his long johns, he caught up to her in the hallway and grabbed her arm. She clamped her hand over her mouth, trying desperately not to vomit.

He began to complain loudly that he had been cheated. Other women and their clients, in various stages of dress, came out of their rooms to see what the fuss was about. Amanda was still trying to wrest her arm from the man's grasp when she lost the battle—and puked all over his shoes, which, yes, he still wore. He looked down at his shoes and back at her, then raised his hand as if to slap her.

Only then did she notice that his red and swollen "mast" was still "hoisted" through the front flap of his long johns. And she began to laugh.

Amanda didn't wait for anyone to tell her she was fired. She packed her meager possessions and went back to her little corner in the alley, crying all the way. But someone else had discovered how comfortable it was in the rear doorway of the shoe shop, away from the wind that seemed to blow constantly. She bedded down as close to the door as possible.

Later that night, she awoke just in time to feel her blankets being pulled away very slowly. "Stop!" she screamed. "That's mine!" It was too dark to see anything but a silhouette.

"Now it's mine," a voice whispered, but she held on tight. "You don't let go, I'll cut you," the voice threatened. And she lost her grip.

She scrambled to get up. The alley was slick with rain, and she fell back onto the ground twice. By the time she ran to the end of the alley, there was no one in sight. She huddled with a group of refugees under an awning for the rest of the night. At least she was sheltered from the rain, but as soon as the owner came to open the shop, they would be run out of there.

A voice woke her in the gray light of dawn. "Is Amanda Armstrong here?" It was a woman's voice.

"Yes," she said, jumping to her feet. "I'm Amanda."

"Hello," the woman said, extending her hand. "I'm Lily. Mr. Johnson told me to find you. He wants to speak with you immediately." The woman had a beautiful face, a swept-up hairdo, and very nice clothes—though they were too revealing for Amanda's taste.

"I have nothing more to say to him," Amanda said angrily.

"He says he has a new proposal he thinks you might like."

"What?"

"I don't know," Lily said impertinently. "He didn't confide in me. Come along, we'll get you cleaned up."

"I'm much better off than you," Lily said, in her room at the Brandywine Hotel. "I have friends who'll protect me if I need them, but it took years to get where I am. For all of Mr. Johnson's rough edges, he's a fair employer—as good as any around here, I'd say."

"Why do you do this?" Amanda asked as she was washing her face.

"I like the money," Lily said, rubbing her fingers together. "Look around you, honey. I'd much prefer to be here than where you just left."

"I can't seem to do it just for the money."

"What other reason could there be?"

"Well, there's this little black boy I keep running into," Amanda said. "I saw him the other day, begging for food, and I didn't have a thing to give him. He'll probably die soon if someone doesn't help him."

"There are people like that all over the city."

"I know."

"They're making a mess of this town," Lily said angrily. "They came here uninvited."

"So did I," Amanda said.

"You'd better take care of yourself, and forget about them."

* * *

Amanda tapped lightly on Mr. Johnson's office door.

"Come in."

"You wanted to see me?" she said meekly.

"Sit down," he said roughly. He didn't look at her.

"Are you angry?"

"No!" he said, apparently louder than he meant to. "I've never known a woman who exasperates me so. You just ran off, and I didn't know what happened to you."

"I didn't think I'd be welcome here anymore," she said.

"Well, I had an idea that might help us both out of this predicament."

"What's that?"

"What if I were to set it up so you had to keep company with only one man, and only when you wanted to? Do you think you could handle that?" he said.

"I don't know," she said softly. "It would depend on who the man was, I guess."

"What if I was the man?"

"Oh!" Her mind was racing. "I don't know."

"Will you, or won't you?" he asked angrily. "That's the only question you have to answer."

"I'll get my room back?"

"Yes, and three meals a day, and no one bothering you but me—just sleep with me at night. All right?"

She paused for a moment, but she could see that he had little patience left. "Uh...all right. Yes, thank you."

"I knew those few weeks of having a warm room and good food would spoil you for street life. It's the goody-goody ones who give in first."

I am simply mortified.

ELEVEN

———◆◆◆———

November 1863

Amanda heard almost daily of events taking place in the counties of Northeast Tennessee. Stories spread rapidly from the soldiers who were returning to Knoxville from that area. She worried about Cinnamon Hill and her decision to leave it. How could she ever get back home? Could she survive another trip like the one that got her to Knoxville?

Amanda and Johnson settled into a comfortable existence. He had a nice suite of rooms on the top floor of the hotel. His employees took care of the cleaning and the cooking, and Amanda had free time to do as she pleased. He had someone to sleep with at night. He was usually too tired to do anything else, which suited her fine.

Josiah Turner came to the hotel one evening, looking for Amanda. Lily told Amanda that the doorman had kicked Josiah out into the street, and she went down to talk to him. He looked about as bedraggled as one could imagine.

"What happened to you?" Amanda asked him.

"I run away from the contraband camp," he said. "It's dirty and smelly and full o' sickness. My Aunt Vinie's baby died," he said sadly.

"Every time I come to these streets, I'm reminded of what I endured here," she said. "But I've come up with some ideas about helping the folks in this city who don't have enough to eat."

She sneaked Josiah upstairs to her room and fed him some bacon she had left from breakfast. He was feverish and exhausted. She laid him on her bed and told him to stay there.

Amanda visited her old friend the kitchen manager at the Brandywine Hotel. "Will you consider donating your leftover food to the poor homeless refugees in this city?"

"We don't have much leftover food, but I'll sell it to you."

"You have a price for everything, don't you?"

"Get out of my office!" he stormed.

"All right—all right, I'm sorry," she said, trying to calm him down. "Do you ever have milk left over?"

"Rarely."

"Coffee?"

"Never."

"Scraps, potato peelings, whatever," she told him. "I'll take it all."

"Very well, I'll work up some prices for you," he said. "You'll have to pay cash money for whatever I have each day."

"Lock it in your office at night, and I'll come get it in the morning," she said, her mind racing. "Can I use the stove in the kitchen if I need to cook something?"

"Only before 5:30 in the morning," he said.

Amanda went to every restaurant owner in town and convinced some of them to sell or donate something. It took weeks to get everything arranged, but it was worth the effort. She was amazed at how much better she felt about herself.

Johnson rarely came to bed before midnight, and Amanda got up at four-thirty in the morning to gather the food contributions and prepare what needed to be cooked. She invited the people she knew from the alley where she had slept and that now included Josiah

Turner. They came to the back door of the hotel, and she served them whatever she had been able to collect that morning. She also swore them to secrecy—if they told others that they were being fed, there would be trouble.

One afternoon, Amanda saw an old man lying in the street. She ran to him and tried to get him up, but he couldn't stand. He didn't speak, but his plaintive eyes begged her to help him. She ran to the hotel kitchen and bought a piece of bread, and filled her canteen with water.

She got down on her knees and held the man's head up. She tried to put a small piece of bread in his mouth, but he grabbed the canteen and tipped it up. Some water went into his mouth; most of it ran down his cheeks and into his ears.

She was trying to get the bread into his mouth again when Johnson arrived.

"So this is how you repay my kindness!" Johnson yelled. "This is food bought with my money!"

"I beg your humble pardon, sir," she shouted, standing up, "but I earned every penny of this money, and no one knows that better than you!"

He slapped her cheek with the back of his hand, with an audible smack. She fell to the ground, almost landing on the old man. Blood flowed from the inside of her cheek and out the corner of her mouth.

"This man is dying of starvation and thirst," she said, covering her mouth to hide the blood. "Do you expect me to walk over him?"

"No, you walk on him! You feel sorry for his kind today, and you'll be down there with him tomorrow."

"We can both live if I give him a little of my food. What's wrong with that?"

"Do not backtalk me!"

A crowd of men had gathered around them, and they were egging Johnson on. She didn't know how many times he hit her after that.

When she regained consciousness, she was still lying in the street.

Two well-dressed women passed by; one of them spat at her. "You finally got what you deserve," she said.

Amanda made it to the alley behind the shoe shop. Josiah was there. He was frightened by her appearance.

"Misty, you're bleeding," he gasped, seeing her swollen face and the terrible gash in her lip.

"Help me to the hotel," she mumbled.

People in the lobby gasped and stared. Leaning on Josiah, she finally made it to her room. He helped her into bed.

"Cold water and a cloth," she whispered.

"Don't die, Misty," Josiah said as he ran to the sink.

"I'm not dying," she mumbled, through swollen and bleeding lips. She rubbed his curly hair as he pressed the cold cloth gently to her face.

Lily came as soon as she heard and found Josiah crying.

"You really love Amanda, don't you?" Lily asked him.

"Yes'm," he sobbed.

"You have to leave right away," Lily told Amanda. "You won't be safe if Mr. Johnson finds out you're still here. I've never seen him this angry."

"I could no longer turn a blind eye to those poor people."

"Well, it was foolish," Lily insisted, "and I hope I can get you out of trouble. Fortunately, I haven't sold my mother's house out on the Kingston Road—not that anyone would be interested in purchasing a property that has been so overrun by the materiel of war."

"Is it dangerous?" Amanda asked.

"I don't know, but it's all I have to offer," Lily said, sounding a little aggravated.

"Forgive me, please. I must admit, I'm feeling quite desperate."

"And well you should," Lily said a little more patiently. "Go back to the alley where I found you. Stay quiet and keep out of sight. I'll send Isaac, my driver, before daybreak. Be ready to leave as soon as he arrives. You'll have no time to dawdle."

"Won't you be coming with me?" Amanda asked.

"I haven't been there since my mother's funeral last year," Lily said wistfully.

"Don't worry; I'll take good care of her," Josiah said.

"You can't take him with you," Lily said. "He won't like staying inside all the time. You'll have to feed him. And I hear General Longstreet's Rebels are all over the place out there. They care even less about little black boys than the Yankees here in town. They'll just haul him off to the contraband camp again."

"I'm sorry, Josiah," Amanda said, "you can't go with me."

He began to wail.

"Josiah, please," Amanda begged.

Lily grabbed his head and clamped her hand over his mouth. "Do you want to get Amanda killed?"

He shook his head, his big eyes bulging.

"Then you have to keep quiet."

He nodded.

"I'll send as much food as I can collect," Lily told her. "What with the Rebels allowing no traffic into the city from that direction, it won't be much. And the Yankees are picking the city clean so that General Burnside has a full table—never mind the rest of us. Everybody's hoarding what little they have."

"Why can't I stay here?"

"Girl, I'm afraid of what Johnson will do if he sees you again."

Amanda began to weep. "Every time I try to make my life better, it only gets worse."

"If you're to live through this, you have to quit feeling sorry for yourself! All of the doors and windows of my mother's house have been boarded up. There's a good supply of dry wood on the enclosed porch, if nobody's made off with it, but you'll only be able to use the fireplace at night. If the soldiers see smoke coming from the chimney, they'll surely come to see why. I know it will be dark and dreary, but it's the best I can do."

Lily displayed one of her loving smiles and touched Amanda's face. She then washed Amanda's wounds and applied some ointment she had in her bag, finally pulling out a black veil to cover Amanda's swollen face. It might be a good disguise; if people thought she was a grieving widow, maybe they would be kind.

They quickly gathered Amanda's belongings, vacated her room, and sneaked out the back door of the hotel.

* * *

Under different circumstances, Amanda would have enjoyed the ride to Lily's mother's house. As it was, she slumped onto the seat and rested her veiled head against the cushioned inside wall of the carriage. They passed through the city streets, then turned onto a narrow country road.

She was conscious of the lack of trees and shrubs one would expect to see alongside such a rural road. It appeared that the entire country south and west of town had been completely denuded of every living plant. Not a bush nor blade of grass remained in the yard of Lily's mother's house. The lawn had been rubbed down to the barrenness of the brown earth.

Lily had told Amanda her family's tragic story. Her father had owned a large plantation in Middle Tennessee, and he had built this house as a summer residence for her mother. Soon after the war began, his slaves deserted him; he lost his plantation and committed suicide. Lily went to work in Knoxville and maintained this home for her mother until her death.

It was a modest wooden structure, a rectangle with the long side facing the road. A one-story porch ran the full length of the front.

There was a large stone chimney at each end of the house. When Isaac turned the carriage onto a path that ran alongside the house, Amanda saw that there was a one-story addition on the back.

"We'll have to enter here," Isaac said, as he helped Amanda down from the carriage.

With a claw hammer, he removed the boards that covered the back door. The door opened into an enclosed porch. He then unlocked the door into the kitchen, which occupied the other half of the addition.

The interior was very nice, but not a shaft of light from the early dawn penetrated the windowpanes. The exterior and interior shutters were closed up tight. The only furniture left in the entire house was a sofa in the parlor and two old beds in the sleeping rooms upstairs. She dragged the sofa and a straw mattress to the kitchen, where she would make her living space. It was small, easy to heat, and she could cook there as well.

After dark, through cracks in the shutters, Amanda saw dozens of campfires. Indeed, there were soldiers everywhere. If she had doubted it before, she doubted it no longer. She cooked what little food she had and rationed it stringently, not knowing how long it would be before Isaac came again. She was lonesome and troubled, sleeping hours on end—anything to avoid having to think.

But in her waking hours, she couldn't help thinking about what had happened in Knoxville. She had been fortunate—though she was reluctant to admit it when the pain in her head was almost unbearable.

After those first terrifying weeks in the city, she hadn't suffered severely for the lack of food or shelter, but she had paid a high price for her comforts. Now that she had hours to contemplate her behavior, she had to face what she had done. She had discovered that, as Johnson so rudely pointed out, she was just like everybody else. She was having a difficult time accepting that. Self-forgiveness would be a long time in coming.

* * *

The cobwebs of deep sleep were beginning to clear. There was a sound. Was there a sound? Amanda gasped and held her breath. Had she been dreaming? What time was it? She let out a breath and sucked in another. She was in total darkness, only a few embers remaining of the fire she had set before lying down. She quickly added a few logs to the fire and lay back down on the mattress in front of the hearth.

She jumped when she heard footsteps on the front porch. She opened the kitchen door and crept through the parlor.

"I know someone's in there," a voice boomed—a male voice.

She didn't know what to do.

"The moon's as bright as day out here, and I see the smoke from your chimney."

Amanda had no idea the moon was shining brightly.

"I'm not here to harm anyone," the voice said. "Any scrap of food would be greatly appreciated. When you're on picket duty, all you do is think about what you'd like to be eating."

She hesitated. If he was on picket duty, he must be a soldier, most likely a Confederate soldier. The thought of opening the door to any soldier caused her great panic.

She crossed to the parlor window. The shutters were closed tightly. There was no way she could see what the man looked like. She stood against the wall, just inside the front door, panicked and frightened, until she heard the footsteps exit the porch.

* * *

She was awakened the following evening in the same manner.

"I'm not leaving this time," the voice said, "so you might as well open the door."

"As you can see, the door is boarded shut," she said in as gruff a voice as she could manage. "Go away!"

"Can't I at least warm myself by your fire?" the man said in a plaintive voice. "It's cold out here."

Something in his voice assuaged her fear a little.

"Go around to the back, and I'll let you in," she said. "And pray you don't hurt me," she whispered, as she grabbed a long cape Lily had given her and put it on over her nightgown.

What she saw when she opened the door was a tall man with a pleasing face and sandy blonde hair. He was dressed in a tattered gray uniform and a thin woolen coat.

"Please be assured, ma'am, I won't harm you," he said as he entered the kitchen. "Are you alone?"

How to answer that question? "For the moment," she stuttered.

He had a very handsome face, she decided after he came into the firelight. She sat down on one end of the sofa; he sat on the other, much too close for her comfort, so she got up and stood by the fireplace. His hands were red and shivering from the cold, and he extended them closer to the fire.

"Captain Ben Braddock," he said, "glad to make your acquaintance, Miss—Mrs.?"

"Armstrong. Amanda Armstrong."

"I'm with General James Longstreet's corps," he said. "We had a spirited fight with General Burnside's troops most of the way to here from Chattanooga."

"I have no food," she said abruptly.

"That's fine. At least I can get warm. We're on short rations until our supply train arrives."

"What time is it?" she asked, still trying to clear her head.

He pulled out his pocket watch. "Twenty past nine, ma'am."

"It seems much later," she said shyly, suddenly remembering that she was in her nightclothes in the presence of a man she didn't know. She wrapped the cape tighter around her.

"I could use some information about some of the lesser-used roads and trails in these parts," he said. "We hear that people are coming and going by roundabout means over here. I need to know where to post my pickets so I can stop this activity."

"I can't help you there," she said, relaxing a little. "This house belongs to a friend. I've only been here a few days."

"Then I'll take my leave now," he said, standing. "Is there anything I can do for you before I go? How about I fill your wood box?"

"Yes, that would be a great help," she mumbled. She kept telling herself she should be frightened of him, but she wasn't.

"Then I'll let you get back to sleep," he said after carrying in three armloads of wood. "With your hair down, I assume you were sleeping."

She nodded.

"Then good night to you, ma'am."

He passed through the kitchen door and waved as he exited the enclosed porch.

Why do I suddenly feel all tingly? she wondered.

* * *

Captain Braddock returned the following evening at about the same time, knocking at the back door and calling out her name.

"Did I awaken you?" he asked.

"No," she said, walking back into the kitchen. She had been unable to sleep.

Was I hoping he would come back?

"Last night I was merely doing my duty," he said. "Tonight's visit is personal."

"What do you mean?"

"I'm sorry," he said, his face reddening. "I sometimes have trouble saying what I mean, especially in the company of women. What I meant was I wanted to see you again, if that's all right with you."

"That's fine," she said shyly. "Your speech is unusual. Where are you from?"

"That's my backwoods Georgia drawl," he said shyly. "I've lived there all my life. I was still living there—with my mother and father—when I joined the army."

"You never married?" she asked. She thought he must be at least in his mid-thirties.

"The love of my life died of scarlet fever at the age of seventeen. After that, I worked hard in my father's store and never courted much."

How odd.

"Most of the women I seen since the war began are those poor fallen women who follow the camps, hoping to find someone who will feed and shelter them. Some are quite beautiful, but I could never take up with one of them. Never," he said, shaking his head in disgust.

Amanda gasped but was able to maintain her composure. She knew she should tell him about her life in Knoxville right then, but she would never see this man again. What did it matter?

He had a prominent nose and the truest blue eyes she had ever seen adorned his face. He was startlingly attractive from head to toe, despite the worn and soiled garments that covered his frame. He caught her looking at him, studying his face in the firelight.

She blushed.

"Isn't it dangerous for you to be out here all alone?" he asked suddenly.

"Probably, but it's the only place I have to stay right now."

He opened his mouth to speak.

"Don't ask," she said quickly.

And he didn't.

"Would it be agreeable to you if we spent some time together?" he asked shyly. "I haven't had an intelligent conversation with anyone in months."

"Why do you think you'd have one with me?"

"Oh, I can tell," he said, looking deeply into her eyes. "You're smart, all right."

She felt the color rise in her face again. She didn't want to tell him that she was just as interested in him. Nor did she want to tell him she was married.

I don't feel married anymore.

Captain Braddock visited her every night for almost two weeks. She had never known a man so easy to talk to, or so kind. He worried about her welfare, brought food when he could, and made sure she always had firewood. He was amazingly well read for a backwoods country boy. He had to check his pocket watch frequently because time easily slipped away when they were together.

One day he came by just long enough to tell her that he had been ordered to take a position farther north in preparation for an attack on the Union detachment that was fortifying a place called Fort Loudon.

"I'm sorry to have to tell you this," he said sadly. "Our visits have been very special to me."

"To me, as well," she said. His visits had made her recent days bearable.

"It won't be easy for me to get away, but I'll come every chance I get," he promised.

"Please do," she said.

At the back door, as he prepared to leave, Amanda was self-conscious. She wanted to touch him, to hug him, to do something to convey her feelings without being too forward. She could see that he was in the same dilemma. Finally, he reached for her hands and clutched them tightly to his breast, and then kissed them with soft sensuous lips. Tears stung her eyes as he walked through the door, pausing to give her one last look.

Later that day, when Lily's driver, Isaac, came to bring her more food, Josiah was with him.

"This boy has pestered me every hour of every day since I brought you here," Isaac said. "I'm tired of it. So here he is. Do with him what you will."

"I can't take care of him here," Amanda said.

"Then, that's too bad," Isaac said. "I asked Miss Lily, and she said to bring him. She sent some extra food along for him."

Josiah followed her every step. When she was cooking the potato skins Isaac had brought, she knocked him on his backside, not knowing that he was standing behind her.

"This has to stop, young man," she said sternly. "I can't even go to the privy without you following me!"

"I'm sorry, Misty—"

"No! I'm not your mistress."

"Sorry," he said, his eyes pleading. "I'm just so glad to be with you."

"Well, you can be with me without walking on my heels." She was trying to be patient, but she wasn't prepared to care for him. Her life was complicated enough, thank you very much! She was missing Captain Braddock already, and feared she would never see him again.

Within a few days, she grew to enjoy Josiah's company. The food Isaac brought wasn't adequate, but they managed. They talked, laughed, and played games. She told him bedtime stories, the same ones she had once told Luke. She thought that living with him in that enclosed dark space would bring her nothing but more problems, but her depression lessened a little.

The following Sunday morning, Amanda and Josiah were asleep in the kitchen. Before dawn, a cacophony of musket fire awoke them, closely followed by a blast of artillery, which sounded very close. They ran as quickly as they could, grabbing clothes and shoes as they went, and didn't stop until they were in the cellar. At least it wasn't as loud down there. A single shot rang out here and there, then they heard not a sound for several minutes, then several cannons going off all at one time. They were relieved when everything suddenly stopped after only half an hour.

Captain Braddock came to the house later that day. He had been occupied with preparations for the assault.

"We were sleeping when it began, but we ran to the cellar in a hurry," Amanda said.

"We?" he asked, a puzzled look on his face

"Josiah is napping," she said, motioning to the mattress in the corner of the kitchen.

"Who's that?"

"This little black boy who's latched onto me. He seems to follow me wherever I go."

Thursday, December 3, 1863

Captain Braddock hadn't visited in several days. Amanda heard his horse arrive that evening and ran to meet him in the backyard.

"General Longstreet's siege of Knoxville has come to naught," he explained. "When he heard General Sherman was bringing Union reinforcements, he announced that we will be withdrawing to the northeast, toward Greeneville."

"Ben," Amanda said excitedly, "that's near my home!"

He grabbed her arms and pulled her close to him.

"In the morning, I will be leaving," he told her. "I want to be with you tonight."

"Oh, I see," she said, turning her back to him, "you are like the rest after all."

"What?"

"Go away!" she shouted, walking quickly toward the house.

She ran up the steps and into the house. Ben caught up to her on the enclosed porch.

"I was cold and starving, sleeping in alleyways in Knoxville. I did what I had to do to live!" She was crying openly now and angry with herself for being brought to tears.

"What are you talking about?" Ben asked.

"How crazy am I?" She laughed out loud. "To think a decent man would want me after what I've become." Tears slid down her cheeks, but she brushed them away as soon as they fell, continually wiping her face with both hands.

"I don't understand," Ben said.

"I'm one of those 'fallen women' you were talking about the other day." She entered the kitchen and tried to close the door, sure that he would be repulsed by her confession.

"No," he said, pushing against the door, "I don't doubt for a minute that you did what you had to do."

"You know and still..."

"Yes, still," he said, grabbing her hands and kissing her fingertips.

Her heart succumbed.

They held each other in the firelight. Ben told her of the disastrous attack on Fort Loudon, and he seemed quite disturbed by what had happened there.

She finally told him what happened to her in Knoxville, about her life at Cinnamon Hill, and her marriage.

"Knowing that you're married, I should leave right now," he whispered.

"Yes, you should."

"You must be the strong one," he whispered, as they embraced. "I cannot bring myself to leave you."

"And I can't push you away," she said softly, before they kissed for the first time.

A few hours later, Ben gripped Amanda's hands tightly as he prepared to leave. "I guess we'll be looking for a place to hole up for the winter," he told her. "Will you stay here until the war is over?" he asked.

"Let me go with you," she said. "I want to go home."

"No," he said firmly. "It's too dangerous."

"I can't go back to what I was, and living in this dark place depresses me more every day. I can follow the army so I don't lose my way, can't I? And you could bring me a little food. This might be the only chance I'll ever have to go home."

"I really wish you'd stay here. The weather's turning nasty, and I'm not sure how much time I can spend with you. It won't be an easy trip, I assure you."

"I've made up my mind. I'm going home, with or without anyone's help."

"All right," Ben finally said. "You can travel behind the army. My regiment's taking up the rear, so we'll be the last to leave. Maybe I can sneak you into camp at night so you won't have to sleep outside. Oh, please reconsider," he begged again. "This whole idea scares me."

"No, I won't change my mind."

"Then I'd rather you come with me than set out on your own."

"Oh," she said suddenly, "what about Josiah?"

"You can't take a child that young on a trip like this. We're gonna be moving out at a pretty good clip. And I don't know how many days of this cold rainy weather we'll have to endure. It looks to me like it's set in for a spell."

"He'll be heartbroken," she said. "He's been nothing but kind to me; it's not fair to desert him now."

"You'll have a much better chance at safe passage if you're alone."

"You're right," she said reluctantly.

"You have to be ready in three hours. Can you get a horse?"

"I might be able to get one from Lily," she said, her mind racing.

* * *

"Josiah, it's time for me to go home," Amanda said firmly, but gently.

"You have a home?" he asked.

"I once did. I hope it's still there, and I have a son," she explained. "Lucas is his name. I should be there in case he comes home."

"You miss him, huh?"

"More than anything, and I would endure hell to have him with me again."

"Can't I go with you? I won't be no trouble," he said.

"No, it's a long, hard trip that I'm not looking forward to myself, and it's much colder now than when I came here in September."

"Please," he begged, huge tears rolling down his brown cheeks.

"I have no way to care for you. If you stay here, you can beg on the streets. With that darling face and sweet smile," Amanda said, cupping his chin in her hand. "I'll ask Lily to help you if you get into trouble."

"I hoped if I was real good, maybe you could be my mama."

"You don't want me to be your mama, Josiah."

"Why not?"

"I'm not a very good one."

"Please, don't go," he pleaded, hugging her legs so tightly she couldn't move. "You're not sick. You can work."

"I can't go back to that life, Josiah. Not ever. If I don't leave this place while I have the chance, I'm afraid I'll never be able to leave. I know you don't understand, and I don't know how to make it clear to you. You'll just have to trust that I'm doing what's best for both of us."

She pulled his strong little arms from around her legs and walked quickly away. She ran out of the alley and down the street until she could no longer hear his heartbreaking sobs.

* * *

"This is Molly," Lily told Amanda at the stables. The horse rubbed her nose against Lily's arm, wanting to be petted. "She's a little sway-backed, poor girl, but kind of heart. If you treat her moderately well, she should be able to see you home. It will be good for her to get out of town, too."

"How much will you take for her?" Amanda asked, digging into the bodice of her dress where she had stashed her last bit of money.

"She was a gift to me at a time when I needed her badly. Now she is my gift to you."

"Oh, I won't take her without paying."

"Yes, you will," Lily said. "You will take her as a favor to me."

"I've spent the last few hours thinking about walking back home, the same way I came," Amanda sighed. "To my tired eyes, she's the most beautiful horse I've ever seen. How can I repay you for such kindness?"

"You just did."

Amanda could see that Molly had once been a beauty, chestnut brown, part Arabian. She rubbed her nose and looked into her warm brown eyes.

"Rest assured that she will be treasured and cared for. I want to go home. I want it more than I've ever wanted anything, and Molly can get me there."

"You might be safer staying in my mother's house, especially now that Longstreet's leaving, but I know it's not safe anywhere," Lily said.

"You've been a good friend, and I will never forget you. If you're ever in the neighborhood of Greene County, come by to see me."

"I wouldn't count on that," Lily said, smiling. "It's doubtful that I will ever leave Knoxville. I have made a place for myself here. Most people would say it's not a good place, but I rather like it."

"If I'm lucky enough to make it back home, I don't intend to ever leave again."

"I bid you Godspeed, Amanda Armstrong."

* * *

Amanda woke up in a small tent at the edge of the woods near the main camp of General Longstreet's army. She tried to sit up but something was tugging at her arm.

"Josiah, what are you doing here?" she said loudly, unable to comprehend how he could have possibly found her.

"I came right behind you and kept you in my sights," he said, nodding his head.

"How did you come all this way?"

"An old slave man rode me in his wagon for a long ways and fed me, too. Then I started off on the run. It's easy to follow a great big army. I knew you'd be somewhere close by. Captain Ben told me where to find you."

"I don't know what I'm going to do with you, young man," she said, rubbing his curly black head, "but I'm glad to know you're safe."

"I just couldn't let you leave me, Misty," he said. "We belong together."

"No, we don't. We come from different worlds. I can't be your mother, and I can't take care of you. I don't know how I'm going to care for myself. Why can't I make you understand that?"

"I just can't stand to be without you."

"You're mighty hardheaded for such a little fellow, you know?" She smiled grudgingly.

"Yes'm, I know, but I always thought when you find something you want you better go after it." He smiled, his eyes twinkled, and there was a look of total contentment on his face.

* * *

"This camp life's not for me," Amanda told Ben later that day. "I'm going home."

"But you'll have no one to protect you along the way," Ben said.

"I can protect myself," she said, but inside she was dreading the trip.

"I'm sorry," Ben said, "I asked for a few days' leave, but my request was denied. A large detachment of Yankees has followed us from Knoxville and may attack us at any time. The least I can do is to provide you with a way to defend yourself," he said, handing her a revolver and a small bag of bullets.

"I'll be fine. I know most of the country from here to Cinnamon Hill," she lied.

"There are soldiers everywhere—ours and theirs. Promise you'll be careful."

"I promise."

"I feel like I'm deserting you," he said, shaking his head.

"No, please. You must do your duty." She reached for his hand.

He surprised her by grabbing her and holding her close to him. Josiah wrapped one of his arms around Ben's legs, the other around Amanda's.

What a pitiful sight we must be. A reformed whore, an orphaned black boy, and a Confederate soldier clutching each other in the fog and damp of a late fall morning in the mountains of Northeast Tennessee.

TWELVE

———◆◆◆———

Amanda was awakened by a strange sensation. She had been sleeping on top of an old oilcloth—the wet ground was unbearably cold. She opened her eyes just enough to see a disheveled man pulling on Molly's reins. Little did he know that she had tucked the lead rope underneath her body before she went to sleep. In one swift motion, she sat up and leveled the revolver at his head.

"If you're intent upon stealing my horse, one of us is going to die this morning," she said coldly.

He grinned at her and bent over, reaching for the handle of a large knife that protruded from his boot top. She knew he meant to cut the lead rope and jump onto Molly before she could get a round off.

"I'm dead serious," she said, raising her other hand to steady the gun. She wanted to stand up but didn't want to expose Josiah, who was still asleep behind her.

"Now just hold on," the man said, holding up a hand in the direction of the gun.

"You think I won't shoot you?" she asked pointedly, stretching her arms as far toward him as possible. She was aiming for his leg, hoping to disable him, but she didn't know if she could pull the trigger. Her hands were shaking violently.

She felt Josiah move. "Be still," she whispered, her eyes never leaving the man's face.

The man tried to peer over her shoulder. "Who's back there?" he asked.

"Never you mind," she said. "I'm feeling a little generous this morning, so if you can make it to the edge of this clearing in three seconds, I might not kill your sorry ass."

The man straightened up and disappeared quickly into the brush.

"What did you say?" Josiah asked.

"Let's get ready to travel."

"I'm hungry," he whined.

"Eat a few of the nuts Ben gave us—but only a few."

* * *

Amanda had no idea how many miles she had walked that afternoon, but it was more than a few. Josiah was suffering from a cold, and probably a low-grade fever. "When Molly gallops, it makes my head hurt," he said.

She placed him on the rear of the saddle, laid him forward onto the seat, and covered him with the oilcloth and the only blanket they had left. Since then she had been leading Molly along deserted mountain trails through very heavy fog. Rain drizzled down all day. She was drenched head to toe. The temperature felt almost cold enough to turn the rain to snow, but she moved on, determined to reach home.

While she walked, she considered the possibilities of all the destruction that might have occurred to her home while she was gone. She knew it was unlikely that it would be in the same condition as the day she left. It might be burned to the ground, which was the fate of some civilian residences she had seen along the way. If the structure was still sound, she would rebuild it—even if it took the rest of her life. If it were destroyed, she would never forgive herself for leaving it.

But when she finally arrived, she abruptly stopped Molly in the lane leading to the house, just before the structure came into view. She was relieved to finally be there, yet dreaded what she might see.

She tugged at Molly's reins and inched a little farther down the lane. Since the foliage had fallen, she could see the shape of the house through the trees. As she rounded the bend in the lane, the house came into full view. She let out a deep breath. *Yes!* The house was still standing.

"It doesn't look so bad from here," she said.

The exterior of the house looked pretty much the same, but every tree in the yard was now a stump.

Josiah sat up and tugged at her shoulder. She helped him down from the horse.

"Is this your house?" he asked, rubbing his eyes.

"Well, it was," she sighed.

"All this for one person?"

"I wasn't 'one person' until last summer."

As she got closer, she could see that the front doors were missing altogether. At first she thought the windows were open, but soon saw that the glass was broken out. The closer she got the worse it looked. She suddenly felt like someone had sucked all the air from her lungs. She stood in the yard for a long time.

When she finally entered the house, she found it incredibly filthy. Not a stick of furniture was left in the rooms on the first floor.

Amanda put Josiah in the small bed in Barbé's cabin and covered him with the blanket. While he slept, she would try to make a livable space in the house.

She discovered that the front doors were still there, but completely off their hinges. She leaned them against the opening, as close together as possible. The door to the sitting room was still attached and the windows intact, so she shut it off from the rest of the house. The heat from a small fire would make the room somewhat comfortable.

She ran upstairs, looking for some furniture. Every room was bare. Nothing was left. She had hoped to find some dresses in her armoire, but the armoire itself was gone. She began to get angry. She cleaned the sitting room and built a fire with wood she found in the side yard. In the parlor, she found one of the legs to her favorite marble-topped table, half-burned. She threw it on the fire as well.

She should have gone right then to see if she could pull off some of the boards in the barn stalls to add to the fire, but fatigue consumed her. She could do no more. She curled up on the cold wood floor in front of the fireplace and fell immediately into a deep sleep.

When she awoke, it was dark. Her body was so sore she could hardly move. She was cold to the bone. Her little fire had almost sputtered out completely. On the raggedy edge of sleep, she thought *Josiah!*

She grabbed a bit of candle from the mantle and tried to light it with the coals from the fire. "Come on," she begged, holding the candle wick in the hot coals, burning her fingers in the process. Finally, it sputtered to life.

She ran to Barbé's cabin and found Josiah still completely covered by the blanket and the oilcloth. She touched his face, which didn't feel as cold as she expected, but his nose was freezing. As she touched him, he began to stir. She reached down to touch his body inside the blankets, and he was warm as could be.

"What's the matter?" he asked, stretching his arms.

"I was scared you'd be frozen," she said impatiently.

"No, I'm warm," he said, pulling the covers up over his head again.

"So I see," she said, smacking him on the behind, through the padding of the blanket. "Get up!" she shouted. "I'm starving."

He laughed out loud. He was like a caterpillar in a cocoon, wrapped in that blanket. He couldn't move without her help.

Amanda had found a small mound of cornmeal in the side yard earlier, where soldiers had been camping. She sifted out as much dirt as possible—the cornmeal being coarser than the sand. She found a small pouch of salt on the kitchen table that someone had forgotten.

The food preparation table was about the only thing left in the kitchen. Her pots and utensils were all gone. The cookstove was in shambles, its burner tops missing. Even the door to the wood box was broken off, and nowhere in sight.

Why would anyone do such a thing?

With water from the well, she made a very small johnnycake from cornmeal, water, and salt. She baked it the old-fashioned way: on a stone in the sitting room fireplace.

"I sure wish we had some furniture," Amanda said as they ate the johnnycake. "A chair, a table... Anything would be nice."

"There's nothing nowhere?" Josiah asked.

"The attic!" she exclaimed.

Chewing on their last bite of cornbread, they raced upstairs. The small door that led to the attic was stuck. After several minutes of pushing and pulling, Amanda put her shoulder into the door and it opened suddenly, sending her flying into the attic stairs. She groaned in pain.

"What is it?" Josiah said in a panic.

"My elbow," she said, grabbing her right arm. "I hit my funny bone." She flung her arm from side to side, but that only increased her discomfort.

"Then why aren't you laughing?"

Even the attic had been ransacked. She found an old upholstered chair. The seat was hard as stone, but it would be better than sitting on the floor. There was an old chaise longue in the corner, under lots of debris. Its brocade cover was stained and worn, but it was comfortable to sit on. Several old rugs were stacked in the corner. They dragged all their findings downstairs.

In the sitting room, she made a bed on the chaise and a pallet out of the rugs in front of the fireplace for Josiah. At last, she laid her weary body down. Her last thought was how good it was to be home.

She was awakened pre-dawn by heavy footsteps in the center hall. Josiah sat straight up and gasped. She grabbed him and placed her hand over his mouth before he could make a sound. Together they huddled in the corner near the back door. Someone was jiggling the locked doorknob.

"Who's in there?" a loud voice asked.

Josiah whimpered.

"You mustn't cry out," Amanda whispered.

"I'm Lt. Quinn from the Union garrison in Greeneville," a male voice said. "We stay here when we come scouting over this way, and I don't plan to be run off."

If his voice was any indication of his size, she and Josiah were in deep trouble.

"You'd best show yourself," the lieutenant yelled. "I'm not going to be very happy if I have to find you myself."

Amanda grabbed the ratty blanket and smelly quilt she had found in the attic. "We're going to sneak out the back door," she whispered to Josiah.

She almost got lost twice, trying to find Gali's hut. She fumbled her way through the hills and forest. Molly, still hidden in the stables, would be of no help in this dark sky. The air was bitterly cold. Finally, she arrived and tapped at Gali's door.

"Who's there?" Gali asked in her gruff voice.

"It's Amanda."

Gali opened the door. She was smiling. "Many nights I worried for you," she said.

"I'm sorry," Amanda said, hugging Gali and gravitating to the roaring fire inside the hut. "You were right. It was a mistake to leave home. Josiah!" she said running back to the door.

"Who?" Gali asked.

He entered slowly, his little head to one side. He walked quickly to Amanda's side and hid behind her skirts.

"Where did you get a black child?"

It took a while to explain all the crooks and turns she and Josiah had made to end up in Gali's home. Gali offered them bread, nuts, and berries to quiet their rumbling stomachs, and then brought a stack of quilts and wool blankets to make a pallet for them in front of the fire. Amanda felt safe for the first time in months.

"Stay here with me," Gali begged after they had eaten breakfast the following morning.

I can't," said Amanda. "I have to get those soldiers out of my house before they do any more damage. It rankles me that they seize property that doesn't belong to them. It's not right, and I intend to protect what is mine."

"Now you know how I feel when Judie Baker tries to take my home," Gali said.

"Yes," Amanda sighed, "I do."

* * *

Amanda and Josiah crept back into the house at Cinnamon Hill. Gali sent what food she could spare—enough to feed them for a few days if they rationed it—and two blankets.

Amanda spent the entire day cleaning. The floors in the center hall were covered with several inches of mud and animal feces. She pushed the slimy dirt out the front door with an old weeding hoe.

At day's end, she and Josiah ate a few bites of bread and beans before they lay down in the sitting room to rest.

Again, the soldiers came and rousted them from their sleep.

This time Amanda marched straight into the center hall and confronted Lieutenant Quinn. She was too tired for another nocturnal journey to Gali's hut. She couldn't see the lieutenant's face, just his outline in the little light that filtered through the open doorway behind him. He was tall and broad-shouldered.

"My name is Amanda Armstrong," she said with all the calmness she could muster, "and this is my home." Her legs began to tremble. If she had been fully awake, she wouldn't have confronted these soldiers in this manner.

"I have impressed this house for use by the Union army," Lt. Quinn shouted.

"I intend to stay here, sir," she said firmly.

"Then, we have us a little problem," he said smartly, "but we won't have it for long. Take this woman and put her in the Greeneville jail," he said to one of his aides.

The soldier grabbed Amanda's arm. She wrenched it from his grasp, ran back into the sitting room, grabbed Josiah, and fled out the back door again. When the cold air hit her, she fully realized how reckless her behavior had been.

They slept in the hayloft, but it was a miserable night. A nasty winter wind kicked up and penetrated every crack in the walls of the barn. It appeared that winter weather had set in for good.

The following morning, Amanda discovered that the soldiers had vacated the property. There were no tents on the lawn and no sign of a fire. Maybe they had gone back to their post in Greeneville. She could only hope.

She was ready to fight for her home, but she couldn't take on a whole cavalry detachment. She closed the exterior and interior shutters on the windows, the ones that were left, and put Josiah to bed on a pallet in a small bedroom at the rear of the second floor. It was the smallest room in the house, and it didn't take much wood to heat it.

She went out onto the second-floor balcony, wrapped in a quilt and blanket, and waited in the darkness. She laid the revolver Ben had given her in her lap. She would tell Lieutenant Quinn that she was holding a gun on them and that they would have to find another house to use for their headquarters. Just the thought of it made her tremble.

The pounding of horses' hooves didn't wake Amanda until they were almost at the gatepost. Startled and half-asleep, she fumbled for her revolver. It fell from her lap, clattered noisily onto the floor of the balcony, and slid over the edge. She heard it fall into the rose bushes below.

"Mrs. Armstrong," Lt. Quinn called from the front terrace. "I don't intend to have any problems with you tonight. If I find you here, I'll send you to jail."

When she heard the soldiers running in the hall downstairs, she panicked. She ran to the bedroom and grabbed Josiah. She threw open the door and climbed the stairway into the attic, Josiah behind her. They huddled together in the corner as they listened to the soldiers enter every room on the ground floor, and then the second floor.

The darkness was pervasive. Amanda told Josiah to get down on his hands and knees, and they crawled slowly up a narrow flight of stairs. When they reached the top of the steps, she pushed on the hatch door that led to the widow's walk on the roof, but it wouldn't budge. The rain had caused the door to swell, and it was stuck tightly in its opening. She sat on the top step and pushed her back against it as hard as she could. It finally opened and slammed against the floor of the observation deck.

She stopped and waited breathlessly to see if she had alerted their visitors.

"Mrs. Armstrong, are you up there?" she heard Lt. Quinn say as he mounted the stairs to the second floor.

She climbed onto the roof, pulled Josiah through the hatch door, and closed it. Her heart was beating double-time.

"Look here, Lieutenant," a voice said from below. "There's a fire in here."

"She must have took off running when she heard us coming," the lieutenant said.

Josiah's eyes opened wider as he mouthed the words: "Someone's on the stairs."

"Sit down," she whispered, trying to hide her trembling hands.

"What did you say?"

"Sit down on the door," she said, sitting down on it herself.

"I can't get up to the roof, Lieutenant," said a husky voice directly below them. They could feel him pressing on the door. "The hatch door is stuck."

"You sleep up here," Lieutenant Quinn ordered, "just in case. If she's up there and tries to come back down, arrest her. I'm going to bed."

She listened while the lieutenant left the house and entered Barbé's cabin.

Amanda and Josiah were trapped on the roof.

* * *

Amanda waited through the night without trying to escape, afraid to re-enter the trap door for fear the guard would find them. If they could survive the night, the soldiers would leave again in the morning.

She and Josiah huddled together against the chimney, trying to pass the time by sleeping.

When Lt. Quinn was ready to leave for a reconnaissance the next morning, Amanda heard him posting a guard. "Hodges, you're it," he bellowed.

"What?" a voice asked.

"You're officially on guard duty at these quarters. Better stake out in the hall, so you can watch the front and back. And you'd better not fall asleep."

"We've got to go down," Josiah said when she told him they couldn't go back inside. "I don't like it up here." He began to cry.

"Do you want me to go to jail?"

"No," he whined.

She didn't frighten him by expressing her other anxieties. Dozens of thoughts raced through her mind as she tried to decide what to do.

What would the soldiers in Greeneville do with Josiah if they arrested me? Would they take him away from me? What right do I have to keep him?

She had to get to her gun in the rosebushes if she had any hope of getting rid of the soldiers. The murky dawn already made enough light to give them away if they tried to climb down. But, with only one guard on the ground floor, she felt safe enough to go into the attic where they could at least get warm and sleep.

Lt. Quinn and his detachment of cavalry returned late that afternoon. Amanda and Josiah were startled, and they climbed back onto the roof. She listened to the activities below for hours, thinking they would never go to sleep. Quinn posted a guard on the second floor again, and another to walk the perimeter of the house all night.

Amanda's hopes were dashed once again. The guard on the second floor would surely discover them if they re-entered the house by the hatch door. If they timed it right, climbing down the rose trellis might be their best chance.

"Josiah, can you follow me?" she asked patiently.

"No, Misty, I'm no good with high places," he stuttered, covering his eyes. He still reverted to calling her "Misty" when he was frightened.

She sat down, pulled his tiny body close to her, and spoke calmly. "If we don't get down, we'll get too hungry and thirsty up here."

"I'm already too thirsty."

"The trellis at the side of the porch is like a ladder," she explained. "I know your legs are short, but I'll be right below you, and I promise I won't let you fall. But you must be very quiet."

She could see the whites of his large eyes even in the darkness. For the first time, she thought about how frightened he must be.

"I wouldn't ask such a thing of you if I had any other choice. Please try," she begged.

At last, he nodded reluctantly.

She climbed over the railing that encircled the deck and lifted Josiah over. The rain had stopped, but the roof was still slippery. She showed him how to sit on his backside and move slowly down the roof, inch by inch, but he whimpered all the way. She shushed him repeatedly, fearing that they would be discovered at any moment.

The porch roof had only a slight pitch, so they were able to move much quicker there. She started down the trellis, coaxing Josiah to follow. She let go of his arm for just a second to get a better hold, and he almost fell. He squealed. She waited, breathlessly.

The guard on the ground came running around the corner of the house. "Who's there?" he shouted. Fortunately, he didn't look up.

Amanda's arm was breaking. Josiah was so frightened that he let go of the trellis completely, and sat down on her shoulder. Then he peed his pants, wetting his trousers and the front of her dress. "Sorry, Misty," he whispered.

"Shh," she said.

The guard continued around the corner of the house. *Thank God for a dark night.*

Amanda let out a full breath. She told Josiah to grab onto the trellis again. She quickly climbed down to the ground and instructed Josiah to jump into her arms.

"I'm scared," he whimpered.

"Jump!" she whispered.

When he finally let go, she couldn't hold his full weight. They fell into the rosebushes with a resounding thud, prompting another alert by the guard.

After the guard passed again, she began to look for the revolver. The thorny bushes scratched her arms and hands, but she finally recovered it. They waited until the guard passed again, and then ran as fast as they could around the house. She opened the door to the summer kitchen and pushed Josiah inside, telling him to stay there no matter what happened. She exited the building as soon as she heard the guard pass by.

Since Lt. Quinn slept alone in Barbé's cabin, she could get to him without alerting his men. He was still sleeping when she pushed the revolver under his nose. He woke up with a start.

"Lt. Quinn," she whispered, "I am a desperate woman, who will do almost anything to save what is left of my home. My menfolk are all in the army. I've already lost my brother and my father to this war, and only God knows where my young son is. So maybe you'd better find another place to house you and your staff."

He sat up and pulled on his boots without a word.

She held the gun to his back as they walked outside.

"Why, you're a fine-looking woman," he said, peering at her in the predawn light.

"What did you expect?" she asked him. "An old hag?"

"I-I don't know," he stammered.

"Why do you hate me so much, Lieutenant?" she asked.

"I don't hate you specifically," he said. "I just hate your kind."

"What kind?" she asked. "I just want to be left alone."

"You might be sorry for saying that," he said viciously. "You're pretty far from the road down here. It'd be easy for someone to come in here and burn your place down."

"Should I take that as a threat?"

"Take it however you want," he said. "It would be so easy to signal my men, and you'd be dead before you took a breath. The only reason

I'm going along with this little game is that little black boy you have here."

She opened the back door and ordered Quinn to call out to his men.

"Come on, boys," he shouted. "We're leaving."

She heard nothing but footsteps as they scrambled for their boots. She waited breathlessly until they rode away.

"You showed them, Misty," Josiah said when she opened the door to the summer kitchen. He laughed and hugged her legs.

"I told you not to call me 'Misty,'" she said irritably.

"What can I call you?"

"I told you to call me Amanda, but your tongue gets tangled up when you say it. What would you like to call me?"

"Mama," he said shyly. "You're my Mama now, aren't you?"

"No, I'm not."

His chin dropped to his chest.

"My dearest friend in all the world used to call me 'Mandy.' Can you say that?"

He recited it repeatedly.

"Let's see," she said, taking his hand as they walked into the house, "what can I call you? Josiah sounds like an old man's name. I'll call you 'Josie.' Is that all right?"

He nodded his approval.

A few days later, the Widow Wilkes came to Cinnamon Hill.

"The Union army is taking the church," she said, almost in tears.

"What do you mean they're taking it?" Amanda asked.

"Something about the War Department ordering them to seize abandoned churches within areas controlled by the Union army."

"What?" Amanda said.

"Since you've been gone," Widow said, "the circuit-riding preacher stopped coming. We haven't had any services for a couple of months now."

"That doesn't mean it's been abandoned," Amanda said angrily.

"They won't listen to me," Widow said. "You can tell them your husband's in the Union army. Maybe that will help."

Amanda rode on Molly to the Crossroads and found a captain and a small detachment of soldiers putting a padlock on the church door.

"You can't take this church. It's mine—ours. There aren't many of us left, but it's still our church," she insisted.

"I have the authority to take this church per the order of Lt. Quinn in Greeneville," the captain said.

I might have known.

"He says it's Baptist property."

"My husband, Jonathan Armstrong, is an officer in the Union army. He was down toward Strawberry Plains, the last I knew. His grandfather built this church, and it belongs to the people of this community. How can the Baptists claim it?"

"All I know is that the order came directly from the Union War Department. Here it is."

"It says here that we have no loyal minister," Amanda said. "Then I'll be the minister."

"Really?" the soldier asked. "Are you ordained? When did you last hold services here?"

"Well...uh...I've been gone, but I plan to have services this coming Sunday."

"Get out of here," he said angrily.

"I'll break that lock," she said.

"And I'll throw you in jail."

Don't you men ever get tired of threatening women?

THIRTEEN

———————◆◆◆◆———————

January 1864

O ne cold January afternoon, Ben came to visit Amanda at Cinnamon Hill. "Sorry I ain't been able to come by. They've kept
us busy fighting off Yanks. Just when we get rid of one bunch, here
comes another."

"You don't have to feel bad."

"Well, I do," he said sincerely. "It's been breaking my heart to
be so close and not be able to see you. We just got back from down
around Dandridge. Oh," Ben said, when he saw Josie in the doorway
behind Amanda, "I didn't know he'd be here."

"Where else would he be?" she asked.

"People won't like this," Ben said, pointing to Amanda and then
to Josie. "It's just not right."

"I had no idea you felt so strongly about this," she said.

"I shoulda told you my true feelings when we were in Knoxville,
but I had no idea he'd follow you. I certainly didn't think you'd bring
him home with you."

"What would you have me do with him, Ben?" she asked, perturbed. "Turn him out into the world all by himself?"

"Saving him from starvation is one thing, but you can't keep him here forever. It wouldn't be fair to him. He won't be a true Negro, and he surely can't be white."

She turned to Josie, whose face looked very sad. "Why don't you go lie down for your nap in Barbé's cabin," she told him. "I'll be there in a minute."

She followed him to the door and watched until he was out of earshot.

"How dare you say such things in front of him!" she said. "This isn't a situation I would have chosen, but he loves me, and I won't treat him badly, no matter what you think."

"Are you ready to announce to all your neighbors that you're raising a Negro child?"

* * *

It was late March when Ben came to Cinnamon Hill again.

"I've been foolish," he said, his head bowed, "to let this thing about Josie keep me away from you. It's been killing me. I talked to our chaplain about it, and he helped me see it differently. If you love this little boy, who am I to say it's wrong?"

"Thank you for that," she said calmly, "but don't force me to make a choice between him and you."

"I'll never forgive myself for letting that keep us apart when we have so little time left. We received orders yesterday to return to Virginia immediately," he explained. "I've come to say goodbye."

They stayed up all night talking. They didn't consummate their relationship, though it was not for lack of desire. They sat on an old quilt in front of the fire. Josie had fallen asleep on the chaise nearby.

"He looks positively angelic when he's sleeping," Ben said, touching Josie's head. When he looked back at Amanda, there were tears in his eyes.

"What is it?" she asked.

"When you went to the kitchen a while ago, he hugged me and begged me not to leave."

"Now you see. He's the most loving child I've ever known. He's lost everyone he's known in his short life, and he's probably afraid he'll lose me, too."

They talked a little, kissed a little, but mostly they held each other.

Toward dawn, Ben begged Amanda to follow him to Virginia. "I'll fix a small tent for you like I did on the trip from Knoxville, and for Josie, too."

"I swore if I ever got back to Cinnamon Hill, I'd never leave it again. I intend to keep that promise. Six months ago, I would have gone with you without a second thought for anyone but myself. But not now."

They were standing on the front terrace. He had already said goodbye three times, but hadn't moved.

"Will I see you again?" she asked, at the same time he said, "Promise me you'll take care of yourself."

She couldn't look at him. It was too painful.

"I could stay here," he said, "hide out in the woods. At least we could spend our nights together."

"We both know you're not the deserting kind, Ben Braddock. If you stayed, it would ruin what we have."

"You're not gonna make this any easier, are you?"

"How can I? We both must do what we must do."

"My faith in the Southern cause diminishes by the day," he said. "So many soldiers are deserting. We've begun to fight each other as much as we fight the Yankees."

"But are you ready to give up on it?"

"No, I committed myself to it."

"And that sense of honor is one of the things I most admire about you."

She clasped her arms around his neck, as much to keep her hands occupied as to ward off the cold. Finally, he pressed his hands on her waist and kissed her on the forehead.

"I'll be careful," she said, feeling tears spring into her eyes.

She abruptly reached for his hand and clutched it to her.

"Do you think we're just clinging to each other because of the war and the desperate emotions it elicits in us?" she asked.

"No, I don't," he said, "but we need some time together."

"I want that time," she said, her voice pleading. "I've lost two of the men I loved most to this war, and maybe my son. I couldn't bear to lose another." She raised his hand and pressed it to her lips.

"I will come back," he promised emphatically.

Before he passed around the curve in the lane, he looked back. She was standing where he left her.

Damn this war.

Spring 1864

Amanda and Josie were surviving, but only because Gali had provided most of their food during the winter. She also gave Amanda seeds to plant in the garden at Cinnamon Hill. The pea plants were already growing, and the corn and beans would soon follow; potatoes would take a while longer. Amanda salivated at the thought of fresh vegetables.

She received a letter from Ben dated May 8, 1864.

I hope you and Josie are well. I miss you terribly every day. When army life gets me down, it's the thought of you waiting for me that keeps me going. We have been involved in the most desperate fighting I have yet seen in Virginia at a place called the Wilderness, and it deserves the name in every way. I am shirking my duties to write this letter to you because a carriage has arrived to carry one of my injured compatriots home to Morristown and he promises to leave this letter at Bixby's.

Not only has my precious General Longstreet been wounded—not fatally, saints be praised—but our gallant General Micah Jenkins has been taken from us as well. I am so hurt I can barely stand it. Jenkins was such a fine gentleman, and so very young.

Yours forever,

B.B. Braddock

* * *

A young Rebel cavalryman came to the gatepost at Cinnamon Hill one afternoon. The underbrush had grown tall in the meadows in front of the house; Amanda hoped that any visitors would assume the house was deserted and go on. She feared that the young rider had been sent by his superiors to take what little food she had left. She didn't dare acknowledge his presence until he called out in a rich tenor tone: "Amanda Armstrong, are you here?"

She learned that he was traveling with a few other soldiers, doing reconnaissance work for the Rebels, and had brought her a letter from Luke. Her hands shook so badly she could hardly get the letter open.

Mother, I am at Hunter House with Grandmother and doing quite well. I have been serving with General John Hunt Morgan, which I'm sure doesn't surprise you. We came to Abingdon after another raid into Kentucky. General Morgan has been given command of the Department of Western Virginia and Eastern Tennessee.

We should be operating in this area for some time to come. I will pay you a visit as soon as I can. Grandmother has given me a sound talking to, and tells me that I have caused you much worry since I left home. I am glad to say that I have grown up since joining General Morgan. He has been like a father to me, and I have learned much *from him. I must go now. Grandmother sends her love and undying devotion.*

    I love you, Mother, and hope you are well,
    Luke

Amanda collapsed in tears on the front terrace. Josie ran to see what was the matter.

"You should be happy," he said when she told him about the letter. "Luke is alive."

"I am happy," she said, drying her eyes.

"Why do you grown folks cry when you're happy?" he asked, a little perturbed.

"It's just too much joy to keep inside, I guess," she said.

* * *

When Amanda arrived at the hut, Gali was sitting in a chair on the porch. She held a piece of paper in her hand, which appeared to have something scrawled across it.

"What's that?" Amanda asked.

"Another message from my friend, Judie Baker," Gali said nonchalantly. "I was not here when he came by, but he always leaves me a message."

"What does it say?" Amanda asked, reaching for the paper. "Do you want me to read it to you?"

"I went to the mission school," Gali said defensively, holding the paper close to her chest. "I can read and write English as well as you can. Sequoyah's Cherokee language, too."

"I know," Amanda said. "I wasn't thinking. What does it say?"

"It is another invitation to remove myself from *his* property."

"I'm afraid he'll harm you one of these days," Amanda said.

"Oh, Judie does not have enough courage to kill an insect."

"Gali, please."

"I will leave these woods only when you carry me to the burial ground."

"Why must I carry you?"

"You are the only family I have," Gali said.

"Well, I have some news that will lift your spirits."

"Tell me!"

"Luke is at Mother's and will come to see us soon!" she cried, dancing around the clearing.

"Many thanks to the Creator!" Gali shouted, raising her arms skyward.

"You are so beautiful when you smile," Amanda said.

"Sure," Gali said, touching her face, "with these old scars?"

"I don't see them anymore," Amanda said.

* * *

"Are you ashamed of me, Miss Mandy?" Josie asked one day.

"No, Josie." She paused and looked closely at him. "Why would you ask such a question?"

"Because I have to hide when somebody comes."

"Well... Uh, some people might not understand about you and me."

He turned his head to one side, scrunched his face up, and asked, "'Cause I'm dark and you light?"

"Yes," she said gently. "Some people wouldn't understand."

A while later, she heard him singing. She crept up to the open door.

"My Mama loves me," he sang. "My Mama loves me."

* * *

Amanda had kept her promise about breaking the lock on the church doors, and she began having meetings at the church on Sunday mornings. She didn't pretend to be a minister, but she could certainly read some scripture and lead the congregation in singing a few hymns. The Widow Wilkes was delighted when Amanda asked her to play the organ. After they sang, Amanda invited the parishioners to stand and talk about the problems they were having or to pass information on to the others.

Amanda had vowed not to be disappointed if no one came, but every week a few more people showed up. She didn't know if it was because they missed church so much or if they had decided she wasn't such a bad person, after all.

She always felt better after the services, but when she got home, all the good feelings quickly vanished.

She knew it was time to do what she had been putting off for months.

Sunday, July 17, 1864

Amanda waited on the front stoop until the noise inside died down a little. She looked down at Josie's inquisitive face.

"Hold your head high, Josie," she whispered to him. "Don't be frightened."

He nodded his head, but he looked terrified.

She opened the double doors, and they marched down the long aisle to the altar of Calvary Baptist Church. Amanda approached the pulpit and faced the congregation. Josie retreated behind her skirts, but she pulled him forward and placed her hand firmly on his shoulder. She cleared her throat loudly.

"I found this little boy on my way to Knoxville, where I lived for a few months last autumn," she announced in a very shaky voice. "His name's Josiah Turner; he's got no family left, so he's staying at my house for food and a place to sleep."

That isn't at all what I meant to say.

Crocker stood up; this was the first meeting he had attended. "Black folks got to set in the back," he said loudly.

"Josie can sit in the Armstrong family pew," she said calmly.

"That's not right," Crocker said.

Amanda ignored Crocker, and he finally sat down.

"For weeks, I've been studying the scriptures, and trying to write a simple sermon." Her hands shook violently as they gripped the pulpit. "Doing Bible readings is fine, but a good sermon can renew the spirit. I'm determined to preach a sermon to you, but please be patient with me."

"This is wrong!" Crocker shouted. "I will not have this in my church!"

"What will you not have?" Amanda asked.

"These people deserve to know the truth about you!" He walked quickly to the front of the church and turned to face the women, children, and old men in attendance.

"Sure, she's all prim and proper now," Crocker continued.

"Sir, I will ask you to take your seat," Amanda said firmly.

"Ask her about that Confederate soldier who stayed overnight at her house."

"We did nothing wrong," Amanda said quickly.

"You are his lover, are you not?" Crocker asked.

"I most certainly am *not!*" she shouted. "The captain has gone back to Virginia with Longstreet's army."

"I observed you from the woods the morning he left, as you clutched each other's hands," Crocker said. "Quite a touching little scene. Almost brought tears to my eyes."

"I don't like your insinuations," Amanda said.

"And you a married woman. Tsk, tsk."

"Get out of here, if you have nothing to say but lies," Amanda said.

She could just walk out, but she was determined to face whatever came.

"And I'm sure she's got money—Yankee money. Ask her how she got it!" Crocker demanded as he turned to look at Amanda, his face full of contempt.

"You should get your facts straight before you make a fool of yourself," she finally managed to say. "I have no money. I'm as poor as the rest of you."

"She was what they call a 'lady of the evening' in Knoxville, but I don't think what she did there was ladylike at all."

The women looked to Amanda for a denial. She just stood there, stunned.

How did he find out about that?

"You may beat me down," Amanda finally said to Crocker, "but you will not defeat me, sir."

"I won't listen to a whore with a black baby! Get out!" he shouted pointing toward the door.

"I will not," Amanda said sounding much more confident than she felt.

"Come on, folks," Crocker said to the congregation. "Let's throw this harlot out."

Nobody moved.

"Then if you won't help me get rid of her, let's leave. She can't preach to an empty house."

He reached the door and noticed no one was following him. "Come on, you cowards! Don't you have the gumption to see her for what she is?"

Crocker finally stormed out of the church.

As relieved as Amanda was to have Crocker gone, his absence left a great void between her and the people in the pews whose approval she needed more than anything else at that moment.

"Yes, I have sinned," Amanda finally said, eyes downcast. "I won't deny it."

Please, God, help me through this.

"Don't condemn me unless you have been in my place," she said, forcing herself to look at the congregation. "I made mistakes while I was in Knoxville. I am sickened now by my actions."

She stopped, cleared her throat, and began again.

"Once you leave behind the world as you know it, you don't come back the same. I have learned things about myself that I didn't see before."

A buzz of whispers spread through the room.

"I thought I was a liberal-minded person. I gave my only slave her freedom because it was the right thing to do. But when it came to this little boy—if he hadn't followed me, he would not be here today. And I shudder when I think about where he might be."

She paused again, trying to clear her mind and say what she had come here to say.

"I brought him home with me, but only because my conscience wouldn't allow me to leave him out there on the road."

She now had everyone's undivided attention.

"Yes, I was ashamed for you to learn that Josiah was living in my house. I admit it!" she said, much louder than she had intended.

She heard Josie gasp.

"I wouldn't let him go outside in the daylight because I was afraid somebody would see him, and I left him at home alone when I came to church. I convinced myself that I did those things for his safety." A knot in her throat forced her to stop and begin again.

"I love this child. I could not love him more if I had given birth to him. You wouldn't believe how smart he is. He has a kind and gentle heart, and there's not a spot of bitterness in him, though he has seen lots of troubled times in his short life.

"This is my son, Josiah Turner Armstrong," she said proudly, urging him forward to stand in front of her. "We will keep Turner as his middle name because of the respect he has for the father who gave him life. All that we ask is to be left alone to live our lives together."

Her throat had become so dry she could barely speak.

"I fed him and gave him shelter in Knoxville, but I was ashamed to tell you that I had a black boy living with me at Cinnamon Hill. How would I explain that to my friends?"

She laughed out loud.

"Don't you see the humor in that?" she said, tears streaming down her face. "I have no friends here. You folks have never liked me."

Amanda grabbed Josie's hand, and they walked quickly out of the church.

The Widow Wilkes caught up to them in the churchyard.

"Don't allow those narrow-minded people to upset you," the woman said. "I think it's a wonderful thing, you saving that boy's life."

"You do?"

"Yes, I do, and you shouldn't allow anyone to criticize you for it."

"Well, thank you," Amanda stammered.

"Why don't we go to my place? I just made some lemonade that will make your dry throat all better."

"All right," Amanda said.

FOURTEEN

———◆◆◆◆◆———

B ack at Cinnamon Hill, Amanda sat on the chaise longue in a
stupor, her legs drawn up, her chin resting on her knees, berating
herself for taking Josie to church.

"Well, Josie, I made a mess of things again," she said with a sigh.
"I wanted to make things better for you, but I might have made them
worse."

"Don't cry, Mama," he whimpered, touching her wet cheek.

"What did you call me?"

"Sorry," he said softly, lowering his head.

"Don't be sorry. I think I'm ready for you to call me Mama."

"For sure?!" he shrieked. He reached up to hug her, knocked her
off balance, and both of them tumbled to the floor.

"Yes," she cried, "forever and ever."

She grabbed him up and cradled him in her arms like a baby,
kissing his face all over. When she kissed his neck, he squealed with
laughter.

"Ticklish on the neck, are we?" she said, burying her face between
his chin and his shoulder. "I'll have to remember that."

"I'm gonna wet myself," he giggled.

"You'd better not," she said, laughing out loud.

* * *

Soon after dark that night, Josie was sitting on Amanda's lap in the chaise before the fire. She was telling him a bedtime story she once told Luke. Suddenly she heard a loud bang on the front door like someone was trying to break it down.

Before she could move, she heard a similar sound at the back door. As if those sounds were a signal of some sort, a whole cacophony of sounds—banging under the floors, tapping on the windows, knocking on the outside walls, and stomping on the roof—began all at once.

Then came the sound of many voices; she heard a Rebel war cry, scary hoots and howls, and a very poor attempt at an Indian chant.

Amanda grabbed Josie and took cover in the corner of the center hall where there were no windows.

"Don't worry, Josie," she whispered. "They're just trying to scare us."

"Well, I'm surely scared," he said, gulping.

Just then a bullet passed through the open dining room door and stuck in the wall nearby.

"That is all I will stand for!" Amanda said as loud as she could, but no one could have heard her above the commotion. She pushed Josie into the corner and ordered him to stay there, no matter what happened.

She crawled to the sitting room and grabbed the revolver Ben gave her from a drawer, shoving extra bullets into the pocket of her skirt. She crawled on hands and knees to the dining room and sat on the floor next to the window that had been shattered by the previous bullet.

Holding her breath, she rose up on her knees in front of the window and fired, almost blowing a man's head off. He had jumped up at the same time she did, but he wasn't able to get off a round.

She saw his body fly backward and land softly on the brick terrace, almost in slow motion.

She turned and sat down on the floor in a panic, unable to catch her breath.

A deep voice from outside said, "Get up, old man. You ain't hurt. She couldn't hit you with a cannonball."

"Do you want to find out?" Amanda shouted. She sprang up on her knees and fired again.

She then heard running, shuffling feet, wagons' wheels, and horses' hooves, getting farther and farther away. Josie was shaking and crying when she got back to him.

"You shot them, didn't you?" he sobbed.

"Luckily, I didn't shoot anybody. I don't want you to think that guns solve anybody's problems. They usually create more."

* * *

The next morning, Crocker came riding in on his mule and wagon. She had previously allowed him to help her with her kitchen garden in exchange for vegetables for his family.

Amanda greeted him from the front terrace. "Don't come any closer," she said.

"What is this now?" he said sourly.

"There's no work for you here," she said coldly, walking out into the oval carriage drive.

"Oh, you mean that—at church?" he said. "Just a little fit of temper. Didn't mean nothing by it."

"I have taken your bad behavior as a consequence of your ignorance," she said calmly. "Now you're hurting people I love, and I won't take that!" She bent over and picked up a rock.

"Now, don't go on like that," Crocker whined. "I need the food. With all my sons fighting in the army, it's hard to feed my large flock."

"You should have thought of that yesterday when you were assaulting my character. I intended to make my past known to our neighbors, but not like that. And I don't appreciate you and your bigoted friends coming here last night. I can take it, but Josie had bad dreams all night long."

"I don't know about that."

"You'd better tell them not to come back. I just might shoot somebody next time."

"I can't tell them, because I don't know who it was," he insisted.

"I don't believe you," she replied.

"Come on now, Mrs. Armstrong."

"I am barring you from my land from this day forward."

"You can't do that. There's still work to be done in the garden, and you'll need my help to get your firewood in for the winter."

She threw the rock she had been holding in her hand, and it hit the mule's hoof. The poor creature was spooked and took off up the lane. Amanda laughed at the sight of the poor little mule running wildly while Crocker struggled to stay in the wagon.

Saturday, September 3, 1864

When Amanda heard Luke call out, she ran out onto the front terrace. He was tethering his horse at the gatepost.

"It *is* you!" she shouted, running to meet him.

"Yes, Mama, it's really me," he said, smiling happily.

He grabbed her and hugged her tightly, kissing her cheek several times. "I've waited a long time to do that," he said.

"Come in," she urged. "You look hot and tired."

"I am that," he said, wiping his brow.

"Your poor face," she said, touching the scars on his cheeks.

"It's all right, Mama," Luke said. "What happened to the house?"

"There's a lot I need to tell you."

In the sitting room, he grabbed her and hugged her again.

"You haven't hugged me like this since you were a boy."

"I know," he said. "Daddy said if he ever caught me fawning over you again, I'd be sorry. I was hugging you the morning he beat me."

"He didn't see us."

"Yes, he did. He walked up behind you and looked directly into my eyes. I knew I was in for it."

"Why didn't you say something?"

"I was going to take my punishment like a man. I had no idea he'd try to kill me."

"He blamed that whole situation on me," she said. "I had hounded him so much about finding you, he lost control of his temper."

"He would have said anything at that point to save his own hide."

Josie came in through the back door. "Mama," he said, and then stopped when he saw Luke.

"Who's this?" Luke looked stunned. "Did he call you Mama?"

"This is one of the things I need to tell you about," she said.

She introduced Luke to Josie and explained how he came to be there. Luke didn't seem too fond of the situation at first, but he came to her later in the day.

"Mama, I thought your generous heart had led you down the wrong path, but the more I'm around Josie, the more I understand. He's like a...a magnet. I don't know how else to say it but that. I could be jealous, you know," Luke said, his cheeks turning pink, "but I'm not."

"I like having two boys."

"When I left you last year—it was an act of selfishness, Mama," Luke said. Tears sprang to his eyes.

"Just seeing you now makes up for all that."

"Can we go to Gali's tomorrow?" he asked. "I want to thank her for everything she taught me when I was growing up. The men call me 'Scout' because I'm so good at spying on the enemy."

"Of course we can go. She will want to see you, too. Where's General Morgan encamped?"

"He's happily ensconced at Mrs. Williams' house in Greeneville. I think he's missed the comfort of a soft bed and a roof over his head."

"One of Catherine's sons is in the Union army, and his wife lives there. That Union general named Gillem stayed there a few weeks ago. It's not safe for General Morgan there."

"I know," Luke said calmly. "We went through all that, and he said not to worry."

"Are you happy being with him?"

"Very happy, but I'm disappointed by the conduct of some of his men. They've looted, stolen, and burned homes, especially on this last raid into Kentucky." Luke sighed and shook his head.

"Then maybe it's time you came home. Josie and I would love to have you here."

"Maybe I should," he said, rubbing his chin, "but I don't think I can leave him. He's still a good man, but I don't think his heart's in it anymore. I think he'd be happy to just go home and live with his wife."

"Then why doesn't he do that?"

"He still has a strong attachment to the Confederacy. I don't think he knows how to get out of it. Those months he spent in prison in Ohio changed him. I'm sure he doubted he would ever see his wife again. He clings to her more than before."

"It seems to me—"

"But my loyalty to the man and what he stands for is as strong as ever."

Amanda sighed and said no more.

September 4, 1864

At some point during the night, Amanda was aware of quick steps and hushed whispers. Probably Luke or Josie going to the privy. They had stayed up late talking, and she was so tired. Come morning, they would have a wonderful breakfast with the supplies Luke brought: salt, flour, sugar, and coffee! She had buried her nose in the little brown bag of beans, relishing the aroma she had missed more than anything else since the war began.

She thought Luke had whispered something in her ear, but she couldn't quite make it out—something about somebody being in danger, but he would be back later. Was she dreaming? She lay in bed for a few more minutes; until something Luke had said jarred her awake. She sat straight up.

She settled Josie, who was sleeping next to her, grabbed her boots and trousers, and ran onto the front terrace. She was hoping to catch Luke, but all she heard was horse's hooves galloping away in the distance.

The almost-full moon bathed the front yard in soft light. As she stood there, wondering if she should follow Luke, her peripheral vision caught some movement near the gatepost. She ran in that direction and soon made out Crocker's form, astride one of his mules. He kicked the old creature, obviously having trouble getting it to move.

"What are you doing here? You told Luke something about General Morgan, didn't you?" she asked, her heart thudding in her chest.

"Might have," he said, clicking his tongue, urgently trying to get the mule to move, but Amanda ran forward, grabbed one of the reins, and held it tightly.

"What have you done now, old man?" she snarled in clipped, overly enunciated words.

"Ain't done nothing," he lied, looking everywhere except at her face.

She tried to remember what Luke had said. Something about General Morgan, that he was... *Think, Amanda, think!* She slapped a hand against her forehead, trying desperately to clear her fuzzy mind.

"The news around these parts," Crocker finally said, "is that somebody is riding hell-bent for General Gillem's camp to tell him that General Morgan is at the Williams house."

"Did you tell Luke that?"

"Might've."

Amanda's feet left the ground when she jumped up and grabbed the old man's collar and pulled his face within inches of her own. "*Did you?!*"

"'Course I did."

"You son of a bitch!" she shouted. She tightened her grip on his collar. "Prepare to die, Crocker, if anything happens to my boy," she growled, in a gritty voice that she hardly recognized as her own. She gave him a good hard shove as she released her grip on his collar, and he fell off the mule with a thud.

"You better pray, old man!" she yelled as she ran for the barn, her boots still in her hand.

At the barn, she struggled with Molly, who didn't appreciate having to move her arthritic legs in the damp pre-dawn. "Come on, old girl," Amanda pleaded. "We have to go. Luke may be in trouble." Molly quickly came right, as if she understood Amanda's words.

What would she do about Josie?

Amanda stopped at the home of the Widow Wilkes on her way to Greeneville. The house was completely dark. She tapped lightly on the door.

"Mrs. Wilkes," she called softly.

"What's happening?" Widow asked as she opened the door. There was abject fear in her face.

"I'm sorry to trouble you at this hour," Amanda said. She quickly explained the situation to the sleepy woman.

"You go on and see about Luke. I'll take care of Josie as good as you would until you return."

"Thank you," Amanda sighed, squeezing Widow's hands.

* * *

The town was full of Yankees when Amanda arrived. A gray murky dawn was trying to break but having little success. She sneaked around the edges of the crowd that had gathered in front of the Williams house.

Just as she reached the edge of the crowd, a Union soldier on a horse came galloping up the alley. He gave a shout, followed immediately by a shot. She saw General Morgan crouched down in the Williams' vineyard. He clutched his chest and fell to the ground.

A bullet fired immediately afterward struck a young man who was trying to help General Morgan get away.

"Oh, Lord—Luke!" Amanda shouted. She rushed forward, trying to get to her son. The man on the horse raised his gun to her.

"I'm the boy's mother!" she shouted.

"Oh… Yes, ma'am," he said. "I'm sorry about the boy. He should have stayed out of the way."

Her perfect child lay in a vineyard ripe with fruit. His blue eyes gleamed in the brightening light. She saw immediately that the bullet had cut his jugular. His warm red blood gushed out onto the bright green grass.

"Somebody help me!" she cried.

She got down on her knees and put one arm under his shoulders, the other under his legs—like one would hold a baby—and tried to pick him up. When she lifted his shoulders, his head fell back. When she lifted his legs, his torso rolled out of her arms.

"Come on, now, Luke," she whispered. "You've got to help me a little bit. You've got so tall, I can't seem to—Luke," she said louder, then her voice softened again. "Come on, sugar, help me just a little. We've got to get you home."

Crocker was suddenly at her side. "Mrs. Armstrong," he whispered, "let me help you."

"Don't you touch him!" she yelled.

"Don't be that way," Crocker whispered.

The man on the horse shouted to some of the soldiers who were standing nearby, "Get that woman out of here. She's pitiful," he said, spitting a stream of tobacco juice that landed on the ground near General Morgan's head.

Some would say that General Morgan surrendered before he was shot; others would say not. Amanda wasn't close enough to hear. Such a tragic figure he was, to come to such an untimely end.

Some of the Union soldiers lashed General Morgan's body to a mule and paraded it around the town. Someone deliberately spooked the animal, and it ran wildly as the general's body jerked and spun.

Crocker brought his wagon and hauled Luke's body to Cinnamon Hill. Amanda followed close behind on Molly. They laid Luke on the old chaise in the sitting room.

Josie began to sob as soon as he saw the blood on Luke's shirt.

Crocker asked the Widow Wilkes to stay with Amanda while he made arrangements to bury Luke. As Crocker was leaving, Amanda ran onto the front terrace. "This is your fault!" she shouted at him with a raised fist.

* * *

Jonathan arrived from Strawberry Plains. Crocker had managed to get word to him. Amanda recalled speaking to Jonathan when he arrived, but she couldn't remember what he said. He cried incessantly. "Stop making such a scene," she told him, not thinking about how heartbroken he must be. He hadn't seen Luke since the day he beat him. Now he was forced to look at his son's scarred face.

Josie cried all day, no matter how much the Widow Wilkes tried to lift his spirits. Amanda sat in a stupor.

"I think you're so sad because your Mama's so sad, aren't you?" Mrs. Wilkes asked Josie.

"No, I saw Luke yesterday, and he was kind to me. He didn't make me feel like I don't belong here, like some folks do."

Amanda's emotions were in a large, crushing ball in the middle of her chest. At times, it almost cut off her breath entirely.

They moved Luke's body to the center hall, where they could gather around the chaise. When Amanda glanced at him at a certain angle, it looked like he was just sitting there. She touched his pale cold face and turned up the collar of his shirt to hide the wound in his neck.

Amanda had planned to read some scripture and lead them in singing a few hymns, but when the time came, she couldn't get the words out. Mrs. Wilkes took the Bible from her, read the marked passages, and led them in singing with her rich alto voice.

After the service, Jonathan came up behind Amanda. He reached out to touch the small of her back. She remembered how much Jonathan had once loved to caress her back, how proud he had been of her slim waist. She sidestepped his advance.

"I will send a request to my commander that I be allowed to remain at home a few weeks—until you are feeling better," Jonathan said.

She floated across the floor to the sitting room door. "I saw one of your precious Yankees blow a hole in my child's neck. I don't want you here," she said coldly.

"I know this is a difficult time," he stuttered.

"If the war ends before we're all killed, I will leave here," she said. "This is your property. Right now, I have responsibilities here: like Josie, to whom you turn up your nose. You might as well say what's on your mind about Josie."

"I have nothing to say about Josie," Jonathan said calmly, hanging his head.

"And I have nothing to say to you."

"Very well," he said softly," I will return to my duties. Take care of yourself, Amanda."

Crocker brought in a nicely crafted pinewood coffin. They carried Luke's body to the family cemetery, where they buried him next to Charles. Amanda was only able to say a few words before they lowered Luke's body into the grave someone had already dug.

She turned to Crocker and said, "You killed my son, just as surely as if you pulled the trigger yourself."

Saturday, September 17, 1864

For the first time since Luke's death, Amanda went downstairs and ate breakfast. She knew how worried Josie was about her, and she made a supreme effort to allay his fears as much as possible.

"I am so thankful, Widow Wilkes, for your help," Amanda said. "I don't know how I would have managed without you, but I don't want to impose on you further."

"You're certainly welcome," Mrs. Wilkes said. "I'm glad to do it, and it keeps me from feeling so lonesome. Don't worry for a minute about imposing on me. When the day comes you don't need me anymore, I'll go back home."

"I'm sure your house needs some attention."

"Josie and I have been there every few days. We went while you napped in the afternoon."

"Really?" Amanda said.

"Yeah," Josie added. "I like to go there. There's a nice big patch of woods all 'round her house. I found some berries and scuppernongs."

"He has a feast every time we go. There's really not much there to tend to: just a few sticks of furniture."

"Furniture?" Amanda said, perking up. "We could sure use some furniture here. Poor Josie ends up sitting on the floor most of the time."

"We can bring it, if you like," Mrs. Wilkes suggested. "Rebels stole my best furniture to burn in their fires. It's nothing fancy, believe me. A small table and a few chairs."

"Chairs! I can't remember the last time I sat in a comfortable chair."

"Well, they're old but still comfortable."

"Let's go get them right now," Amanda said.

"Why don't you let us do that?" the Widow said, patting Josie's head. "You're still mighty weak, and you shouldn't overdo."

That afternoon, Amanda and the Widow were sitting in the rockers they had brought from Widow's place, in front of the fireplace in the sitting room. Josie was napping on the old chaise in the corner.

"Do you mind being called Widow?" Amanda asked.

"It don't matter much," the Widow said. "I've been called that so long... I've been widowed twice, you see, the first time when I was very young. I doubt most people around here remember my real name."

"What is it?"

The Widow hesitated a moment.

"I think you've forgotten it, too," Amanda said, smiling.

"No, I've not. It's Eleanora."

"That's a beautiful name. Why don't people call you that?"

"You'll have to ask somebody besides me," the Widow said, shaking her head. "I was Jeb Long's widow, then Arthur Wilkes' widow. They started calling me the Widow, then just Widow."

"You don't mind?"

"Not really. It's just funny how people can be sometimes."

"Amen," Amanda said.

Widow's appearance was a little old-fashioned—she was probably in her fifties—but she was always neat and clean. She wore her hair in a tight knot at the crown of her head. Amanda thought there was something elegant about her, something in the way she carried herself. Despite the difficulties of her life, her self-confidence seemed never to waver.

"I still miss Mr. Charles a right much."

"That's right," Amanda said, remembering that long-ago day when she and Widow talked in the churchyard. "You really loved him, didn't you?"

"More than anyone I've ever known. I lost two children when I was young—one in childbirth and one to smallpox—but his loss affected me more even than that."

"Were you ever in this house?"

"Lord, no," Widow said. "Evalinda would have killed me—and him!"

"Do you think she knew about your relationship?"

"I can't say. She never went anywhere, and she didn't have any friends. Charles was discreet; he didn't want to hurt her. I respected him for that. He'd come to my bed in the middle of the night, then rush back so he'd be in the kitchen when she came down. He did say she questioned him at first about his sudden habit of getting up so early. At Charles' funeral was one of the few times I ever saw Evalinda."

"Were you at the cemetery that day?" Amanda said. "Oh, I remember seeing a woman clothed all in black with a veil over her face, leaning against a tree. It never occurred to me at the time that it was you."

"I didn't know whether to go or not go, in case Evalinda did know about the affair...but I couldn't stay away completely. My whole body was shaking. I thought if I let go of that tree, I'd sink right into the earth."

"It was a sad day, made doubly sad by the drizzling rain."

"Mr. Charles was a wonderful man, kinder to me than either of my husbands."

"How sad," Amanda said wistfully.

"You know, I don't have a thing to remember him by—not that I need a reminder. Rarely does a day go by that I don't have some thought of him. Did he leave any personal things? It'd be comforting to have something of his to hold to my heart when I'm hurting."

"My Lord, I forgot!" Amanda jumped up and hurried out of the room.

By the time Widow caught up to her, she was in the library. "What did you forget?"

"There's a loose board in here somewhere," Amanda said, squatting down. "Charles showed it to me a long time ago and made me promise I wouldn't tell anyone about it. There was a metal box he hid under the board, but I don't know what was in it. I don't come in here very often. Out of about three hundred books, I salvaged only thirty-two after the war. I often wonder if maybe I could have saved his books if I'd stayed here."

"And maybe you'd be dead," Widow said bluntly.

"Maybe so."

"Where is the loose board?"

"I think it might be by the fireplace. It's hard to remember."

"Here?"

"No. I think it's the other side," Amanda said. "It sounds hollow when you step on it."

They both started stepping heavily, and they couldn't hear a thing.

"One board at a time," Amanda said, laughing.

Widow looked as gleeful as a child.

"Wait," Amanda said, listening to Widow's footsteps, "step on that board right there again. Yes, that's it! We need something to pry the end up with."

"Would my pocket knife work?" the Widow asked, fumbling at the waist of her skirt.

"You carry a knife?"

"A woman alone can't be too careful."

"True enough."

After several minutes of work, Amanda finally lifted the board and pulled out a long narrow metal box. She set it on a bookshelf and opened it. The first thing she found was a tress of brown hair mixed with a lot of gray, tied with a pink ribbon.

"Evalinda's?" Widow asked.

"I'm sure it's not," Amanda said. "Probably his mother's."

Next, she pulled out a gold pocket watch. "That's strange," Amanda said. "We buried him with his pocket watch."

"This was his father's," Widow said. "He showed it to me once. He adored his father, and he was a hard man to love."

"Would you like to have this?"

Widow took the watch into her hand as if it were priceless. She carefully opened it and discovered why he had kept the watch hidden. It held a picture of her. She carefully removed it, and another piece of paper floated to the floor.

"Saints be praised," Widow whispered. Tears welled in her eyes.

Amanda picked up the paper that had fallen to the floor. It was a picture of a man. "Is this the other half of that picture?" Amanda asked, handing it to Widow.

"Yes," Widow sighed. "My second husband, Arthur."

Widow's legs gave way; her face went white. Amanda grabbed her and helped her sit down on the floor.

"I thought..." Widow stammered. "I thought he..." she began again.

"You thought he used you for his own pleasure?"

Widow's tears kept coming, spilling down into her lap. "I gave up crying a long time ago," she said, roughly wiping the tears from her face. She tried to stand but Amanda held her down, afraid she would fall.

"I can't..." Widow said, slapping at Amanda's hands. "Let me go."

"Listen to me," Amanda said firmly. "This is a blessing."

"What blessing?" Widow said angrily. "I've looked for that picture for years. Why would he steal it?" She threw the watch across the room. It thudded against the wall.

"Maybe he decided he couldn't continue to see you. Knowing Charles as I did, he must have felt terrible about his infidelity. He probably took that picture to have something of yours with him, just like you want something of his to keep."

"That makes no sense," Widow said, drying her eyes.

"Wouldn't you have enjoyed having a picture of him? Like you said, on your sad days?"

"Of course."

"Then there's your answer," Amanda said. "Charles loved you, Widow."

"Surely not," Widow protested, shaking her head.

"Then how do you explain this?" There was an envelope in the box with Widow's name on it.

Widow grabbed it and clutched it to her breast. "I don't understand."

"At some point in time, he must have written this letter to you. I'll let you read it in private."

"No, stay with me." Widow's hands trembled as she opened the envelope and began to read the letter aloud.

"My dearest Eleanora—he remembered my name!"

"See?" Amanda said.

"My dearest Eleanora, I pray that someday this letter will find its way to you, though I can't say how even God could make that wish come true. But I need to put down these words. I must unburden my heart. I've loved you so long, before you became aware of it, long before I came to your bed. But it's unfair of me to mistreat you the way I have. You deserve so much more. I'm just a foolish old coward who has never had the backbone to go after what I want. I sit and wait for life to come to me..."

Amanda tiptoed out of the room.

FIFTEEN

Monday, September 19, 1864

"You must let the past go," Gali told Amanda. "You are pale as a ghost. You cannot continue to relive Luke's death every day."

"Pray, tell me, how do I stop?" Amanda asked.

"I know," Gali conceded. "It is easy enough for me to say, but you have to do it."

"I've tried, but his dead face is the last thing I see before I go to sleep and the first thing in my head when I wake up."

"Not only do you barricade yourself in that house, but that poor child, too." Josie was playing at the edge of the woods. "Has he eaten today?"

Amanda reluctantly shook her head. "A little."

"Come, Josie," Gali called, "beans and bread." He hurried into the cabin.

"Our food supply is low already. We'll be on very short rations just to make it through the winter. Widow brought some potatoes and cabbage, which we buried in the ground to cook later, but that doesn't give you strength like meat does."

"You have forgotten my teaching," Gali said. "You must hunt rabbit and squirrel to supplement your diet."

"You know I can't kill an animal, not even the ones you say God gave us to eat. I've tried, but I just can't pull the trigger."

"Wait, I thought of something after you were here last. You said some of the women who left home because of the war are returning now that things have settled down a bit?"

"Yes, I saw three of them at church yesterday."

"The Cherokee grew gardens communally—beans, corn, squash, potatoes. Everyone who worked the gardens got a share of the food. You can gather these women at Cinnamon Hill and plant a garden large enough to feed everyone."

"Do you really think that would work?"

"I do. And you could be the leader. It might be just the thing you need right now. You will be too busy to dwell on the past."

"I don't know," Amanda said. "I'm not good with people."

"You are better than you know. Are these women in your same situation?"

"I guess. Since they're coming back, they've learned what I learned: that there is no better place than home."

"A woman alone can't grow enough corn for meal, fruits to preserve, and root vegetables for the cellar to last the winter."

"But it's autumn."

"I think autumn would be a good time for you to come together. There are nuts and berries to collect, wild yams to dig, squirrel and rabbit to hunt, and firewood to cut for the winter."

"I doubt if anyone has guns to kill small game. I've only managed to keep my revolver," she said, patting the waist of her skirt, "because I keep it on me at all times."

"They can make bows and arrows. I will teach them."

"You hate being with whites."

"Most women are tolerable," Gali said, smirking.

"And you would do that for me?"

"I will take the chance if you will."

"How is it you always have the right solution?"

"I am very wise," Gali said, a look of total satisfaction on her face.

* * *

At church the following Sunday, Amanda invited all women who were living alone to come to Cinnamon Hill the next morning. Sally Jensen came, as well as Dorothy Jacobs, Althea Davis, Nell Jones, Rachel Harris, and Rebecca Brown; Becca, people called her.

"Ladies," Amanda said from the front terrace, "who knows how long the war will last? If we pool our resources, maybe we can make our lives better in the meantime. We will share everything equally. I can accommodate up to ten women in my house, if you bring your own bedding.

"There's room enough for a nice garden in the forest behind the cemetery. There's a sizeable clearing that gets sun most all day long. Maybe back there we can keep it out of view of foraging troops and hungry civilians. It's too late to plant anything now, but we can get the ground ready to plant in the spring."

Amanda paused, trying to read the women's faces. "What do you think?" she asked, hesitantly.

"A commune—is that what you're proposing?" Sally asked.

"Yes," Amanda chuckled, "I guess I am. Some will say it's a crazy idea, that I'm crazy to suggest it. Planting, tending, harvesting, and gathering... These are the rhythms of rural life. I miss that. So I am pledging my time and property to the women of Armstrong Cross-roads. Come again tomorrow morning. Bring whatever you have to contribute to the larder. If you have any poultry or livestock, please bring it."

The same six women arrived at Cinnamon Hill the next morning, carrying, leading, and dragging their last worldly possessions. Nell brought a rooster, Becca two hens, and Rachel, a horse and wagon. *Oh, the luxury of a wagon!* Amanda thought. They would use it to gather furniture from the women's homes and haul much needed firewood to Cinnamon Hill.

"We have among us," Amanda announced, after making an inventory, "not a single plow; two horses, but only enough harness for one; two puny weeding hoes, one with a broken handle; and a rake. We'll have to make everything else we need."

Sally brought five little pigs, one male and four females. "The sow died before the pigs were weaned," she explained. "I don't know if the pigs will live."

"We'd better make sure they do," Amanda said. "Our future depends on them."

"The first thing we have to do is build safe housing for our animals. Livestock will be stolen if they can be found in the usual places. So, I propose we build pens in the woods near the garden. After we plant there next spring, everything will be in the same area and easier to guard. Those on duty will be safer if they're not out in the open, too. As with any group, we have to have some rules of conduct.

"One," she began, "we don't go anywhere off the property alone, not even in daylight. It's too dangerous.

"Two, I have vowed to neither help nor hinder the Yankees or the Rebels. Each of you must pledge to do the same, and you must sign your name to this document," Amanda said, holding up a single piece of paper. "I will not inquire about your politics, nor should you ask that of each other.

"Three, everybody must take their turn at guard duty. There will be three eight-hour shifts a day. I know the nights will be frightening; I'll make it as safe as possible for you, and you will have a weapon with you at all times.

"Four, you may volunteer for jobs you like to do or do well, but for those nasty jobs no one likes, everyone must take a turn.

"Five, if you hear the bell above the summer kitchen ringing, come running. We will only ring it in times of emergency.

"Last is regarding my little Josie: If any of you object to living with a black child, you must leave right now. If you take the time to get to know him, you will find that he is anxious to do his part to make this commune a success.

"Any of you who feel you cannot live under these rules must leave now."

No one moved.

* * *

The Cuthbertson house was a plain, two-story, frame dwelling. Except for the kitchen, the entire ground floor was one big room. Amanda crept slowly up onto the porch.

"Emily," she called softly. "It's Amanda Armstrong. If you're here, please show yourself."

No answer.

Amanda entered the barn and called Emily's name several times. Just as she was turning away, she heard a sob.

She found Emily in a horse stall with only a fireplace grate covered with a piece of iron grid for heat. She lay on a straw bed in the corner. The place was smelly, cold, and damp.

Amanda rushed to her. "What are you doing out here?" she asked.

"I'm too scared to stay in the house," Emily answered, beginning to cry.

She was so weak that Amanda held on to her securely and helped her to the wagon.

"Bless you for thinking of me," Emily said. "I thought you still hated me."

"I never hated you, Emily. I was very disappointed in you, but I've learned that our heart won't always let us do what our head knows is right."

Crocker passed the word through Sally that he would like to join the commune: not to live there, of course, but to help with the garden and the livestock.

"I think he's afraid to ask you," Sally said.

"I haven't seen him since Luke's funeral," Amanda said. "He's just looking for an easy way to feed his family, without doing a lot of work. I know he's getting up in years, but sometimes he's just lazy."

A few days later, Sally came to Amanda again about Crocker.

"I know how you feel about the man," Sally said patiently, "and I know why, but I think he's got a good idea this time."

"What?" Amanda barked.

"He wants to run Mr. Charles' mill. He says there's some people around here who have a little corn saved up, but no way to grind it into meal. Since nobody has any money, Crocker says a small portion of each customer's corn meal be taken as payment to the commune— and Crocker would take a small portion for his family."

"Well, of course he would," Amanda said with contempt. "I knew there was a hidden motive in there somewhere!"

"But it's only fair."

"It will take a lot of work to get that thing running again."

"He says he's prepared for that," Sally said. "It would help the commune and other people in the community." Sally was a petite woman, but she was as feisty as a bulldog.

"All right," Amanda finally said. "Just tell him to stay out of my sight. He can come and go and run the mill without being in my presence."

Charles had built the gristmill on Bottom Creek a little way downstream from the house. It used water power to grind corn and wheat into meal and flour. Jonathan had worked at the mill when he was a boy, and he detested it. He closed the mill down the day after Charles died.

* * *

One afternoon, a thunderstorm came rolling over the mountains, bringing horizontal rain and hailstones the size of a fist. A flash of lightning struck a large tree in the middle of the pigpen. Sally, who was on guard duty, rode quickly to tell Amanda that the lightning had killed all five piglets.

Widow wept openly. "I bottle-fed two of them for weeks," she told Amanda.

The commune women were up all night in the summer kitchen, rendering fat, cooking the meat that couldn't be preserved and making sausage. The liver, innards, and brains were processed too; almost every part of a pig was edible. The hams and bacon were hung in the smokehouse to be smoked with hickory wood.

Everybody around Armstrong Crossroads ate very well for several days. Amanda sent Emily and Sally to deliver fresh meat to everyone they found at home.

Amanda visited Gali and gave her a ham and a large cut of bacon to hang in her cave.

"How are you?" Gali asked, always anxious to hear about the commune. "You are looking better every time I see you."

"Well, I must say I'm feeling better than I have in a long time."

* * *

At dusk one evening, Amanda heard a voice calling her name at a far distance. She went to the front windows in the dining room and looked out. The shadows had begun to recede into the darkness. She squinted her eyes but saw nothing.

On her way back to the sitting room, she heard the voice again.

She took a candle from the hall table and stepped out onto the front terrace. "Who's out there?" she called.

"It's me, Mrs. Armstrong. I'm over here."

"Crocker?"

"Here I am," he called, "down in the dirt. And feeling lower than a sow's belly."

Yes, there he was by the gatepost.

"Stand up."

"I'm afraid you'll shoot me."

"Then why are you here?"

"It's my baby girl, Pearl. She's had the fever almost a week now. She won't take no nourishment a-tall." He sounded like he was a mile down a well.

"What do you expect me to do?"

"You've learned how to use Gali's medical roots and things. I know you can save her—if you will."

"Well, look at the shoe on the other foot," she drawled. "You sent my only child to his death. Now you have the gall to come bawling to me to save one of—how many children do you have now, Crocker? A dozen?"

"I've done everything I know to do."

"That wouldn't take long," Amanda mumbled.

"And she's not a bit better. I'm begging, for her mother's sake if not for mine. She's the sweetest thing you ever saw, my little Pearl. Looks like an angel with pretty yellow ringlets all over her head."

"Shut up," Amanda shouted. "Let me think a minute."

She stepped back into the house. The other women were gathered in the hall.

"What's going on?" Widow asked.

"It's Crocker. How dare he come begging me to help his sick little girl!"

"Amanda!" Widow scolded. "It's a sick *child*."

"Of course, you're right. The child can't be held responsible for the deeds of the father," Amanda whispered.

"I'll be there shortly," she called to Crocker. "You just stay out of my sight."

"Yes, Mrs. Armstrong, I surely will. Can I stand up now?"

"I don't care what you do."

* * *

When Amanda arrived at Crocker's cabin, his wife was angry. "I told you I don't want her here," she said, glaring at Amanda. She stood in the doorway of the cabin and wouldn't let Amanda pass.

"Do you want to save your daughter's life?" Crocker asked his wife. She moved aside.

Toward dawn, Pearl's fever finally broke. She took a few sips of herbal tea before going back to sleep. Amanda stepped out onto the front porch for some fresh air. Crocker was there. He had been peering in the window all night while she cared for Pearl.

"I know," he said, turning away, "you don't want to see me."

"Why is your wife so hostile toward me?" Amanda asked before he could leave.

"She hates you."

"Why? I've never so much as spoken to her."

"Yes, you have," he said. "She came to your Saturday tea years ago, remember? Our son is the one who broke your Granny's china."

"Oh," Amanda said.

"You broke her heart that day," Crocker said. "She wanted to learn from you, but you brushed her off like she was a pesky housefly. Sometimes you don't consider other people's feelings before you speak."

"That would make me pretty much like you then, wouldn't it?" Amanda said.

Crocker shook his head but said nothing.

"Was she the one with all the children? She said her husband was at the tavern drinking with Jonathan."

"I was," Crocker said.

"You were one of Jonathan's drinking companions?"

"Yes," he said, "I was at your house every weeknight and at the tavern on Saturdays, and I'm not proud of it."

"Where is your wife?" Amanda asked. "I want to apologize to her."

"She's probably listening," he said, nodding toward the corner of the house. "That was a hard time for her. She was very young and had just married me, and got a ready-made family. She had no control over my children; they were still missing their mother. She thought you were the grandest lady who ever existed."

"Then please tell her I truly am sorry, but that doesn't mean I'm anywhere near ready to forgive you for what you did to Luke."

"I didn't expect you would be."

Amanda was taken aback. It wasn't like Crocker to take her sass without giving her the same in return.

December 1864

In answer to Josie's call, Amanda stepped into the center hall. Crocker was standing in the open doorway. Josie was hiding behind the door.

"Oh, it's you," she said.

Crocker nodded, holding his hat in his hand.

"Come on out of there, Josie," she said, pulling him out of the corner. "You have nothing to fear from this man. Isn't that right, Crocker?"

"Certainly not. I love children."

"I haven't seen you in a while, which is exactly the way I like it. What do you want?" she asked.

"I'm sorry to have to bring such bad news, Mrs. Armstrong," he said, twirling his old hat in his hands, "but there's been quite a little cavalry fight over at the Crossroads—"

"Yes, is that what we heard a while ago."

"And your husband—"

"Some of it sounded quite close by."

"What I'm trying to tell you," he stated loudly, "is that your husband has been wounded."

"Jonathan's been wounded? What's he doing here?"

"He was riding with Stoneman's cavalry out of Knoxville."

"Is he hurt bad?"

"I don't know," he stuttered. "The major in charge sent me to fetch you. He's waiting for you at the church."

"The church?"

"That's where most of the fighting took place. Looks like the church caught quite a few rounds. There's holes in the walls everywhere."

"Dear Lord," she said, shaking her head, "is nothing sacred?"

"Is there something I can do to help you?" Crocker asked.

"No," she said absentmindedly. The full comprehension of what he had said suddenly registered in her mind.

Amanda rode quickly to the Crossroads. Union soldiers and their horses filled the churchyard.

"Are you the major?" she called to an officer.

"Yes, ma'am," he said, walking toward her. "You must be Mrs. Armstrong."

She nodded, out of breath.

"He's at the edge of the woods beyond the church there."

"Is he severely wounded?" she asked, peering through the smoke of battle in the direction the major had pointed. She tasted gunpowder on her tongue.

"Yes, ma'am," he said. "He asked me to tell you if he should die before your arrival. He's been going on about it for three-quarters of an hour. Frankly, I don't know how he's still alive, except for his determination to speak to you before he..."

Tears filled her eyes. "Please, just tell me." Her voice came out in a gruff whisper.

"I've known Colonel Armstrong since he came into our camp at Cumberland Gap, over a year now. And I've never known anyone so afraid of death. His conduct in battle has been controlled by that fear."

She began to walk toward the church. The major fell in step beside her. Someone took Molly's reins from her hand.

The major stopped and looked into Amanda's eyes. "We were trapped in the woods there," he said, pointing at the rear of the churchyard. "Nothing behind us but a creek too deep to cross, and nothing in front of us but Rebels. Colonel Armstrong went flying out of the woods and rode deliberately toward the enemy, drawing their fire away from the rest of us. He fell almost as soon as he entered the clearing, his breast riddled with bullets. He saved our lives," the major said, his voice trembling. "That's what he wanted me to tell you."

Before they reached the corner of the church, the major said, "You must prepare yourself, ma'am, for...his appearance."

Amanda walked on past the church. She recognized Jonathan immediately. He was propped against a tree at the edge of the woods. As soon as he saw her, he began to cry.

"I did it, Amanda," he said, weeping. "I did it. Did you tell her, Major?"

"Yes, sir," the major said humbly. "I told her everything."

She got down on her knees beside Jonathan. The full front of his uniform was soaked with blood. It had even penetrated the heavy winter coat he wore. A thick line of red spittle drooled from the corner of his mouth. Drops of perspiration covered his face and sopped his hair in spite of the cold. Her emotions suddenly boiled up and settled in her throat.

"Yes, Jonathan," she said, trying not to cry. "He told me, and it's the bravest story I ever heard."

His eyes brightened as he talked about the battle. She begged him to be quiet, to conserve his strength.

"When I learned those Rebels were part of General John Hunt Morgan's old command, I wanted to kill those bastards for what happened to Luke."

"There's nothing to be done about that now," Amanda said patiently.

"General Stoneman gave us strict orders to chase them down and to kill or capture as many as possible. He was just up here three weeks ago, and he didn't want to contend with them again."

"We must carry him to the hospital," Amanda told the major, pointing toward a group of wounded soldiers she saw in the shade of a cluster of oaks in the meadow beyond the church.

"There's no doctor here. Only a medic," the major said. "He examined him before you arrived."

"What can we do?" Amanda asked. "Surely there's—"

"There's nothing we can do," the major said patiently, but firmly. "It's a miracle he's still alive."

Amanda thought Jonathan hadn't enough air left to speak again, but he fooled her. "We got this little detachment on the run, you see," he said, excitedly. "They'd ride on a little, then stop and look back to see if we were coming. They thought they were baiting us; all the time I was baiting them. I left a few men on the road to make them think we were still coming.

"The rest of us veered off onto the old wagon road along Bottom Creek, so we could ambush them at the Crossroads. Of course, the wagon road hasn't been used much in recent years, and it's grown up in thickets. Our horses kept getting tangled up in it, but I was sure we'd make it in time to ambush them."

"Don't try to talk," she said softly into his ear as she kissed his cheek.

"They beat us here. It was my mistake, so I had to rectify it."

"Please, Jonathan," she whispered.

"You know how you hated it that you had to be dependent on me. You never saw the truth."

He tried to rise up, but she held him against the tree trunk, sure that every word would be his last. "I was the one who needed you, but I couldn't tell you that—except when I was drunk, and you didn't want me then."

Her face reddened.

"Please forgive me for failing you so miserably," he whispered.

"Shh," she said. "It sounds like you failed yourself."

"I've missed you so," he said. He grabbed her hands and clutched them to his bloody chest as if she were his last hold on life.

He began to cough. Blood gurgled up in his throat. "I'm sorry for Luke, for Emily, for the woman in the tent. For everything I did that caused the disappointment I saw in your eyes."

"In my eyes?" Her heart suddenly felt heavy in her chest.

"The disapproval was always there, but I deserved it all."

"Why did you not tell me of your feelings back then?" she asked.

"I thought you hated me," he whispered.

"It sounds like you should be forgiving me."

"You did everything right, Amanda. I didn't have the gumption to be the man you deserved."

"You changed today," she said, smoothing the hair on his forehead. He was sweating profusely now, his breathing shallow, his lips as transparent as paper.

"Can you forgive me?" he cried.

She nodded. "I forgive you, Jonathan, for all of it."

He pressed her bloody fingers to his lips as tears welled in his eyes. "Bury me beside Luke," he said weakly. "I can't wait to see him in Heaven—if God is kind enough to let me go there. I love you, my wife," he whispered.

His eyes suddenly went wild.

"Are you frightened?" she asked.

"No," he said, suddenly calm. "I find it quite comforting to know that my life will end here, where it began."

"You've done everything right here today," she said, "and I admire your courage."

"Bless you," he said and took one last shaky breath. She wiped his tears away, and gently closed his vacant eyes.

Amanda wanted to honor Jonathan's last wish, but how could she transport his body to Cinnamon Hill? The cavalry detachment was traveling light. They had no ambulance with them, not even a wagon. By the time she brought the wagon from Cinnamon Hill, it would be long past dark, and too dangerous for women to be out on the road, but the thought of wild animals attacking his body during the night filled her mind with horror.

"We can put his body across your horse," the major offered.

"No," she said, shaking her head violently, the vision of General Morgan's body being paraded through Greeneville on a mule flashed through her mind.

"We can bury him in the church cemetery here—inside the wrought iron fence," the major said. "I'll mark his grave, so you can find it later and give him a proper burial."

"Yes," she whispered, "his great-grandfather is buried there."

Amanda remained until Jonathan's body was interred. She touched the mound of earth under which his body lay, whispered a prayer for the salvation of his soul, and promised to carry him home to Cinnamon Hill as soon as possible.

When there was nothing left to do, she walked trance-like toward Molly. "I have so many regrets," she said.

"I have a lifetime's worth of regrets from this war," the major said.

"If you mark the graves of the other soldiers who have died here today, I'll try to find their families, in case they should want to carry their remains home."

After she mounted Molly, a young man handed her Jonathan's personal possessions, tied up in a bundle.

* * *

At Cinnamon Hill, Amanda tried to explain another death to Josie.

"Josie," she asked, "do you feel like I don't like you sometimes?"

"Sometimes," he said sadly.

"How does my face look when you feel like that?"

"Mean."

"You know I still love you, don't you? Even when I look mean."

He shrugged his little shoulders.

"Well, your Mama's not very patient sometimes. She needs to ask God to help her with that."

"He will if you pray," Josie said.

"Do you pray?"

"All the time."

"What do you pray for?" she asked.

"That we don't go hungry, that no bad soldier men come to hurt us, that you don't get sick again—all kinds of things."

"Really?"

"But I really pray we don't get stuck on the roof no more."

Amanda laughed out loud. "Promise me one thing. No matter what Mama's face looks like, I always love you in my heart."

* * *

Among Jonathan's possessions were a clean Union uniform and a knapsack. Inside the knapsack, Amanda found a journal he had begun to write shortly after leaving home. Interleaved in the pages of the journal were several letters and parts of letters. Apparently, he had begun to write to her many times. Behind one page, there might be another, with the same beginning as the one previous. He had swiped harsh scrawls across some of them. Some of them had been balled up, and then carefully flattened out again.

In the back of the journal were several complete letters. The dates ranged as far back as October 1863, not long after she saw him at Strawberry Plains. Some of them were attempts to beg her forgiveness. In those writings, she became reacquainted with the man she met in 1841.

A profound sadness overcame her. She retied the bundle and hid it in an old trunk in the attic. Maybe someday she might find it easier to look at its contents.

SIXTEEN

———◦◦◦———

Sally came to the house to get Amanda one afternoon. There was a small woman with dark stringy hair standing near the gatepost.

"Can I help you?" Amanda asked as she approached the woman.

"My husband was a Rebel, ma'am," the woman said, her eyes pleading. "Killed at the second Manassas. I know most of you folks here are for the North, but can I still join your commune? I've nowhere else to go."

The woman wore a mere shred of a dress, and underneath it an old pair of badly tattered men's trousers. Her arms were bare from her elbows to her fingertips, and she was shivering so badly that her teeth chattered when she spoke. On her feet were pieces of an old rug that she had cut up and tied to her feet with twine.

"Are you going to harm me because my husband was a Yankee?" Amanda asked.

"No, ma'am," she stammered.

"Then I won't worry about your husband being a Rebel. Our only requirement is that you take an oath not to help either side."

"Then I swear."

"It's not quite that simple," Amanda said. "Come inside. You must sign the oath."

"I don't know..."

"Then, I'm sorry, you can't stay here."

"Is that the only way?" the woman asked.

"Yes, I'm afraid so."

Emily had told Amanda that a certain woman might be coming to join the commune, and she didn't know if she could be trusted. Amanda disliked disqualifying people based on rumor, but she had to be careful.

"Are you Velma Parker?"

"Yes," the woman said. "How did you know that?"

"There are people who tell me about such things."

"They told you some things about me, didn't they?" Tears welled in the woman's eyes. "It probably won't do no good to tell you I'm a different person than I was a year ago, but I am. I won't hurt nobody."

The woman began to sob. The way her collarbone protruded from the neck of her loose dress told Amanda that she was already close to starvation.

"Listen," Amanda said, "I'm willing to take a chance on you, but you'd better not disappoint me."

"I promise I won't," the woman nodded, wiping the tears from her cheeks. "Then, can I stay?"

"Yes, but I'll be watching you. It's hard work here. Can you do your part?"

"Yes, ma'am," Velma answered, "I'm stronger than I look."

"Come inside, and we'll find you some warm clothes."

Amanda still had that prickly feeling at the nape of her neck, wondering if the woman was hiding something.

"Do you have anything to contribute?"

"Yes ma'am. A few apples," she said as she drew them from the deep pocket of her trousers. "It took all my strength to keep from eating them, but I was told that I would be expected to bring something."

"Apples? How did you save them from the foragers?"

"I buried 'em under the privy," she said shyly.

"Oh, my," Amanda said, jerking the apple away from her nose.

"They ain't nasty or nothing," Velma said quickly. "I had 'em in a paper sack inside two burlap bags, and I washed 'em real good in the creek."

"Clever girl," Amanda said.

Several days later, Amanda asked Velma to help her dig some potatoes near the root cellar. Velma had kept to herself since she joined the commune, and some of the members were suspicious of her.

"I've been troubled about something since I came here," Velma said as they worked. "I was afraid you'd send me away if you knew." A look of fear and shame crossed her face.

"What is it?" Amanda asked, sitting down on the cold ground.

"I was here that night when them people come to scare you and your little black boy. Since I'm so small they made me crawl under the house and beat on the floor with rocks."

"I knew there was something not quite right with you, but you work very hard, and you never cause me any trouble."

"Believe me, I'll never do anything like that again," Velma said.

"I believe you."

* * *

Rachel Harris came running into the kitchen early one morning. "Velma's in the hayloft with a black man," she said excitedly.

They're curled up together asleep. Looks like they been there all night."

"I'll handle this," Amanda said, brushing past Rachel.

Amanda climbed the ladder to the hayloft and crept quietly to the corner where they lay. Just then, Velma opened her eyes. The daylight and the sight of Amanda standing over them caused her to panic.

"Elias, wake up," she whispered as she jostled the man's shoulder. He quickly sat up, fear in his eyes. They moved apart and crawled backward.

"Oh no, no, no, no," Velma stammered, as she retreated. "I'm sorry, ma'am. We didn't do nothing wrong."

"Who is this man, and what is he doing in my barn?"

"This's Elias Powder," Velma said. "He's a slave from Georgia. I happened upon him in the woods one night on my way to guard duty at the pigsty. He'd been beat up real bad by some Rebel soldiers who kidnapped him and was gonna make him their slave. But they beat him so bad he weren't of any use to them, so they left him to die. By the time I come upon him, his back, where they slashed him with a whip, was full of infection."

Velma couldn't explain fast enough. The words poured out of her mouth, one on top of the next.

"I been taking care of him, and he'll be able to travel real soon. He's trying to get to Kentucky; he's got family there. There's a cave he's been staying in, but last night was so cold, and he didn't have no wood for a fire. When my turn at guard duty was over at midnight, I sneaked him in here to get a few hours of sleep and laid down with him to help him get warm—we got no blankets."

"I see," Amanda said.

"I think God meant me to find him," Velma said, "or he'd be dead by now. When I have guard duty in the woods, he goes with me. I feel so much safer with him there, and he stays on the lookout so I can sleep a little while."

What am I going to do about this?

The man looked back and forth, from Velma to Amanda. Though he was sitting, his hands and feet were all on the floor, prepared for a quick escape.

"Please, don't tell the others," Velma begged.

"I'm afraid they already know, or soon will."

"We got to get Elias out of here quick," Velma said in a panic.

"I'll talk to the others," Amanda said, kneading her brow. "It's too dangerous to have him wandering about. Is the cave safe?"

"I think so," Velma said, "but he'll need help getting firewood."

"Go in the house for breakfast as if nothing's happened. Then you can help him get settled in the cave, but he won't be safe here."

"Just a couple more days, and he'll on his way," Velma promised and headed toward the house.

"And, Velma," Amanda called to her.

"Yes, ma'am?"

"You really have changed."

"Yes, ma'am." Velma smiled with satisfaction, showing her crooked teeth.

"You must be very careful," Amanda told Elias. "Wait in the back of the barn, and I'll bring you some breakfast."

"Bless you, ma'am," the man said, his large hands trembling.

* * *

Food began to disappear. Just a little at first. Widow was in charge of the kitchen, and she knew exactly how much food was left from the night before. Amanda gathered everyone on the rear terrace one morning after breakfast. She stood on the porch so she could see their faces.

"You all know food has gone missing over the past few days. It will make this matter easier if the guilty party will step forward and take her punishment."

The women looked suspiciously at each other, but no one moved. Amanda watched everyone closely. Any person with a conscience couldn't sustain a lie of this magnitude very long. It was soon evident to her who the culprit was.

"Everybody go to your work," Amanda said. "I'll deal with this later."

"But," Emily stuttered, "who is it?"

"Go to work," Amanda said firmly.

* * *

Amanda went to the pigsty that afternoon. Becca had found an old sow and two young males wandering aimlessly in the woods a few weeks earlier. The women had finally managed to capture them and put them in the pen in the woods. The stench of hog manure assaulted Amanda's nostrils. She had rather smell anything but pig shit.

"Come over here," she called, pressing her left index finger under her nose to block the smell.

"How could you?" Amanda shouted. She slapped the woman's cheek. "I believed in you."

"What?" Velma cried.

"Don't even try to deny it."

"How did you know?"

"You couldn't look me in the eye."

"I'm sorry," Velma whimpered. "I stole the food, yes ma'am."

"Why?" Amanda said, her voice filled with rage. "Are we not feeding you enough? Or are you feeding someone else?"

"It's Elias, ma'am," Velma whispered.

"You told me he was long gone from here."

"He would be if not for me."

"I don't understand," Amanda said.

"I love him," she said, averting her eyes.

"Are you crazy?" Amanda shouted.

"Yes ma'am, probably am," Velma sighed, nodding her head. "I love a black man."

"You know what people think of this kind of thing!"

"He's so kind to me, ma'am," Velma said. "I never knew a man so kind. I just keep coming up with excuses why he can't leave yet."

"Don't think you're the first," Amanda said. "I've heard there lives a white man with his former slave on one of the high ridges east of here.

They live mostly off the land. He makes occasional trips to civilization for flour, sugar, and such."

"It wouldn't be so bad if we could get to Kentucky," Velma said. "He's got relatives living free up there."

"Will they have a problem, you living there with him?"

"I asked him that very question, and he says not."

"It will be dangerous for a black and a white traveling together all that way."

"I've come to love y'all, and it'll be hard to leave you." Velma began to weep.

"I wish you had come to me before you resorted to stealing food," Amanda said. "I told the others Elias was leaving, and I trusted you to keep your word. Now they'll know. I'll have to give you some punishment."

* * *

Amanda stumbled across the bricks of the rear terrace in the light of early dawn, stretching her arms and trying to coax her eyes to open. Ben had visited her dreams again, looking as strong and handsome as the day he left. They did in her dream what they had been too shy to do before he left.

Half-conscious and cold, she continued toward the privy. Her eyes were trained on the ground to keep her from tripping, and she noticed some odd brown stains on the terrace. It looked like paint. On the white stone walk that led to the privy, the spots became larger and looked more red than brown. Fully awake now, she followed the trail from the stone walk to the fencerow.

"Velma!" she cried as she knelt beside the slumped form, half-hidden by some evergreen bushes at the edge of the yard. Amanda pressed two fingers to Velma's neck and was surprised to find a pulse.

Velma's face was puffed out grotesquely, both eyes swollen shut. Blood covered the bodice of her dress and had spilled out on the ground. Her head wounds bled profusely. Amanda ran back to the terrace and called for Emily.

Emily came running. Widow was behind her. They carried Velma to the sitting room and put her on the old chaise. Amanda retrieved her kit of roots and herbs and made bandages for Velma's wounds. There was a deep cut in her throat, which had clearly been made by a knife or some other sharp instrument.

"Who did this to you?" Amanda asked Velma when she opened her eyes.

Velma shook her head slightly.

"You didn't see them?" Widow asked.

Velma shook her head again. Amanda wasn't convinced.

That evening after supper in the kitchen, some of the women rose to tend to their chores.

"Wait just a minute, ladies," Amanda said. "I've been thinking all day about the attack on Velma Parker and what I should do about it."

Amanda paused. The women began looking at each other.

"This was a vicious assault," Amanda continued. "I have told you that you cannot attack your fellow members because their beliefs are different from yours. That's the only way we can live together peacefully."

She paused again.

"When I checked the boot box in the sitting room this morning, only one pair had fresh mud on them—like somebody had been walking in the yard out there. And this somebody must have attacked Velma when she left the house to take her turn at guard duty. Who got off guard duty this morning?"

"Rachel," Emily said.

Rachel's face went white. "I didn't do it."

"I know you didn't," Amanda said, "but somebody hoped you would be blamed for it."

"Who is it?" Emily said, looking around.

"It was you, wasn't it, Nell?" Amanda said.

"No, ma'am," Nell said with conviction.

Nell was a large woman, close to six feet and a hundred and eighty pounds. She was a good worker, and she did the heavy chores that some of the smaller women couldn't do.

"Let me see your hands," Amanda said calmly.

Nell held out her hands, palms up. "I've got a few blisters from cutting wood."

"Turn them over," Amanda said.

"You're trying to blame me for something I didn't do," Nell said, but she finally turned her hands over.

"Why are the backs of your hands so dirty?" Amanda asked.

"I didn't take time to wash them good, I guess."

"Bring that basin of water over here," Amanda told Emily. "Wash the backs of your hands, Nell."

When Nell washed the caked mud off of her hands, every knuckle was split and bloody.

"All right!" Nell shouted. "I did it! And she deserved every lick I gave her. God's law forbids the mixing of the races. I'm only sorry I didn't kill her!" She paused for a minute and then said in a lower voice. "I thought I had."

"Now you know what I must do," Amanda said.

"You can't throw me out!" Nell screamed.

"You're a big girl, perfectly capable of taking care of yourself. Go back to your cabin in the hills. You can hunt and trap to get through the winter. We'll send a little food with you."

"I'm not leaving!"

"Yes, you are," Amanda said, pulling her revolver from her pocket.

* * *

When Velma and Elias were well enough to travel, Amanda and Emily escorted them to a Union encampment a few miles up the Greeneville Road. The colonel there promised that they would receive safe passage to Elias' home in Kentucky. Amanda bid them a sad farewell. The commune had done all they could for the couple. God would have to see to the rest.

Amanda believed that what happens to us in this life is what we need to balance out our past lives here on earth. Too much joy would cause complacency and the expectation of only joy to come. Too much pain and grief would cause us to despair.

I must have had plenty of joy in my previous lives.

Christmas 1864

"Josie, stop doing that," Amanda said, opening the door to the center hall. "Why are you being such a bother today?"

He had been running from one end of the hall to the other.

"I'm cold," he whined.

"Come in here where it's warm."

He came slowly, stomping his feet all the way, his lips in a pout.

"It's Baby Jesus' birthday today. Have you forgotten?"

"Baby Jesus forgot me," Josie whined. "I didn't get any presents."

"Christmas is not just about presents. We had a wonderful dinner with our friends, didn't we?"

He nodded grudgingly. "It just isn't the same without presents. No orange. Not even candy."

"What about that nice slingshot Gali made for you?" Amanda said.

"I can't go outside because I don't have a coat," Josie continued, "and I can't play with it in the house."

"No, you certainly may not. You might hit somebody. You can't always have things your way, my little man."

"Am I your little man?" He smiled and clasped his hands together.

"Who else would be, if not you?"

"I don't want to be a bother."

He acted so grown up most of the time she tended to forget he was still so young.

Amanda went to the attic and carried a large wooden box downstairs to the sitting room.

"You remember Luke?" she asked Josie.

"He's dead," Josie said. "I saw him."

"Yes, darling, I know. These are the toys he played with when he was a little boy. I know he'd want you to have them."

The box contained every toy Luke had played with as a child: a spinning top, wooden blocks, a cloth storybook, and little metal trucks and whirligigs that Juba had made for him. And with that thought, Barbé came to her mind. How was she spending Christmas? She missed her old friend every day, and prayed that Barbé was well.

Amanda and Josie sat near the hearth and played with Luke's old toys for hours.

SEVENTEEN

───◆┼◆───

January 1865

A manda hadn't told anyone, but her health was not improving as she thought it should. Her heart had begun to beat with great intensity at times, rattling around in her chest like an old wagon with a bent wheel. She agonized over every little decision, knowing that everything she did would have an impact on the women of the commune. Fatigue was her constant companion and her emotions sometimes went out of control, which was hard to hide from the women—especially Widow.

Some mornings she could hardly get going, and this was one of those mornings. It was Sunday. There wouldn't be much activity in the commune; they honored God by attending church and resting on the Sabbath.

Amanda decided to walk to the livestock pens in the woods while Josie napped. She needed to build up her strength if she was going to be ready for spring and all the work that season entailed. The size of the garden in the woods seemed to increase every time she saw it. The women had done an admirable job of getting the ground ready for planting.

Amanda chatted a while with Rachel, who was on guard duty, before leaving. She was beginning to feel the fatigue gnawing at her limbs. As she reached the main path leading back to Cinnamon Hill, she heard something. She looked around but saw nothing. She climbed a little embankment beside the path and looked across the field.

There was a dark-clothed figure at the Armstrong Cemetery, its silhouette in stark contrast to the leafless trees behind it. She thought it was a child at first, or someone very short in stature. Then she realized that the figure was kneeling. It looked like this person was at Luke's grave, but it was hard to tell. There was no gravestone there yet.

She crouched down, crossed quickly to a nearby tree, and stood behind it. She saw what looked like a head bowed and hands clasped together as if in prayer. The figure stayed in that position for quite some time. Then came the sound of great heaving sobs.

Who could be weeping at Luke's grave?

Finally, the figure stood up with some difficulty, trying three or four times before it became fully erect. When the figure turned to walk away, Amanda saw that it wore an old slouch hat. She knew someone who had a hat like that.

It was Crocker! She could see now—the slow halting stride, the manner of throwing his head back and looking at the sky, reaching into his shirt pocket for his corncob pipe.

Crocker had stayed away from Cinnamon Hill recently. Amanda tried not to be bitter and begged God to help her get past the anger she had toward Crocker for his part in Luke's death. She was thankful that Crocker's little girl Pearl had survived her illness. Amanda saw her at church every Sunday, and she was as lively and bouncy as ever.

February 1865

Emily rode to the house one afternoon to find Amanda. "I heard an awful commotion coming from the direction of Gali's hut. It sounded like gunshots."

Amanda grabbed Molly's reins from Emily and rode quickly to the mountains. She found Gali on the ground outside her hut, naked from the waist down. The front of her shirt was soaked with blood. A few feet away lay a man who was obviously dead. Amanda recognized him immediately. He was one of the men she had seen with Judie Baker on the trail that day.

"No!" she shouted, running to Gali's side. Amanda thought Gali was already dead; but when she cradled her head in the crook of her arm, Gali opened her eyes.

"They did it, didn't they? Judie Baker and those animals who travel with him."

Gali nodded.

"I'll kill them all!" Amanda screamed in a voice full of rage.

"You cannot avenge me," Gali whispered. Gali had told Amanda years earlier that the spirits of the Cherokee dead couldn't go to the "darkening land" until their death was avenged.

"What do you mean, I can't? How can I not?"

"They will kill you."

"I don't care!" Amanda shouted.

"But you must," Gali said. "You have so many who need you now."

"Please don't leave me! I love you."

"And I love you, my sister," Gali whispered, "but I am ready to be with my tribe again."

"Wait!" Amanda cried. "Where shall I bury you?"

"Long Island," Gali said and exhaled her last breath.

"How can you take her from me, too?" Amanda shrieked, looking skyward. She let out a wail that sounded more feral than human.

She felt a stirring in the air as Gali's spirit passed up through the trees.

Someone was riding hell-bent for the clearing.

Probably Judie come back for me.

It was Emily, her hair wild and flying—obviously frightened by Amanda's scream.

"Is she…"

"Yes."

Emily began to cry.

"I don't know what to do; I can't think," Amanda said, but a certain peace had come over her when Gali's spirit rose up.

"First, we have to get her to Cinnamon Hill," Emily said.

"We'll build a dray."

"What do we need?"

"Two long limbs, and some strong vines."

Amanda finally dried her eyes and began to prepare for another burial, wondering how she would find the strength to live through it. She brought a large leather cape from Gali's cabin and they lashed it to the limbs with the vines. They gently placed Gali's body on the cape and tied it securely. In an odd way, Amanda felt that Gali was still with her. She was still warm to the touch, and her face looked completely serene.

Amanda remembered Gali telling her about Long Island, sacred ground to the Cherokee. It was in the middle of the Holston River, up toward Virginia. Gali's ancestors were living there when the whites moved in and began to push them off their land.

* * *

When Amanda reached Cinnamon Hill, all the women were soon crying. She hadn't realized how much they had grown to love Gali.

Emily offered to bathe Gali, but Amanda refused. "I want to do it myself," she said. "I owe her so much."

"We all owe her," Emily said.

Amanda lifted Gali's petite body and placed it on a makeshift table the women had built in the kitchen. She was surprised at how little Gali weighed. Amanda washed her body and cleansed the wounds on her chest. She placed a bowl of fresh water on a chair beside the table and washed Gali's hair, mostly gray now. Amanda brought the better of the two blankets she slept under and wrapped Gali's body tightly from head to toe, leaving only her face exposed.

"Just us, you and me, will go to bury Gali?" Emily asked later.

"I guess," Amanda stammered. She hadn't thought that far ahead.

They would leave the next morning. It would be a long and arduous journey. As weak as she was, Amanda wanted to personally grant the last wish of a woman who had richly blessed her life.

* * *

It was long before first light when Amanda stumbled to the barn. She had been unable to sleep. Every time she closed her eyes, she saw Judas Baker's face, and she had to get up again. She would let Emily sleep a while longer.

As she neared the barn, she heard a voice. "Crocker, what are you doing here?"

"I'm going with you to bury Gali," Crocker said, stepping out of the barn door into the moonlight. "Her medicines saved my child. I understand how you feel—"

"You haven't the slightest idea how I feel!"

"You'll never forgive me for Luke, will you?"

"Not as long as I draw breath," she whispered, glaring at him.

"At least be sensible. You'll need a man out there."

"I'd rather be in danger than to be with you," Amanda mumbled.

"You can be spiteful and refuse my help, but should you risk Widow's life, too?"

"Widow?" Amanda said.

"Emily's not going," Widow said and stepped out of the shadows. "I am."

"Who decided this, now?" Amanda asked.

"I did," Widow said firmly.

"Widow, you're too old—I didn't mean that," Amanda said, wishing she could stuff those words back into her mouth. "I meant to say you're too fragile for such a long journey." That still wasn't the right word.

"Beg pardon," Widow said haughtily. "I've lived alone since I was twenty-eight years old. I have farmed, raised hogs and chickens, cut wood, and maintained a good home in these Godforsaken mountains. Ain't nothing fragile about me."

"What I meant was, why would you want to go on such a long trip in the company of two bullheads such as us?" she said, pointing at Crocker. "We'll most likely be bickering all the way."

"I don't trust you to take care of yourself," Widow said. "You won't eat or rest properly unless you're forced, and I'm the only one who can force you."

"You're just getting to know me too well for my comfort," Amanda mumbled.

And then, she remembered seeing Crocker at Luke's grave.

"Crocker, get those horses hitched."

"You mean I can go?" Crocker asked.

"Not if you don't get a move on," Amanda said.

Just then, Emily walked up. She was dressed and ready to go.

"Emily, I'm sorry to leave you out," Amanda said, "but Widow's going."

"Sure you are," Emily said angrily.

"But there's a very special job you can do for me," Amanda said.

"What's that?" Emily asked.

"Take care of Josie for me. He'll be lost without me and Widow, and he's grieving terribly for Gali. If anyone else dies, the rest of you will have to tell him. I just can't do it again."

"He won't make up to me," Emily said.

"He loves you as much as the others. You just don't know it yet. Give him a chance to show you, and you will be amazed by his powers of persuasion."

* * *

Amanda crawled on her belly to the top of a knoll to get a better view of the encampment. She had seen their campfires in the distance. The soldiers had obviously meant to catch all passersby by placing their tents astride the road. Night was falling and Amanda's little group was trapped, with no other way out except in the direction from which they had come.

They were hoping to find a nice dry barn to bed down in until morning.

"There's only a few of them," Crocker said. "We'll wait for them to fall asleep, skirt the road through the edge of those woods, and be on our way."

"Those are pickets, which means there's a large body of soldiers camped somewhere nearby. And they're right in our path. I can't tell if they're Rebels or Yankees, and I'm afraid to trust them. We have to get Gali to the burial ground. If they were to detain us..."

"But we can't go on, not with them in our front," Crocker said.

"We might be able to find an alternate route—if you're up to it," Amanda said.

"I'm going no farther," he stated firmly.

"I guess we'll have to put it to a vote."

"No more voting," he whined. "I always lose."

"I'm going to knock your heads together," Widow whispered, "if you don't stop this infernal bickering."

"You were warned about this," Amanda said.

* * *

They were traveling slowly down a little gully when they heard the trickle of a stream up ahead. Amanda was riding the lead horse, which was pulling the wagon carrying Gali's body. She saw a wooden structure ahead, but couldn't see that the bridge's planks were gone until it was too late. She panicked and pulled Molly to the left. Horse, wagon, and all went headfirst into the water.

"Good navigating, Crocker," Amanda screamed when she resurfaced.

"I might have known it'd be my fault," he grumbled. "You told me to find an alternate route, and I found it."

"Well, you might have made sure there was a bridge across this creek while you were at it."

"Can't I do anything right?" he said loudly.

"Keep your voice down, before you get us taken prisoner by those soldiers back there," Amanda said.

"You opened your big mouth first," he said.

"Why don't you both shut up!" Widow said.

"In case you haven't noticed, I'm standing elbow-deep in water," Amanda said a little quieter, "and Gali's body is—oh, no—floating down the—"

Amanda lunged and caught the end of the blanket she had wrapped around Gali's body, and it began to unwind in her hand. By this time, Widow and Crocker had jumped in the water and grabbed Amanda, but the cloth continued to uncoil.

Crocker finally got a firm hold on Gali's body, and pulled it to the side of the creek, out of the current. He waded out to Amanda and helped her to the shore. Amanda began to laugh. Soon they were all giggling and splashing around in the water.

"Quiet," Amanda whispered, which only made them laugh harder.

When they finally got out of the water, everyone was soaked, and cold. They had to build a fire and dry out, making the alternate route hardly a shortcut.

* * *

At the burial ground, Crocker dug a small burial pit next to a large mound, which Amanda hoped was the resting place of Gali's ancestors. It looked like the place Gali had described to her long ago. Crocker made a sling out of his saddle blanket, and they each held a part of it as they lowered Gali's tiny body into the grave.

They slept that night at the edge of the woods. Amanda wasn't ready to leave this place quite yet. As long as she remained in that place, she wouldn't have to say a final good-bye to Galilani. The next morning, she stood at the gravesite and read some passages from her favorite Wordsworth poem.

"The Rainbow comes and goes,
And lovely is the Rose,
The Moon doth with delight
Look round her when the heavens are bare,
Waters on a starry night
Are beautiful and fair;
The sunshine is a glorious birth;
But yet I know, where'er I go
That there hath past away a glory from the earth. ...
Our birth is but a sleep and a forgetting:
The Soul that rises with us, our life's Star,
Hath had elsewhere its setting,

And cometh from afar:
Not in entire forgetfulness,
And not in utter nakedness,
But trailing clouds of glory do we come
From God, who is our home ...

What though the radiance which was once so bright
Be now forever taken from my sight,
Though nothing can bring back the hour
Of splendor in the grass, of glory in the flower;
We will grieve not, rather find
Strength in what remains behind ...
Thanks to the human heart by which we live,
Thanks to its tenderness, its joys, and fears,
To me, the meanest flower that blows can give
Thoughts that do often lie too deep for tears."

Amanda read in a calm voice, but at the end, Widow saw that she was on the verge of collapse. Widow reached for Amanda, put a strong arm around her waist, led her to the wagon, and helped her into the seat.

"That's all you can do for her," Widow whispered.

On their way home to Cinnamon Hill, a moist snow began to fall, the kind that settles in little white tufts on evergreen boughs and hurts your eyes when you look directly at it because it is so bright.

* * *

A few days later, Amanda went to the hut and gathered Gali's possessions. To anyone else, it might look like so much trash, but to Amanda it meant everything. She took the leather pouch her friend had worn around her waist, to hold special little goodies she found in the forest. She wrapped Gali's tools in a large piece of leather; they would use them in the commune.

Being in Gali's hut made her so sad and lonesome she could hardly bear it—and angry! She had been so busy since Gali's death she hadn't had time to think about Baker and his men, but she thought of them now. Angry bile rose in her throat. It was physically painful to be filled with so much rage.

* * *

In the dark of early morning, she walked quickly and quietly in moccasins and soon reached the gap between the two huge boulders that provided the only access to the bushwhackers' camp. It was a natural fortress, and much too beautiful to be inhabited by such animals. She climbed undetected onto one of the boulders and stuck her gun into the back of the guard who slept there.

"Don't shoot," he yelled. He dropped his weapon and jumped down off the rock.

"Quiet, you cretin," she whispered, jumping down in front of him, thrusting her pistol into his gut. "I don't want anyone to know I'm here just yet."

She could feel the trembling of his body through the gun that she jabbed into the soft flesh of his belly. "It's your boss I want," she said.

"Major Baker?" he whimpered, his round eyes large with fear.

"Oh, a major, is he?"

"He once was," the man said.

"Go get your 'Major' so I can have a word with him—if he's not too much of a coward to come out and talk to a woman."

"He's sleeping."

She transferred the pistol from his stomach to under his chin and pushed it up so hard she could no longer see his face. "Get him," she growled. "*Now.*"

"No, ma'am. I mean, yes, ma'am. I'll do that right now."

"Tell him to come alone."

The man nodded as he ran into the forest.

Morning was coming on; the sky was lightening. The timing was perfect, just as she had planned it. She readied herself for what would happen next.

Judie Baker came creeping up to the gap between the boulders, gun in hand, half a dozen of his men several paces behind him, their weapons drawn as well. She jumped down from the boulder and stuck her gun in Judie's ear. He dropped his weapon.

"Tell your men to drop their guns and walk on out of here, or you're a dead man. You see, *Major* Baker," she said, her voice as cold as stone, "the fact that one of them might shoot me after I kill you doesn't scare me in the least, but we need to have a personal conversation."

"Go back to camp," he said softly, motioning to his men. They didn't move. "Get out of here!" he yelled.

"Don't dawdle, boys," she said, or make any sudden moves. I'll blow his head right off."

They took off at a run.

"Now, isn't this a comeuppance? Not so brave by yourself, are you?" she asked, her gun still in his ear.

"Woman," he said, "you will die if you hurt me. It might not be today or tomorrow, but my men will kill you. What's this about anyway?" He looked sideways, trying to see her face.

"You killed Galilani."

"Who told you that?"

"Oh, Judie, I've learned more about you than I ever wanted to know."

"She killed one of my men," he said.

"And what did he do to cause her to kill him?"

"Nothing."

She jabbed the pistol harder into his ear. "Not the correct answer," she said, teeth clenched.

"He was just trying to be nice to her. He liked the old squaw, for some reason."

"He raped her!"

"No, not that," he stammered. "He was just being nice to her."

She thrust the pistol even harder against his head. "He raped her, didn't he?" she shouted.

"I guess that's what he did," he whined.

"You know it, don't you?" she yelled.

Her hand began to tremble uncontrollably. The gun was banging against his skull.

"That thing's gonna go off, you keep hitting me with it," he said.

"You know he raped her, DON'T YOU?"

"Yes!" he yelled. "All right? He told me he was going there to give her some—uh-uh—loving. He didn't mean her no harm. She stabbed him to death for no good reason."

"Did it ever occur to you that she didn't want what he gave her?"

"All women want it," he mumbled.

"What did you say? All women want it? You rotten son of a bitch!"

"You all want it. You're just too uppity to admit it."

"You *dog!*" she shouted and banged the gun hard against his skull.

An explosion left her temporarily deaf. Her shoulder jerked back so hard it felt like somebody was ripping off her arm. Judie Baker's head flew back violently. In slow motion, she watched his face float to the ground in a spray of red. It looked so funny she was tempted to laugh, but something was wrong. Where did all the blood come from?

Then everything went dark.

* * *

Her vision suddenly snapped back into focus, and the realization of what she had done slashed through her mind like a whip. She stood for a minute, a minute that seemed to go on forever, until she heard footsteps running through the woods. She urged her legs to move, but they were paralyzed. She couldn't stop looking at Judie Baker's head.

The sound of running feet, getting closer, brought her back to reality. Someone was calling, "Major! Major!"

A searing pain seized her back, like a thousand nerve endings grating against each other. It was the closest to unbearable pain she had ever experienced, pain so intense that she thought if it didn't stop at that very instant, she would go mad.

Move! Move! Follow the creek. Leave no trail.

The water that trickled down the gradual slope of the hillside was a clear blue-green, changing to an opaque white as it cascaded over the rocks. Thin spindly branches arched out over the creek, getting caught in her hair and slowing her down.

She stumbled and flailed through the water, sometimes on all fours, unable to stand upright, hunched over, panting like a dog, trying to stretch the pain out of her back. Finally, slowly, it began to subside. Finally, she was able to take a deep breath. As she raised her body up, relieved that the pain had passed, she was assaulted by nausea, wave after wave of sickness. She clasped her hand over her mouth, trying to keep from retching.

She stopped and stood still for a moment, listening intently. At one point, she thought she heard dogs barking. Now everything was quiet—too quiet.

Move! Move!

The water was cold; it quickly soaked through her moccasins. Her legs, then her whole body, began to tremble. Weakness overcame her. The water was becoming deeper and deeper, but she stumbled on.

Her toe hit a large stone underwater, and she fell face first into the creek. She soon came up out of the water, arms flailing, gasping for air, and making entirely too much noise. Her fingers located the source of the pain in her head: a large, bloody bump protruding from the center of her forehead.

She lay down on her back in the creek bed, her head just above water level. The blood flowing from the wound blinded her completely in one eye, partially in the other. She tried to wash it out with water, but the blood kept coming.

Deep woods with dense underbrush grew right up to the creek bank here on both sides. The creek changed its course every several yards, making sharp turns left and right and rising and falling in elevation.

Still, she could barely see. She crept to the edge of the creek and positioned herself up under the eroded bank, below the roots of a massive tree. Afraid to leave and afraid to stay, Amanda lay there, cold and wet, for what seemed like thirty minutes. She heard nothing but normal forest sounds. No dogs. No voices. No footsteps.

Suddenly, she heard the sounds of leaves being crushed and underbrush being trampled.

Hurry! Hurry! They're coming for you!

EIGHTEEN

———◦◦◦◦———

"What happened?" Emily asked Amanda at the barn. "You're soaked and shivering."

"Just take care of Molly for me, please."

"Your head's bleeding!"

"Leave me alone," Amanda mumbled. She walked toward the house. Emily followed right on her heels, questioning her all the way.

Amanda just wanted to escape to her bedroom. She didn't want to explain her condition or where she had been, but Emily persisted. At the bottom of the stairs, Amanda spun and glared at Emily, almost knocking her down.

"He's dead, all right?!" Amanda shouted.

"Who's dead?" Emily asked.

"Judie Baker's dead! I shot his face right off his head. Does that satisfy your morbid curiosity?"

Emily gasped.

"And it wasn't just for Gali. It was for Father and David, for Jonathan and Luke, for your sons and husbands, for everyone from these mountains who has suffered or died for this foolish war at the hand of such animals as Judas Baker!"

"The world will be a better place without him," Widow said, coming forward and putting her arm around Amanda's shoulders.

"No!" Amanda screeched, trying to escape the hold Widow had on her.

"What is it?" Widow asked calmly. "What's troubling you?"

"Aren't you glad to know that Gali's killer is dead?" Emily asked.

"No! Gali is still dead, and now I am a murderer. I'm just like Judie Baker!"

"Now you listen to me," Widow said, turning Amanda's face toward her. "Judas Baker deserved to die. I should have killed him years ago, after he murdered my husband."

Amanda stopped struggling for a moment. "He killed your husband?"

"He came into our home and shot him as he slept beside me."

Amanda tried to raise her arms to hide her face, but Widow held them down.

"If you have to justify it in your mind, think of the other lives you've saved by killing Judas Baker."

Amanda broke free and ran up the stairs.

For three days, she did not leave her bed. She slept fitfully and woke up weeping. She dreamt horrible nightmares and was awakened by her own screams. Her body temperature rose to dangerous levels, then plummeted again.

On the fourth morning, Amanda opened her eyes and spoke to Widow, who was sleeping on a pallet beside the bed.

Too soon, the memories came flooding back and she began to cry. "What did I do?"

"Hush, now, hush," Widow said firmly, grabbing her hands. "You don't want to go back to that dark place you just came from, do you?"

"No," Amanda sobbed.

"Try not to think about it for right now," Widow said. "Are you hungry?"

"Starved," Amanda said, drying her tears.

"Wonderful," Widow sighed.

Widow helped Amanda get dressed in the old blue calico, the dress she had worn the day Gali was killed. She wondered how they got out the bloodstain; upon closer examination, she detected a faint brown splotch on the bodice, just above the gathered skirt. The edges of the stain feathered out, but the center of it was still quite brown, and she knew that it could never be separated from the fabric.

Widow helped her down the steps and into the sitting room, holding onto her all the way. She was very weak.

Widow summoned the other women of the commune.

"Our leader has returned," Sally said amid a round of applause.

"Welcome back," said Becca.

"We've been praying for you," Emily said.

"I'm all right now," Amanda said.

Josie came running when he heard Amanda's voice, climbed into her lap, and kissed her face incessantly.

"What did I do while I was delirious?" she asked Widow after the others left. "Did I behave badly? There's so much I don't remember, but I remember you were always there."

"Exactly where I want to be."

"I believe there comes a time in almost everybody's life," Amanda said, "when you realize you've made the wrong choice—a life-changing choice that cannot be undone. You say, 'Wait. I didn't mean that. Let me go back.'"

"Please don't be so hard on yourself," Widow begged.

"But there is no going back," Amanda said softly. "Then the weight of that decision settles upon you, and you must learn to live with it."

For several days, Josie stuck to Amanda like a second skin.

"I'm sorry to keep scaring you, Josie," Amanda told him.

"You can't help it," he said, patting her shoulder.

"I believe some people have special souls, and you're one of those people."

"Me?" He bowed his head shyly.

"Yes, you," she said, touching his nose with her fingertip.

"Where did I get it from?"

"God must have given it to you."

"When you were sick, I felt like you were leaving me." His large brown eyes looked very sad. "But I kept telling you everything would be all right 'til you believed me."

"See there, that's how special you are."

"I made Miss Widow mad at me sometimes for bothering you too much."

"She'll get over it."

* * *

Later, Widow found Amanda in tears.

"Don't tell me you're still torturing yourself about Judas Baker."

"I don't want to forget it. I want to remember that sick feeling I had after I killed him, in case I ever get that desperate again. I had no right to kill him. God should be his judge, not me."

"Why don't you try to focus on all the good you've done here? These women respect you and admire your courage."

"Why, for heaven's sakes?"

"You've shown them how to take care of themselves. How to live, really. They can be on their own now, without being paralyzed by fear. You've given them faith in themselves. That's powerful medicine."

* * *

One afternoon, Amanda was helping to prepare supper. Her strength was coming back, but not nearly fast enough for her comfort. She thought she heard someone calling, "Mandy." There were only two people in the world allowed to call her by that name, and it certainly wasn't Josie's voice. Amanda ran through the house, not yet knowing why she was running.

Barbé was just reaching the carriage drive when Amanda ran out the front door. Barbé was running so fast and Amanda grabbed her so strongly, they almost tumbled to the ground. They cried and clung to each other, too emotional to speak for several minutes.

"Can I come home?" Barbé asked.

"You are home," Amanda said softly.

Then they stepped back and looked at each other, and wiped the tears off each other's face.

"My dear girl," Barbé said, "what's happened to you? I've never seen you so thin and pale."

"It's a long story, which I will tell you later. Right now, I want to know what happened to you."

"Things weren't like we thought they would be in the North. I guess we expected too much. And I was so homesick. People didn't understand why we missed the South, but why shouldn't we miss it? We were born and raised here. Everything's so different up there. It's like going to another country altogether."

"Darling," Amanda said, touching Barbé's face, "I'm sorry. I know how much Juba wanted it to work out. Where is he, anyway?"

"There," Barbé motioned toward the gatepost. There he sat with his horse and wagon.

"He's going on to the Crossroads to see what might be left of the blacksmith shop. He said he'd stay the night there. And I can stay here with you!" Barbé shrieked.

For a minute, they danced around like schoolgirls.

"What's happened to the shop?" Barbé asked.

"Oh, it's still there, but I can't say what condition it might be in. What tools you couldn't take were stolen. Everything of any value that isn't nailed down soon disappears around here. I'm glad you weren't here to see it all."

"The only work I could get up there was cleaning for white women a few hours here and there, and they don't want to pay you enough to earn a living. I tried to hide from Juba how unhappy I was. Then one day he come home and looked like a totally different person. Something in his face had shaded over. The man who owned the blacksmith shop where Juba worked... His brother came home from the war, and they threw Juba out of his job. And then, I told him how much I missed you."

"Bless your heart," Amanda cried. "I've been worrying about you since you left. Are you well?"

"It was a hard trip. Lots of good people sympathize and help you when you're leaving the South, but they don't understand why you would ever want to come back. They wouldn't give us no papers. We had to hide like runaways. Some days we didn't eat, and we had to sleep in the wagon in the woods. My poor feet won't never be the same after this journey," Barbé said, looking down at her worn-down shoes.

"Go with Widow," Amanda told her. Widow was standing on the terrace, waving to them. "I want to have a word with Juba."

"Juba, wait," Amanda yelled as she ran up the lane. Maybe he couldn't hear her above the noise of the wagon wheels.

"Wait!" she called again, louder.

He finally pulled on the reins, stopping the wagon.

"Juba," she gasped, as she caught up to the wagon. "Thank you for bringing her back to me."

She said his name again, but he didn't look at her. She moved forward, near the small, jittery horse. She stared at Juba, willing him to look at her. When his gaze finally met hers, she saw the heartbreak in his eyes.

"Just so you know," he said through hard tight lips. "I don't like nothing 'bout this. Weren't my idea to come back here." The muscles in his jaw twitched.

"I know how hard this must be for you," she said gently.

"You don't know nothing of it. A man takes his wife away from a hard life, and she's still not happy." He looked off into the distance.

"You're right. I don't know, but I remember how I felt when you took her away from me. I'll do almost anything not to ever feel that again."

He looked at her inquisitively.

"It hurt me so bad," she whispered, tears close to the surface, "I swore if I ever got the chance, I'd handle things differently."

Some of the pain left his face.

"You're a proud man, Juba, and I respect that. I'm a proud woman. Just don't be so proud that you shut people out of your life. I've learned that I can live without my pride, but it's hard to live without the people I love. I've lost almost everybody." Her throat choked off those last few words.

"Mr. Armstrong?" Juba asked.

"Yes. He was killed at a cavalry fight down at the Crossroads, and..."

"Not Luke."

She nodded.

He covered his eyes with one large brown hand and stayed like that for a few minutes.

"I'm sorry. I truly am," he finally said.

"I know you are," she said, trying not to cry.

"I hate it I can't give Barbé a child. That's the one thing she wants more than anything in this world."

"Why do you think it's your fault?"

"Just do, I guess. Always have."

"Nobody knows why some people can't have children," she said. "Maybe it's God's will.

"If I had a child, and it got taken away from me like your Luke, I'd surely lose my mind over it."

"I did, for a while."

A long moment of silence passed between them.

"Juba," she said plaintively, "I'm sorry for all the times I didn't consider your feelings when Barbé and I shut you out. I didn't see it then, but I see it now. I thought I needed her more than you did, and that was wrong of me. But you're wrong if you think she loves me more than you."

Juba's jaw clenched.

"It's hard to explain the connection Barbé and I have. We were born only a few months apart, and from our earliest remembrance, we've been together. What with Barbé's mother being a house servant—"

"They were slaves," Juba said, but not too harshly. "Have the decency to call them what they were."

"Yes, they were slaves, but I didn't know what that meant. Barbé and her mother lived on the third floor of my home, and I thought she was part of my family. We did a very childish thing—after she came here to live." Amanda chuckled, remembering it. "We pricked our fingers with thorns and pressed them together so our blood mixed and made a little ritual of it. 'You are the blood of my blood, the heart of my heart, and we will never be separated.'"

"Why didn't she ever tell me about things like that?"

"I expect there are many things she didn't tell us about each other—because we already disliked each other so much."

Juba jerked on the reins and urged the horse to move, but she grabbed his arm and said, "Don't leave yet. Please."

He looked at her face and then at her hand on his arm. She removed it at once.

"There's more I need to say," she stammered. "Maybe the best I can do is tell you how I feel, and you can think about it."

He nodded begrudgingly.

"I've been jealous of you since you and Barbé met at church that day—more so after you bought your freedom. Then you could take her away from me. I guess that's why she didn't tell you when I freed her, for the same reason."

Juba turned his head completely away from her. She had no idea how he was reacting, and she suddenly became scared—cold fingers ran up her spine. But she continued, trying to talk faster, to get it over with, and let him be on his way.

"Maybe the only good thing this war has given me is time—time to reflect, to see myself as I was back then, which certainly hasn't always been pleasant. I was selfish, willful, and inconsiderate."

He turned and looked at her, but she couldn't look at him while she made her last confession. "And I haven't always spoken kindly of you. At times—when you upset her—I criticized you terribly. The only reason I spent so much money to get the blacksmith shop for you— well, it wasn't for you. It was to keep her here."

She nudged a rock with the toe of her shoe.

"But I'm pleading with you not to take her away from me again. It probably sounds ridiculous for me to say that Barbé's absence has been more difficult for me than the death of my own son. I saw what happened to Luke with my own eyes, and I put him to rest in the cemetery on the hill. It was the not knowing about Barbé that has troubled me so much, realizing that I might never know what happened to her—it made me quite desperate. Desperate people do foolish things, and I have done my share."

Two teardrops fell to the ground; two tiny puffs of dust flew up. "Well, enough of this," she said, trying to sound carefree, wiping her tears away with both hands before looking at Juba.

"If I do something that upsets you, tell me, please," she said. "And try to remember that I'm trying to do better, and I'm not very good at it yet. We've been fools all these years, and we've hurt her more than she deserves. Maybe it's time we tried to get along."

He finally met her gaze. She thought she saw relief in his eyes, and maybe a glimmer of hope, which was no small thing for a man who had been kept down by white folks all his life.

"Maybe so," he said. He clucked at the horse, and the wagon slowly pulled away.

* * *

Amanda found Barbé in her old cabin.

"Oh no, darling, we don't want to go through this again," Amanda said.

"What?" Barbé asked, a frown on her face.

"I hope I just patched up things with Juba—or at least I made a start. I won't be responsible for keeping the two of you apart. You have to live with your husband at the Crossroads—if Bixby agrees to let him run the shop again. We'll just have to hope that Juba will let you visit often."

"All right," Barbé sighed.

"From now on, you're sleeping in the house with me. Let's go. There's someone I want you to meet."

"Who?" Barbé asked.

"It's a surprise," Amanda said.

They found Josie napping on the old chaise in the sitting room.

"Who's this?" Barbé whispered, wonderment in her voice.

"Shh, he's my son."

"What!"

Just then, Josie looked up at them. "Who are you?" he said, rubbing his sleepy eyes.

"Do you remember all the stories I told you about Barbé?" Amanda said.

He nodded.

"Well, this is Barbé. She came home."

"Can I pick you up and give you a great big hug?" Barbé said.

Josie raised his arms. Barbé lifted him and held him close, his head resting on her shoulder. Amanda had never seen the joy that came over Barbé's face.

Barbé and Amanda clung to each other and talked late into the night. It was the talking they had missed the most.

"How's Luke?" Barbé asked. "Does he write to you?"

"Darling, I hoped you would save that question for tomorrow."

"Why?" Barbé instantly looked worried.

"Well, there's no easy way, so I'll just say it straight out. Luke's buried up on the hill."

"No," Barbé screamed. "It can't be true." Amanda held her while she grieved for the boy she had loved as if he were her own child.

* * *

Barbé found Amanda crying the next morning. "What's wrong?" she asked.

"They're threatening to take Cinnamon Hill away from me," Amanda said, looking at a letter she had just received.

"Who?" Barbé asked.

"The county government."

"How can they do that?"

"I owe hundreds of dollars in back property taxes," Amanda explained. "Jonathan hadn't paid them in years—one last slap in the face from him. I shouldn't say that; Jonathan was wonderful to me the day he died."

"That doesn't mean you should forgive him for all he did to you," Barbé said.

"Yes, it does. I told him I forgave him for all of it," Amanda said. "But I have no money to pay the taxes."

"That's not fair," Barbé said.

"Maybe I should leave Jonathan's bones at the church. When I leave here, I'll be leaving my son up on that hill," she said, nodding toward the cemetery.

* * *

When Juba came back that evening, he was in high spirits. Bixby had been overjoyed that Juba wanted to run the blacksmith shop again. Bixby had fared no better than many others during the war, and he needed the income.

When it was time for Barbé to go to the Crossroads with Juba, Amanda hugged her for a long time. "I'll see you soon," Amanda said.

Barbé's eyes filled with tears.

"What if I bring you back here tomorrow morning," Juba said to Barbé, "before I open the shop and pick you up tomorrow evening? Then I'll bring you every other day during the week. And we can all have dinner together on Sundays after church."

"I think that's a wonderful idea, Barbé," Amanda said, smiling at Juba.

Barbé hugged Juba and thanked him.

The next morning when they returned, it was obvious that Barbé had told Juba about the back taxes.

"I worked hard while I was in the North," Juba told Amanda, "and put back a good bit of money. Cinnamon Hill was once my home, too. I'll be glad to do what I can to help."

"I won't let you do that. That money is for your future—yours and Barbé's. I won't be able to—" Amanda quickly covered her mouth to hide her trembling lips. "I won't have a home for her anymore."

NINETEEN

April 1865

A soldier fell wounded on the last day of fighting near Petersburg, Virginia. Shrapnel shattered his leg.

"Am I dead?" the soldier asked.

"Be still, son," the gray-haired surgeon said. "I won't let you die."

"I'm dying I tell you. My leg!" he screamed. "Where's my leg?"

"I had to amputate it to save your life."

"Just let me go on," the soldier cried. "The woman I love—I won't be fit for her now."

* * *

"The war is over! The war is over!" Crocker shouted, riding in on his old mule and wagon. When he saw the women coming out the front door, he urged the mule on, ran right onto the front terrace, dirty hooves, muddy wheels, and all.

"Crocker," Amanda yelled, "you're ruining my yard!"

"I don't care a whit," he said.

Everyone was elated, jumping around and hugging each other, but Amanda couldn't find the joy in it. The war had already taken everything it could take from her. Then she chastised herself. At least Ben was still alive, or so she hoped. She hadn't received any news from him in months. He hadn't answered her last letter, and she had no idea where he was.

A few nights later, the women of the commune held a dance in the forest by firelight. Some dressed as men and danced with the other women. Amanda wore Jonathan's uniform, the one she had received the day he died. They laughed, cried, and celebrated the end of a war that some thought would never come.

Late in the evening, Amanda stood on a tree stump and addressed the group.

"We have survived the war. We have learned to live with no one's help but our own. We are sisters!" she shouted. Cheers went up all around.

"I must try to tell you what your presence has meant to me all these months," Amanda said, "and I'm having some difficulty finding the words. In the past, I was shamelessly judgmental, and I didn't exactly like women as a rule. During my girlhood at home in Virginia, I only knew the women of the upper class—and I found them empty-headed and entirely too impressed by their own importance. That's the way I was raised.

"You have shown me another way of life. You are strong, fearless, and you don't wait for someone else to do for you. You do what needs to be done. You can remain with us for as long as you please. After you go back to your homes, don't forget about me. I hope you will visit often, and I will always be available for whatever you need of me.

"You saved our lives—mine and Josie's," Amanda said.

"That ain't right!" Becca Brown said. "You saved us! Maybe we saved each other."

"I love you all more than you will ever know," Amanda said, her voice cracking.

The women gathered into a tight-knit group and wrapped their arms around Amanda.

On the way back to the house, Sally said, "I'm almost sorry the men are coming back. I enjoyed us women being in charge."

"Don't speak too quickly," Amanda said. "We don't know yet how many will be returning." A few women didn't know if their husbands were alive or dead, Sally among them. "I'm sure it won't be easy, but you want to return to your homes and take up your lives as they were before, don't you?"

"I'm not wanting it to be like it was," Rachel sighed.

A pall fell over the crowd.

* * *

The following week, Barbé and a few other blacks who had returned to Northeast Tennessee held a huge celebration at the church, like the socials of old. They cooked all of the food and invited everyone in the neighborhood to attend. Amanda was leaving Cinnamon Hill when she met Emily in the center hall.

"Emily, aren't you going to the party?" Amanda asked. "The others have gone ahead to help."

"I thought it was a party for the blacks." Emily wasn't the only one still learning how to deal with the newly-freed slaves.

"They're our friends and members of our church."

"You certainly have changed," Emily said.

"How do you figure that?" Amanda asked. "In some ways, I'm as lost and scared as ever."

"Then you hide it well," Emily said. "You've taken on so much responsibility. I hardly know you now. Where do you find the confidence?"

"It's hard to explain. I value myself more," Amanda said.

Emily nodded, but her face was vacant.

"When you don't get the approval from others you strive for every day, you have to find it in here," Amanda said, touching her chest. "We can't love others until we learn to love ourselves."

"Oh, God," Emily groaned and turned away. "How horrible I must have made you feel when you found me and Jonathan together. I'm so sorry."

"I forgive you," Amanda said.

"I don't deserve your forgiveness."

"Yes, you do," Amanda said, putting a hand on Emily's shoulder. "You made a mistake, but I don't think you'll do it again."

"No. Never," Emily said as she turned to face Amanda. "If I have to live the rest of my days alone, I will never do that again. To hurt another woman..."

"I understood your need to reach out for comfort because of Franklin's mistreatment of you, but Jonathan was so busy trying to hold himself together he had nothing to give to anyone. We allowed our husbands to take away our love for ourselves. It was our fault as much as theirs; we let them do it."

"But Jonathan seemed so..."

"Strong? I know, but he was flawed. Heavens, we're all flawed to some extent." Amanda laughed. "But I didn't know the depths of his self-doubt until the day he was killed."

"Oh," Emily said, nodding.

But Amanda knew she didn't truly understand. And that was fine. What was important was that Amanda understood, and that she had let go of all that.

"Now let's go to the party," Amanda said. She put her arm around Emily's waist, and they skipped out the door and down the steps, laughing all the way.

And it felt so good.

* * *

A few weeks later, Amanda finally received a letter from Ben.

Dear Amanda:

The war is over. The Confederacy has been lost, and I can't make myself feel too sorry for that. If that makes me a traitor, then so be it. I learned today that my lieutenant shot himself out of despair over the outcome of the war. He left a note stating that he couldn't go on, knowing how many lives he had sacrificed for the Confederacy—only to have it come to this. I am greatly saddened by his passing.

Please continue to be careful in your daily activities. There are still stragglers and refugees everywhere who are desperate for food and shelter. I don't know where I may be going once I am released, or what I might do. I have not yet decided. You will find at the end of this letter the address of my parents' home in Georgia. If you should like to keep in touch, I am sure they will be glad to forward your letters to me.

With greatest affection,
Captain Benjamin Braddock

After waiting all this time for news of Ben, Amanda almost wished she hadn't received this puzzling letter.

"When is Captain Ben coming?" Josie asked.

"I don't know if he will."

* * *

"There's a man at the door asking for you," Widow told Amanda one afternoon.

"Jed Palmer!" Amanda exclaimed. "How wonderful it is to see you."

"And I, you," he said, clasping her hands in his. "Looks like you've come through the war just fine."

"I don't know about that," she said, "but I consider myself lucky." She invited him into the sitting room.

"I've often wondered how different our lives might have been if I'd had the courage to tell you how I felt about you years ago," Jed said shyly.

"I knew, Jed."

"Well, if that isn't the worst thing you'd ever want to hear," he said softly, his cheeks turning red.

"I was always in love with Jonathan. Even when I denied it to myself."

"Then, what about now?" he said. "It doesn't seem to me that you and Jonathan have much of a marriage left."

For a split second, the thought of sleeping safely inside the warm, strong arms of a man caused her heart to flutter.

"I'm waiting for someone else," she finally said.

"Oh," he said, obviously disappointed. "Then I guess I should be going."

"Don't rush off. I hope we can remain friends."

"Yes, I'd like to very much. There is something I wanted to ask you about."

"What's that?"

"What you said the day we left to join the army, about Jonathan doing something to Luke. While we were riding up to Kentucky, I asked him about it. He pulled his horse up close to mine and knocked me onto the ground, and then he rode away and left me there. I didn't see him again until I got to camp, and he never spoke to me again."

"I can't say I'm surprised."

"What did he do to Luke?"

"Apparently you haven't heard, Jed. Jonathan was killed in a cavalry fight at the Crossroads last winter."

"No," he whispered. His face went white as cotton. Tears sprang to his eyes. "We've been friends as long as I can remember."

"I know, Jed." She put her hand on his.

"I know he must have been a difficult man to live with, but he's the only true friend I ever had," he said, wiping his eyes.

"Do you know what strikes me most about you?" Jed asked as he was leaving.

"What's that?"

"How calm you are."

But Amanda wasn't feeling at all calm. She thought more and more of Ben. The war was over. Why hadn't he contacted her?

* * *

At the supper table one evening, Sally told the group that Franklin Cuthbertson had returned and was living in his old house at the crossroads.

"He don't look nothing like himself," Sally said. "He's thin and gaunt—he lost an arm and got shot up pretty bad, I hear."

Amanda looked to Emily for some reaction to the news.

"I know," was all she said.

Franklin came to Cinnamon Hill a few days later to speak to Emily.

"What should I do?" Emily asked Amanda.

"You don't owe him anything," Amanda said. "But if you want to talk to him, that's fine."

"I guess it wouldn't hurt to hear him out," Emily said. She asked Amanda to wait inside the front door. "Just in case I need you," she said.

Emily spoke to Franklin on the front terrace.

"I'm sorry for the way I talked to you the other day when you come by the house," he said, sobbing with every word. "I can't do nothing like I used to, but I'll be a good husband to you—if you'll have me."

"You won't yell at me and call me stupid?" Emily asked. "I won't take that anymore, Franklin."

"I swear," he said. "I won't."

"Wait here," she said.

"Well, I guess I'll be moving home now," Emily told Amanda.

"What will you do about Franklin?"

"Take care of him."

"After the way he treated you, I didn't think you'd ever go back to him."

"He needs me now," Emily whispered.

* * *

The men of Greene County began to straggle home. Of the fifteen men from Armstrong Crossroads, ten returned, and some of those were so demoralized by their experiences during the war as to be of little use to their families. The women of the commune slowly moved back to their previous homes, after many tearful good-byes.

Rachel's husband came home, as did Sarah's. Becca Brown and her widowed sister moved in together. Becca's two children, who had been sent to live with relatives in Ohio during the war, came home to their mother.

Amanda waited for Ben.

For many people, the great relief that the war had finally ended soon turned to despair and frustration. Family members who had taken opposite sides in the fight were still alienated from each other.

Amanda learned that Catherine Williams, in whose yard General Morgan and Luke were killed, was heartbroken over her sons. The son who fought for the Union came back to Greeneville to live with Catherine and his wife. The other son was so embittered because the Confederacy had been defeated that he vowed never to visit his mother as long as his brother lived there.

Though Tennessee was the first state readmitted into the Union, its civilians were still under military control—like the other seceded states—until federal authorities were satisfied that there would be no further rebellion. Food and supplies were agonizingly slow in coming to remote regions, such as Armstrong Crossroads.

* * *

Amanda worried every day about Ben. Since her housemates had gone home, she had much more time to think. She had to fight every day to keep thoughts of his possible death from her mind. When the weight of her burden became too great, she mounted Molly and rode for the mountains. There she screamed his name and beseeched God to bring him back to her.

Amanda knew she must prepare for long endless day after long endless day until a day like no other would force her to accept that Ben had been killed and that she would never know how or where. The weight of that loss was almost too heavy to bear, but she kept it to herself. She had scared Josie and Widow too many times; this she would suffer alone.

During the early hours of the morning, she sat, sleepless, on the balcony outside the second-floor hall, praying that she might live to see the sun rise again without going completely mad. And when noon arrived, she began to pray that she might live to see the darkness, when she could hide away from everyone and allow the pain to show on her face again.

Thus Amanda's days were survived in increments. Amanda knew she had to get past torturing herself like this before her health failed again. She didn't like feeling helpless again, and cursed Ben for it. If he had changed his mind about returning to Cinnamon Hill after the war, why would he not tell her?

Summer 1865

One sunny afternoon, with humidity thick enough to cut with a knife, Amanda dragged a rocking chair to the front terrace, trying to rest while Josie napped on a pallet in the center hall. The front and rear doors were open waiting for stray breezes, which gently moved the curls on Josie's head. Widow was working in the garden, insistent that Amanda rest. She hadn't slept much the night before. She closed her eyes and settled into the chair.

"Mrs. Armstrong," someone called.

She raised her eyes, shading them from the sun, and was astonished to see Lt. Quinn.

"What are you doing here?" she asked angrily.

He dismounted and tethered his horse at the gatepost. "Just passing through, ma'am, and thought I'd say goodbye. I've been called back to Richmond to help with the Reconstruction there."

He reached the terrace and passed to her a few overripe peaches and two little shortbreads that had obviously been hoarded in his haversack for days.

"In case you haven't heard, Lt. Quinn," she said, "the war is over."

"How are you?" he asked meekly.

"We're still here," she said in a strong voice.

"It's sad to see how devastated your valley has become. I haven't been over this way in a while. It's worse than I remembered."

"I'm sure you have better things to do than to pass pleasantries with me, Lieutenant."

"I thought I might try to explain myself if you'll give me the chance," he said, sitting on the bricks of the terrace.

"If you feel you must."

"When I received my lieutenant's commission and was put in charge of this area," he said, "I thought I could finally do things my way. I let that go too far."

"You certainly did!"

"I learned later that I was wrong about you."

"I appreciate that. Most men have a hard time admitting it when they're wrong."

"I didn't say I was liking it."

They both laughed.

He scooped up a stone and pitched it into the overgrown meadow.

"I respect you for defending your home," he said so softly she didn't understand at first what he had said. "Your menfolk home from the war?"

"Lost them all: father, brother, husband, and son."

He took in a gulp of air so suddenly he choked on it. "I'm sorry to hear that," he said when he finally regained his voice.

"I'd offer you some refreshment, Lieutenant, but I have nothing but water. Not even sassafras for tea."

His face suddenly brightened. "How about some coffee?" he said.

"You have coffee?" She felt like a child at Christmas.

They sat on the terrace in the warmth of the waning evening, sipping the coffee Widow made from the lieutenant's stash. Fireflies began to appear as the sun began its descent behind the high ridges. He insisted that she take his last little bag of ground coffee. She would honor him by keeping it, he said.

"I have put off the main purpose of my visit as long as I can," he said, sighing heavily.

"The reason I treated you so badly, Mrs. Armstrong, was that one of your neighbors told me that you were a Confederate spy," he said, clearing his throat. "And I believed it. That's what I meant when I told you I didn't like your kind."

"I'm no Rebel," she shouted. "And certainly not a spy!"

"I deliberately chose your house as my headquarters when I traveled over here, and I didn't care how much my men destroyed it. I wanted to punish you."

"Shame on you, Lieutenant!"

"An officer always wants to believe that people in his jurisdiction are on his side. It took me a long time to realize that not every person residing in Northeast Tennessee was a Unionist. One man in particular, I trusted too much."

"Crocker?" Amanda asked.

"That's the one," he said, averting his eyes. "I told him too much, and he got me in a right smart of trouble for it, too."

"Dear Lord," she sighed. "That's how he always knew so much! I'd like to go box his ears, but I'm learning to forgive, with God's help."

"Oh, he made a big fool of me—and I helped him do it," Lt. Quinn said. "He came to Greeneville to visit me whenever he could. I stopped at his cabin every time I was over this way, brought him newspapers, and talked to him about what was happening with the war. I finally learned that he did the same with the Rebels when they were in control here."

"I wouldn't feel too bad about that, Lieutenant."

"Don't worry about any more trouble from that one. I warned him that if he ever bothered you again, I'd come back and deal with him myself. I scared him so bad I think he piddled down his leg." The lieutenant chuckled.

"I'm sorry I didn't get to see that," Amanda said, laughing.

"It was a good thing you did here for those women, Mrs. Armstrong. Some would have starved if not for you. And here you are," he said, rising from his chair, "and I must say none the worse for wear. Thank you for your hospitality. I have another hour to ride before I reach my stopping place for the night."

"Thank you for coming by, Lieutenant."

"My pleasure, Mrs. Armstrong. Good luck to you."

She watched as he quickly mounted his horse and rode out of sight. As she turned to go inside, he rode back just as quickly.

"Almost forgot," he said. "There's still a small detachment of soldiers in Greeneville: occupation troops, staying until we can be sure there is no danger to those who favored the Union during the war. The commander—Sykes is his name—will be out to see you one of these days. He'll give you no trouble. I told him about you and your little fellow there." He nodded toward Josie, who still lay on the pallet in the hall.

"Thank you, Lieutenant," she called as he rode off again.

"I guess there still are a few surprises left in life," she mumbled as she entered the hall. "And, might I say, quite happy ones," she said as she picked Josie up and kissed his little brown face. He was still half-asleep and cozy warm from the afternoon sun that had reached his pallet. "I love you, sleepy Josie," she whispered and buried her face in his neck. He squirmed and giggled, but allowed her to hold him for a very long time.

* * *

One evening, Amanda left Josie catching fireflies on the front terrace and went to Barbé's cabin. Though Barbé slept in the house now, she still liked to spend a little time in the cabin that had been her home for so many years.

"I can see you're troubled again," Barbé said in her easy way.

"Still. Yet. Always. I love Ben," she finally said, "but I don't think he's coming back here. I know I haven't been the best person, but I hope God won't punish me anymore. I don't know if I could face another loss."

Just then, Amanda heard Josie scream and immediately panicked. She rushed to the front terrace, Barbé on her heels.

"He's coming!" Josie yelled, as he ran down the lane. "He's coming!"

"Who?" Amanda asked. "You know you're not supposed to leave this yard," she said harshly.

"Captain Ben is coming," Josie said.

"Are you sure?"

"Yes, he saw me. He called my name."

Amanda ran past Josie and up the lane. It was Ben!

As she got closer, she noticed the crutches under his arms, one pant leg pinned up to his knee. When she reached him, he fell into her arms. His face was pale as ash.

"Horse fell a few miles back," he said breathlessly, leaning heavily on Amanda's arm.

Barbé ran to his side and looped his other arm across her strong shoulders. Josie carried his crutches.

"You poor soul," Amanda said. "You're here now. That's all that matters." She wanted to grab him, hug him, and never let go.

"Well, at least for the moment," he mumbled. When she looked at him, he turned his eyes away.

"What do you mean?" she asked, as they helped him to a chair on the front terrace.

"I shouldn't have come here, but I couldn't stop myself. Please," he said softly, tears in his eyes, "just tell me you don't want me and let me go on to Georgia."

"I will not! I have waited all these months for you. I plan to never let you out of my sight again—not unless you want to be out of my sight."

Even Ben had to laugh at that.

"You're the best thing I've ever seen!" she cried, as they helped him through the front door.

"Then we must get you some eyeglasses," he said, tears streaming down his face. He gently kissed her cheek.

"It's your heart I love, not your leg," she told Ben.

"Well, I'd become quite attached to it, myself," Ben said sadly.

A chuckle escaped from Amanda's mouth before she could stop it. Ben smiled, acknowledging the humor in what he had said.

After they had settled him in a chair in the sitting room, Ben called for Josie. "Come sit in my—on my leg. There's something I want to tell you."

Josie ran to Ben. "What is it?"

"Thank you for taking such good care of your mother while I was gone," he said.

The look Amanda saw in Ben's eyes dispelled any lingering uncertainties she might have had about his feelings toward Josie. *Your mother,* he had said. Ben held Josie for all of thirty minutes; they talked and giggled, and Amanda sighed with relief.

* * *

Ben ate ravenously from their leftovers from dinner, beef stew—minus the beef. Amanda found some of Jonathan's old clothes packed away in the back of the attic. She filled an old washtub with water for him. It wasn't as good as an actual bathing tub, but he could sit on a chair next to the tub while he bathed.

Widow lighted every candle they could spare in a large circle in the middle of Amanda's bedroom with all their blankets arranged inside. Amanda and Ben sat across from each other on the floor.

"You were always such a proper lady in Knoxville I really didn't think you'd want me after I lost my leg."

"Benjamin Braddock!"

"I don't see that in you now," he said. "Those fancy dresses Miss Lily gave you must be a bit worn by now."

She raised the bodice of the dress she was wearing and showed him where the skirt was separating from the blouse. If not for two strategically placed safety pins, it would have fallen to the floor when she stood.

"I will always want you, no matter what. And if you hadn't come back to Cinnamon Hill—as you promised—you would have broken my heart!" Pent-up emotions came to the fore, and she shrieked as a torrent of tears flowed down her face.

"Sorry, I don't mean to hurt you," he said softly.

"You fool," she scolded Ben, "I love you more than I ever dreamed I could love any man."

Scooting across the floor, Ben positioned himself as close to Amanda as possible and reached out to embrace her. She resisted at first, but not for long.

"I was a fool for not making my feelings plain to you before I left here that day, and I have prayed every day that some other man hadn't stolen your heart before I could get back."

"Just say what you feel," Amanda said.

"I just don't have the ability to tell you how I feel about you. It overwhelms me and leaves me tongue-tied." He paused for a moment. "My life growing up wasn't easy. My daddy is a bully; he enjoys making people feel uncomfortable. Thank you for saving me from going back to that," he said in a whisper.

He touched her hair, her face, her lips.

"I adore everything about you," he said with great emotion. "If I have to live one day on this earth without you, I will not survive."

"Then why did you ask me to let you go on to Georgia?"

"To save you from this imperfect body and mind I am now." Silent tears oozed from his eyes. "I'm not the man who left you here that day. The carnage I saw in Virginia... It's not something you get over. I will carry it with me for the rest of my life!"

She touched his face and wiped his tears away.

"The word *love* meant nothing to me until I met you," he said. "You *are* love to me."

They lay down on the blankets and wept as they held each other, but Ben was still visibly upset.

"I can't love you with this," he sobbed, gesturing toward his empty pants leg.

"Please forgive me for being far too forward," Amanda said, "but I can solve that dilemma."

She pushed Ben onto his back and settled on top of him.

The next morning, Ben asked Amanda for some fishing poles, but she could find none. She rigged a long, thin limb with some string and a large safety pin as a hook. She watched as Ben and Josie walked down to the creek, sat on the footbridge and put their line in the water. They actually caught two hand-sized fish, and Widow cooked them for dinner.

* * *

One hot summer evening, Amanda Armstrong saddled Molly and rode to the Calvary Baptist Church Cemetery. She entered the enclosed area where Jonathan was buried. The wrought iron gate's hinges creaked when she opened it. The hairs at the nape of her neck stood on end. She was disappointed with herself because she had not yet moved Jonathan's remains to Cinnamon Hill. She decided she would kneel a while there, and maybe her mind would be eased.

Something caught her peripheral vision, something she had forgotten: a neat row of pine bark markers. Six in number, they marked the graves of the other soldiers who also died that day. The major had buried them in the corner, as promised.

She crossed the enclosure and began gathering the markers in her lifted apron. The pine bark markers had survived the elements, but the information on them had not. An occasional letter, a dig here, a line there, but not one name could she discern. Again, she berated herself for not coming sooner. The identities of those soldiers were lost forever now, to all but God.

As she turned to walk away, her head bowed with sorrow, a name came into her mind: "Donald Brooks from Scituate, Massachusetts." That was odd. She knew no one by that name. She turned back, stood at the foot of the same grave, and received the same response. She walked to the foot of the next grave, and heard, "Hezekiah Moffatt from Norwalk, Connecticut." At the next, "James Elcott from Sandusky, Ohio." Then, "William Martin from Waldoboro, Maine."

Darkness would descend soon, but Amanda couldn't leave. She not only knew the names of the soldiers, she also heard them in her head—each one in a different voice. One voice came to her so clearly that she thought someone was standing behind her, but no one was there. Were the dead speaking to her? No. She was just so disappointed that the names had been destroyed that she imagined all of it.

But she couldn't forget about the soldiers. On subsequent nights, their voices inhabited her dreams. She felt compelled to send a letter to each family telling them where they could find their loved one's remains. She asked Mr. Bixby, of all people, to help her. He received and forwarded the mail for Armstrong Crossroads at his store, and he quickly volunteered to help Amanda with her "noble deed."

With the help of Jed Palmer and some volunteers among the commune women, Amanda gave Jonathan a proper funeral and buried him next to Luke, fulfilling his final wish. Her breathing came a little easier knowing his remains were finally at home.

Amanda returned to the church cemetery, this time with pencil and paper. She stood at the foot of the first grave again. Donald Brooks was the name she heard. Just as before. She wrote down all the names and the towns where they had lived.

The following day, she asked Ben to make a list of the places where soldiers were buried during Longstreet's long, slow trek through East Tennessee.

"Why?" Ben asked.

"I'm hoping to locate their graves and let their families know where their remains are."

"How are you going to do that?"

"I'm not quite sure yet," she said noncommittally, not wanting to tell him about the voices. She might never tell anyone.

"Will you be wanting me to list the burial sites of Confederate and Union soldiers?" Ben asked.

"Anybody," she said. "I don't care who they fought for, do you?"

He paused for a moment. "No," he said firmly, "it doesn't matter. They gave their lives for their country; you can't fault a man for that. And why are you taking this upon yourself?"

"I'll just feel better if I can let their families know where their remains are. Who knows how long it will take for government officials to sift through all the records, especially in remote areas such as this? I'm lucky: I know exactly where the men I lost are interred. I can visit their graves and talk to them when my heart is heavy. I can't imagine how incredibly difficult it must be for families who have no idea where their loved ones were buried."

"Better yet, I'll draw you a map," Ben said.

She might not be able to visit all of the burial sites, but she would continue as long as her health permitted. It was emotionally draining, but she feared that if she didn't continue, their souls would never rest. Widow, of course, accompanied Amanda on every trip.

* * *

She stood alone on a remote mountain road, words flowing quickly through her mind. She reached into her pocket for her last scrap of paper and a pencil that was so short she could barely write with it; writing materials were still in short supply.

Going by the list Ben had made for her, Amanda found many graves in out of the way places. A round mound of earth or a long narrow trench indicated a common grave, one which often contained the bones of many men. How could she ever hope to identify each soldier? She could only try.

When Amanda and Widow went looking for burial fields along the Holston River, they visited Galilani's grave and found it to be undisturbed. Violets grew rampantly over her resting place, and there was not a weed in sight.

TWENTY

———◆———

Autumn 1865

The war will always be a part of those of us who survived it, and we will never forget those who did not. It has forever altered my life, but I find something to be thankful for every day. I try not to dwell on what I have lost, but to focus on what I have left:

Barbé and Juba

Juba finally understands that the connection between Barbé and me can never be broken, but he is no longer tortured by it. When I learned that Juba had paid the overdue taxes and saved Cinnamon Hill from the auctioneer's gavel, I opened the last jar of fruit the commune had canned and baked an apple pie, Juba's favorite. We celebrated everything that night: home, family, and friends. Juba has built a home for Barbé down the creek from Cinnamon Hill, near Charles' old mill. He's going to build a blacksmith shop there as well. I plan to deed fifty acres there to Juba and Barbé as a Christmas present.

Widow

Widow is my constant companion. She shadows my every step from the time she awakens me in the morning until she tucks me safely into bed at night. I tell her that my strength is coming back. Her answer to that is, "I'm not taking any chances." I can't account for her devotion. She says that taking care of me has given her a new purpose in life. I think she's trying to compensate for my losses and to make me feel safe again. She is doing quite a nice job at both.

Josie

He truly is my son, and he continues to amaze me every day. I am still in awe of his goodness, his intelligence, and the gift God gave me by making sure we ended up together. "We will share this little boy," I told Barbé. "And he'll grow up to be so spoiled no one will be able to stand him but us." We laughed heartily. Occasionally, I send Josie down the creek to spend the night with Barbé and Juba. I watch him until he reaches their house; he turns to wave at me at least a dozen times along the way. I miss him when he's gone, but I feel no jealousy. I am satisfied knowing that they love him as their own and that they will teach him of his African heritage. On the days when I miss Luke most, I stay even closer to Josie. I'm thankful that Luke and I shared those few precious hours before he was taken from me. When I close my eyes, the memories flash through my mind like pictures in a book.

Ben

He is slowly becoming the man I met in Knoxville once again, if not externally, certainly internally. I sometimes wish I'd never seen Knoxville, that I could wipe the experiences I had there from my mind and the shame from my heart. But if I hadn't made that trip, I would have never met Josie or Ben. With Crocker's help, Ben has fashioned a tree limb into a leg, which he lashes to his thigh with a band of leather. It's crude, but it will do until we can get a better one.

Crocker

The Crocker of old is no more, and I'm learning to know the new one. He still runs the mill, and he has spent untold hours working on Barbé and Juba's new house. Occasionally, Juba pushes a few coins in the pocket of his overalls; Crocker always protests, saying payment isn't necessary. Then Juba says, "You've got a large family to support." And Crocker says, "That I do!" And that's the end of it. Crocker brings his whole brood to our picnics at Cinnamon Hill. We had two this summer. The women of the commune bring their families, and those times are some of the most joyous of my life.

Women of the commune

Thanks to the lessons we learned together, we all are coping well enough. We've discovered that we aren't quite ready to be completely independent just yet. The structures of our homes and farm buildings have suffered from age and neglect. We have leaky roofs, broken-down steps, and chicken coops that have to be rebuilt. Now, if we only had some chickens! If he's feeling up to it, Ben joins our work crew. He splits fence rails on one leg every bit as good as any man on two. He works tirelessly, helping us with whatever project we have going.

We spend one day each week at one member's home, doing whatever needs to be done. We will continue this rotation until the work is finished. Our work parties have also repaired local roads and bridges. Josie is in his element on those days, when his family of "Mamas" is together again. Our best times are spent in the kitchen. I think everybody misses that the most. We cook, talk, and laugh—Lord, do we laugh! We are comforted by the knowledge that we are linked for as long as we may live. The women continue to look to me for leadership as they attempt to return to some normalcy in their lives. I hope they always do.

Amanda

I am finally coming back to myself, what I can only assume to be my true self. I've discovered a new Amanda, one that I've never known—or at least, one that I haven't known for a very long time. I have a new confidence. Instead of panicking in frustrating situations, with a deep breath and a few seconds of silence, I can invoke a calmness that I do not recall ever having. If I am to pass the remainder of my days as I presently do, I will consider my life a great success. We have a pretty good stand of corn at Cinnamon Hill, and my kitchen garden is especially productive this year.

My family is complete: Barbé and Juba, Widow, Josie, Ben, and me. We share at least one meal a day, usually at Cinnamon Hill, where Barbé often ends up in the evening. She enjoys having her own home and working in her flower and vegetable gardens, and it's wonderful to see her so happy.

The six of us are as true a family as I can imagine. We cherish each other because we know how quickly life can slip away. We ride to church together every Sunday morning, and the six of us sit proudly in the Armstrong family pew. If some church members find our little black and white family peculiar, they know better than to say anything about it.

Some of my life's most precious moments happen when I'm doing everyday things. I look at the sky and nod my head to God and thank Him for that one lucid moment that began as nothing special but will stay with me forever. Having that little slice of time in my memory comforts me. In sad times, I can call it up, and it will help me get to the other side of trouble.

I can't say the transition in our little family has been easy for any of us, but especially not for Ben. Many days he curses his leg, or the lack of it, as he tries to participate in activities around the farm. I feel his frustration, and I allow him the freedom to express it.

When the struggle becomes too much, we strap him into the saddle, and he and our sweet old Molly—God love her heart, we have put upon her so much—head out for a ride. I've shown him all my favorite places. He finds freedom and serenity in the mountains, where it matters not if one's body or mind is intact.

Josie tries hard to understand why Ben gets so frustrated and seems to fear that we'll lose him yet.

"How can he live with one leg?" Josie asks.

"Ben's still learning to live without his leg," I tell Josie, "and he gets upset when he can't do the things he once could. But he can't just give up and sit in the house all day."

"That's what I'd do," Josie says, "if I lost my leg."

"Josie," I say, pointing, "see that gnarled old apple tree down there by the barn? I don't know how it came to be there, but every year I've lived here I think it surely doesn't have the strength to produce one more apple. Every year I vow to cut it down if it doesn't, and every year it surprises me; there were almost a dozen on it this year. It's not the best tree, but it's still doing what God put it here to do."

"Papa Ben says you are the most remark'ble woman he's seen in all his born days."

"He does, does he?" I answer with a chuckle. "Don't worry about Papa Ben, Josie. We'll take real good care of him, and he'll be just fine. I believe that, don't you?"

"Yes'm, I do," says Josie, sliding his little hand into mine as we walk slowly toward the house on a beautiful Tennessee morning.

About the Author

Maggie MacLean has an autoimmune disease, but she has never allowed it to prevent her from accomplishing the goals she set for herself. She raised two children and spent her business career working in management positions, including plant manager. While doing research for this novel, Maggie fell in love with the people and the history of Northeast Tennessee. She has turned that passion into a blog, Northeast Tennessee in the Civil War, which is available at northeasttennesseecivilwar.com.